DECEPTION'S WEB

THE DEIZIAN EMPIRE: BOOK THREE

BY
CRISTA MCHUGH

1

As soon as Claudia Pacilus heard the engine of her father's airship die down, her pulse quickened. He'd sent her back to Tivola weeks ago, his displeasure at her inability to capture the attention of Emperor Sergius evident without him saying a word. Now, the emperor had married that Alpirion, Azurha, and she was left to deal with the punishment for her failure.

She pulled her palla tighter around her chest as though it would drive away the chill forming in her soul. Her gaze traveled to the cliffs on the far end of the moonlit garden. *Will I be the next person tossed over the edge for my father's pleasure?*

The waves crashed against the rocks in reply, and a shiver coursed down her spine. Her mind screamed for her to run and hide, but pride kept her feet planted firmly in the center of main atrium. She was a Deizian, and such cowardly behavior was beneath her. She would greet her father like a dutiful daughter and pray to the gods that his ire had lessened during the weeks of imperial wedding festivities.

Her father, Gaius Hostilius Pacilus, provincial governor of Lucrilla, strolled into the villa with a regal bearing that rivaled that of the emperor himself, surrounded by slaves carrying torches to illuminate his way. Fine threads of silver shimmered in his golden hair, hinting at his age, but his body remained as well

1

muscled as any member of the Imperial Army. He fixed his cold blue eyes on her, his mouth pressing into a tight line.

Claudia lowered her head and dipped into a curtsy. "Greetings, noble Father, and welcome home."

He stopped in front of her, but said nothing. She could feel his eyes upon her, dissecting each of her flaws, from the loose strand of hair that had slipped free in the ocean breeze to the wrinkle that creased where she'd gripped her palla moments ago.

A tremor worked its way into her bottom lip, but she dared not move from her position of subjugation. She stared at his sandals and waited for him to give her permission to stand. She was little better than the slaves who served them. Her father owned everything, from the jewels she wore to her freedom. If she left, she'd have to leave everything behind. It was far better to try to appease him than to be cast out with nothing but her name.

Another step of footsteps approached her with quick strides on the tiled floor. Her body tensed a second before the back of a hand connected with her cheek, knocking her to the ground. Blood filled her mouth. She wiped it away and glared at her younger brother, Asinius.

"Washed up whore," he growled before he kicked her in the stomach, knocking the air from her lungs and leaving a burning ache that made her wonder if death wasn't close behind. "If you had done what you were supposed to have done, you would be empress now instead of that slave."

He drew his foot back to deliver another blow but froze when their father said, "Patience, Asinius. The emperor will fall in due time."

Then Hostilius peered down at her as if she were a puzzle for him to unravel rather than his flesh and blood. Seconds passed in silence. Claudia gulped in a breath, but other than that, remained as still as a statue.

"Pity," he said at last, as though he'd just discovered a smudge on his pristine white toga. "It seems like she has outlived her usefulness to us."

Anger tempered the fear chilling her blood. How dare he not show any concern for her welfare! She, the daughter whose three marriages had helped him gain control of the province with the death of each of her husbands and had elevated him to governor. Her jaw tightened, and she reached up to pull her palla back over her shoulders.

"What should we do with her?" Asinius asked as though she were a disobedient slave. The perverse note in his voice hinted that he would love to be the one who flung her over the cliffs. Even though he was the favored son, he'd always borne a grudge against her, especially when she reminded him that their father's rise to power was due to her, not him.

"Time will tell." Hostilius continued past her on the way to his study. "Come along, son. We have much to discuss before we act again."

Her brother followed him like an eager puppy who had been offered a juicy bone to chew on. Whatever they were planning, blood would be spilled when they carried it out. The slaves followed them with the torches, leaving her alone in the darkness.

Claudia spat out the last of the blood and pushed herself off the floor. So it had come to this. She had lost her father's favor, and her life hung on the thin string of his mercy.

For years, she'd been a pawn in his political games. She'd warmed the beds of three men she loathed in order to strengthen her family's position, hoping for the day she'd satisfy her father's thirst for power long enough to be allowed to live out the rest of her days at a country estate. She'd watched her father claim her widow's dowry each time and add it to his coffers, leaving her with nothing more than his approval and the ever-tightening noose of guilt from association, should the truth about her plots ever come to light. She'd even agreed to lower herself to the level of a concubine as part of her father's plan to gain imperial favor. And now she was left wondering when her body would slam against the rocks below and be carried off to sea.

The muffled voices of her father and brother floated out from under the closed doors of the study, fueling her anger. If they wanted to cut her out of their plans now, so be it. But that wouldn't keep her from discovering their plot. Perhaps she could use it to her advantage.

She moved to the gardens, keeping her steps silent as she crept closer to the open window of her father's study. She clung to the shadows and listened.

"Pontus was arrogant to think he could kill Sergius," Asinius said.

"Pontus had hired the Rabbit. He thought she would succeed as she has numerous times before. None of us imagined Sergius would succeed in seducing her."

"And now that she has her lips wrapped around his dick, it's only a matter of time before she convinces him to free all the slaves, even after that slave uprising in Alpiria last month."

"Emperor Sergius is too cautious to make such a sweeping change. He'll start slowly because he knows that such a drastic measure will crush the economy of the empire." Hostilius's chair creaked like it did every time he leaned back in it. Claudia pictured him steepling his fingers together and pressing them against his lips as he thought. "His marriage to the Alpirion has endeared him to the lower classes."

"All the more reason to destroy him as quickly as possible." Her brother's sandals slapped against the tile floor as he paced. "Who's the next best assassin in the empire?"

"You're not thinking clearly. The Legion will be guarding Sergius more closely than ever, and even if an assassin gets past them, the Rabbit will already have placed measures to protect him. You forget that she knows many ways to kill a man, and she will have made sure that another assassin could not gain access to him."

"Then how are we going to get the throne?"

Her father's chuckle caused her gut to clench. It was too cool, too collected, too calm. "An emperor is only as safe as his popularity. If the people fear he is placing them in danger, they will demand his head."

A pause filled the room, followed by Asinius's laughter. "The barrier."

"It will take careful planning. Sergius outwitted us once. And the barrier appeared stronger than ever when I was there. This time, I will not act until I am certain I will succeed."

Claudia bit her bottom lip to keep from gasping. She'd heard rumors that the barrier had been weakened after the death of the prior emperor, but she had no idea her father was behind it. Why would he risk having the empire overrun by the Barbarians? Those creatures knew only death and destruction. They could not be reasoned with, and if the barrier fell, thousands of lives would be lost.

"How shall we start?"

"Slowly. I need to make sure the device is at its maximum potential."

"That will mean more ore."

"What do you think I was discussing with Minius last week? The first shipments should start arriving in less than a month. But we must be discreet. If the emperor catches wind of our plan, we'll suffer the same fate as Pontus."

"I doubt that, Father. You are far more cunning than him."

"As you can see, there's no need to bloody our hands. The masses will do it for us."

"And when we save them from the Barbarians, they will demand we assume the throne." Asinius's laughter drifted outside again, this time with a musical note of insanity in it. "It's perfect."

"Would you expect otherwise from me?" The chair creaked again, followed by footsteps. "Remember, patience is the key here. We wait until everything is ready." Their voices faded as they left the study.

Claudia slid along the wall and rubbed the chill from her arms. How long would her father allow the barrier to fall before he restored it? Hours? Days? Weeks? How many lives would be lost in the process? Whatever his plans included, they didn't include her. What was to keep him from selling her to Minius in exchange for more ore? Or worse, for him to shift the blame on her should they fail?

I refuse to be his pawn any longer.

She took a deep breath, cleansing her fears from her mind. Her father had made a mistake when he called her useless, and he would pay for it. If he feared the emperor would discover his plan, then perhaps she should capitalize on that.

She stood, straightened her clothes, and went to her room. In careful block letters to disguise her handwriting, she wrote:

If you wish for the barrier to remain intact, you should monitor the ore shipments from Gracchero.

There. Nothing too precise. A hint, and no more. Just enough to clue the emperor in to her father's plan and hinder his efforts without giving everything away. No one would ever suspect the note came from her. And when her father's face turned red from frustration, she would have the start of her revenge.

"Zavi," she called to her slave, "could you please fetch Kafi? I have a task for him that requires his unique talent for discretion."

2

Eight Months Later

"Are you certain that's him?"

Galerius Metellus cracked one eye open when he heard the man's question, then immediately shut it. He had no idea what time of day it was, but the sun was still shining brightly enough to double the throbbing in his head.

"Yeah, that's him," another man answered. "Check his wrist."

Eight months ago, Galerius would have tackled any man who touched him without permission, but today, he was too hungover to care. One of the two men lifted his right arm, turning it over to find the insignia of the Legion that was tattooed on the inside of his wrist.

His arm dropped to the ground as the first man cursed. "I never would have thought it was true."

"The truth is ugly, isn't it?" A pair of arms wrapped around Galerius's waist, pulling him off the ground. "And it stinks, too."

"No kidding."

"You've had your fun," Galerius croaked, his throat dry. The taste of stale, cheap wine lingered on his tongue. "Leave me alone."

"Sorry, Captain," the first man replied. "We've got

orders to bring you in."

Upon hearing his former title, a wave of anger rolled through his gut. Or was it nausea? Either way, he shoved the men away and stumbled until he collided with the wall of the alley. The cool stones eased the ache in his forehead as he leaned against them. "I said leave me alone."

"Like he said, we have orders to bring you in, sir," the second man replied.

There was something familiar about his voice. Galerius risked opening his eyes again and found himself staring right into the Legion insignia on the man's chest. His graze traveled upward until he recognized the man's face. Fabius, one of his former lieutenants. A curse flew from his lips. "What does Horatius want from me?"

"It's not Horatius who wants you." Fabius grabbed his shoulder and spun him around. "It's the emperor himself."

Galerius's gut lurched, and the horizon wavered. If it had been the new Captain of the Legion, he might have been able to talk his way out of the meeting. But when the emperor commanded it, the Legion was obligated to obey. That didn't mean *he* had to follow orders, though. "Can I have a moment to make myself presentable, then?"

Fabius shook his head. "I'm not taking a chance on you slipping away, or risking the emperor's impatience. He said he wanted to see you as soon as possible." He shoved Galerius forward. "Let's go."

"Not that you're getting any pleasure ordering me around," Galerius muttered.

"It's not often a lieutenant gets to tell a captain what to do, even if it's a former captain."

The two members of the Legion flanked him, guiding him through the crowded streets of Emona toward the imperial palace. Galerius combed his fingers through his matted hair, not wanting to think about what was mixed in with the dried mud that crumbled onto his shoulders. The last thing he remembered was leaving the bar after what he had hoped was enough wine to dull the shame that had been eating away at him for months. Based on where they found him, he didn't make it out of the alley.

His hand traveled to the three days' worth of stubble on his cheeks. He lifted his arm and sniffed. By the gods, he reeked. And he had thought he couldn't sink any lower. Not the way he wanted to be seen by the emperor after all these months.

Thankfully, Fabius and his companion didn't say another word until they deposited him in the middle of the imperial throne room. They bowed and left as though they might be reprimanded for the filthiness of their prisoner. The doors closed with a resounding thud that mimicked the sound of the pulse in his ears.

Galerius kept his eyes down as he knelt in front of Emperor Titus Sergius Flavus, the man whose life he was once charged with protecting. Whose life he'd failed to protect twice—once when a scheming Deizian had managed to lock himself in the emperor's quarters and tried to murder him, then less than a month later when Alpirion rebels poisoned him. Thankfully, he'd been spared the public shame of losing another emperor under his watch, but the personal shame at his failure to protect the previous emperor had prompted him to resign from the Legion months ago. Emperor Decius had been poisoned, even though no one realized it until the same poison had sickened the current emperor, and he carried the full responsibility for the murder as though he'd been the one who slipped the poison into the emperor's oil.

You'll never be anything more than a disappointment to me.

His father's words cut into him like a knife, driving the guilt deeper into his soul.   He clenched his jaw and bore the blow without showing any of the pain he inwardly felt. He'd spent his whole life proving his father wrong, but at times, he wondered if he'd reached the breaking point. Would he ever live down his lapse in judgment?

"Galerius Metellus, we thank you for coming before us," Sergius said as though he were welcoming him to dinner.

9

As if I had any choice in the matter. His gaze fixed on the mud that caked his tunic from his night in the alley. "The emperor sends for me, and I come, although I have no idea what use I may be to you."

"See? Even he agrees he's not worthy of serving us."

Empress Azurha's words ripped away his self-pity, leaving a new raw emotion in its wake. He jerked his head up and saw her sitting on the throne next to emperor, her glittering blue-green eyes never wavering from him. The cold hostility in her face reminded him she was more than some nobleman's daughter who'd captured the title of empress. She was the Rabbit, the deadliest assassin in the empire, and her recent marriage to the emperor had done little to dull her reputation. Her black hair and coppery skin declared her Alpirion heritage, but the gleaming gold bracelets around her wrists did more than proclaim her status a freed slave—they also concealed the tattoo of the Legion on her right wrist.

"Please, Azurha," Sergius said, laying his hand on her arm as if to soothe her, "let me speak and hold your censure until I'm finished."

"As you wish, but you already know my thoughts on the matter."

Galerius curled his fingers into the flesh of his palms. Already, his enemies were lining up against him. It was bad enough to know she was the one who twice had saved the emperor's life, not him, but to have her belittle him front of the emperor was too much. "What do you require of me, Emperor Sergius?"

A smile curled up the corners of the emperor's mouth, the first sign of warmth Galerius had noticed since he'd entered the throne room. "As a member of the Legion, you loyally served my father for many years. As the Captain of the Legion, you served me without fail. And now, we have one more favor to ask of you."

Please don't let it be falling on my sword. Such punishment was expected for captains who let an emperor fall under their watch.

"And what is that?"

"We've received a series of dispatches from Tivola about a plot to overthrow me. I'm asking you to go there and investigate them."

"Why me?"

"Because the dispatches are addressed to you."

A bead of sweat formed along the nape of his neck and trickled down his spine. His gut had always warned him when something smelled like a trap, and this practically reeked of it. "Are you certain, Your Majesty? Why would someone be writing me with such important information?"

"Why indeed?" Azurha curled her hand around the arm of her throne and leaned forward. "Is there something you're hiding from us?"

Galerius jumped to his feet. "On my honor, I know nothing of this."

"I believe you." The calm tone of the emperor's voice soothed the stinging accusation from his wife. "What's strange about these dispatches, is that they're addressed to Captain Galerius Metellus. Whoever sent them doesn't know about your resignation."

"If he doesn't know about that, then how accurate can the information be?"

"Very accurate so far." Marcus Flavius Lepidus, the emperor's closest friend, stepped out of the shadows. A sailor by trade, he had access to the underworld of the empire and usually acted as the emperor's spy when there was a rumored threat to the empire. His blue eyes revealed his Deizian blood, but his dark brown hair and beard proclaimed his Elymanian ancestry, making it easier for him to blend in with the crowds. "Everything I've been asked to investigate has been proven true."

"Then why don't you continue to investigate since you have more knowledge of it than me?" Logically, none of this made sense, even to his still half-drunk mind. "Bringing me on will surely slow down your efforts."

Marcus lifted the sleeve of his tunic, revealing a freshly

stitched wound snaking up to his shoulder. "Because I got too close."

Another trickle of doubt ran down his neck. "Marcus is one of the best men in the empire when it comes to ferreting out information. How can I possibly succeed where he failed?"

"How indeed?" Azurha turned to Sergius. "Titus, dear, listen to him. Even he expresses doubt in his ability. Why should we trust him with such an important mission? It's obvious he's fallen from the man you once knew."

A wave of nausea rolled through him, and he couldn't tell if it was from the cheap wine he'd drank last night, the stench clinging to his clothes, or the fact that the empress's assessment hit too close to home. *Have I fallen too far to ever recover?*

"I disagree with you. I think he's the best man for the job."

"Be reasonable. Just look at him." She stood, stepped down from the dais like a lygress approaching her prey, and circled him. "He's barely a shadow of the man who once served you. He's a filthy, disheveled drunk. He has more mud caked in his beard than the bricks of this palace. And the gods only know when the last time he had a bath was."

The wrinkling of her nose set every nerve on end, yet he managed to keep his anger in check and his face devoid of emotion. He knew how to handle her taunts. They were no different than those his father had hurled at him throughout his childhood, and he'd proven him wrong by rising through the Legion to become the youngest man ever to hold the rank of Captain. He just had to wait until the emperor dismissed him so he could leave and forget this nonsense.

But he made a note to head straight for the public baths after this encounter. Even he couldn't remember the last time he'd bathed.

Azurha turned her back to him, standing between him and emperor. "Titus, I beg of you, reconsider. There's nothing redeemable left in him."

Something in Galerius snapped when she said that. If it

had been any other day, any other circumstance, he would have agreed with her. But this morning was different. The emperor had summoned him. Not the current Captain of the Legion. Not Marcus. Him. And if Emperor Sergius selected him for the mission, then perhaps he saw something in him the others didn't. Perhaps he hadn't fallen so far that he couldn't regain some of his pride.

"You're wrong."

His words, hardly more than a low growl, surprised everyone in the throne room, especially the empress. She spun around, her lips parted as though no one had ever dared to disagree with her.

He stepped around her to stand in front of the emperor again, his shoulders squared like they were when they were covered with the armor of the Legion. "Your Majesty, I have made it my life to serve the empire, and if you have need of me, then let me know what I can do."

"Are you certain you want to accept this mission? We haven't told you what is required."

He shook his head. "If you have faith in me, then that's all I need to know."

As soon as the said that, he knew it was true. Sergius was not like the other emperors before him. He was a man of books, a man of strategy, a man who thought about every conceivable option before choosing a course of action. If he had chosen him, then there was a good reason for it. Add in the fact that even the empress could not sway him, how could he not accept the mission?

"Excellent. We knew you would not refuse us." Sergius stood and held out his hand for his wife.

Galerius just realized then that instead of using the "we" in the imperial sense, the emperor had used it to include his wife, elevating her to his equal, his co-ruler. Change was already happening in the empire, starting from the throne itself.

As Azurha passed him, he caught a glimpse of a sly smile on her lips, so very different from the look of disdain she'd worn

13

from the moment he'd entered the room.

His mouth went dry. He'd just been had.

She took the emperor's hand, her voice now calm and inviting. "Thank you, Galerius. Return tomorrow morning, and we will share all we know with you."

His feet remained glued the mosaic floor while the imperial couple left the throne room followed by Marcus. Everything, from the members of the Legion dragging him to the palace to Azurha's insults, had been part of an elaborate ruse to trick him into accepting the mission.

"Don't look so upset, Galerius," Varro said from the doorway. He stood at attention like the solider he'd been before the tip of a sword had cut his military career short and turned him the Head Steward of the imperial palace. A leather bracelet covered the tattoo that marked him as a former Captain of the Legion, but traces of his command still radiated in his bearing. "You've been given a second chance to prove yourself."

"But why all this?"

A grin carved more lines into the older man's face. "If they'd sent you a letter, would you have accepted?"

"Probably not," he admitted. Since he'd resigned, he had tried to distance himself from the emperor as much as possible.

"Then cheer up. At least they've given you an opportunity to make yourself more presentable the next time they see you."

Galerius ran his hands over his clothes. "You wouldn't know where I can find a clean tunic?"

Varro nodded, the twinkle in his brown eyes hinting that he was as much a part of this ruse as anyone else in the room. "I do indeed, along with a good barber. Perhaps I can even find a way to sneak you into the Legion's baths."

Galerius followed him out of the throne room. Only the gods knew why he'd been given a second chance, but he was determined not to squander it.

3

The next morning, Galerius strode into the throne room behind Varro a changed man. A day at the baths had removed the months of filth that had covered him, and the hour-long massage had eased the tension and stiffness from his muscles. His cheeks were clean shaven, and his hair was cut short in the style required by most members of the Legion. If it wasn't for the lack of armor and the missing sword on his side, he would have felt like his old self.

Unlike yesterday, the throne room was dim and empty, though. Varro continued to lead him to the side room where the emperor commonly met privately with his friends and confidants. He didn't think it was anything out of the ordinary considering the matter at hand, but he was shocked to see the empress waiting for him instead of the emperor.

"Thank you for bringing him, Varro."

"Of course, Your Majesty," the steward said with a brief bow. "Do you require anything else from me?"

"No, thank you. We have everything we need."

As Varro left the room, Galerius studied the new empress. The long black hair that hung to her waist was worn in a casual style favored by Deizian women these days, but her strangely colored eyes shone with a magical light all their own. Although he doubted she was of Deizian blood, he'd twice witnessed her strange powers—once when she'd managed to blow away the locked doors that he and three of his men had failed to ram open, and then again when she had extracted the poison from the emperor after the most talented healers in the empire had failed.

She, too, seemed to be studying him with equal interest. The hostility from yesterday had been replaced with a mixture of approval and curiosity. Her dress today was simpler than the elaborate gown she'd worn yesterday while she was seated on the throne, her jewels noticeably absent as though she wanted to appear lower than her status as empress to put him more at ease. She sat beside a small table with a chest and several scrolls on it and beckoned him forward.

He knelt before her. "Good morning, Empress Azurha."

"Good morning to you, too, Galerius. I trust Varro was able to assist you adequately yesterday."

He smoothed his hands over the clean tunic and nodded. "It was much appreciated."

"Please come closer so I can share with you what we know."

His gut told him this was not a trap. He stood and approached the table, feeling less cautious than he had before.

"What do you make of these?" she asked as she opened the chest.

He estimated that there were about twenty letters inside, each written on the same fine paper. He picked one up and studied the carefully written block letters that spelled out his name on the front. "Whoever wrote these has access to someone with money. A common man would've used coarser paper."

She nodded, and he continued his assessment, sniffing the paper. The slight hint of incense clung to it, much lighter than the heavy scent that followed priests and priestesses. "It came from a household, not a temple."

"Good. Now tell me what you think of the contents."

He'd been dreading this moment from the second he'd heard the dispatches were addressed to him. He glanced at the broken wax seal, noting that it did not bear any insignia, before reading the few cryptic lines inside. "Have you been monitoring the shipments of ore from Gracchero?" he asked.

She nodded again. "Marcus was able to intercept two of the shipments that were trying to bypass the customs officials by coming in late at night. And these were sizable shipments—several tons, by our estimation."

"But who would need so much ore? It only takes a mere coating to act as a conduit."

"Read on," she replied before taking a sip from her goblet.

Each dispatch contained a subtle hint, a clue that something was a potential threat to the empire. As the letters continued, the writer acknowledged the emperor's intervention, showing he was aware of plots being foiled, and yet he did not know that the one person he was writing to was no longer the Captain of the Legion. He frowned. "Something doesn't add up."

"What do you mean?"

"Whoever wrote these letters is close enough to the plotters to gain access to this information, but is not high enough in rank to know of my resignation. And yet the paper suggests the writer has access to money, and the writing reveals the person is well educated—no spelling mistakes or sloppy penmanship."

Azurha raised a brow, the corner of her mouth rising in a half-smile. "Based on this information, who do you think might have written it?"

"A scribe, possibly. Maybe a high-ranking servant in a Deizian household."

She nodded again, keeping her face blank. If she wanted to play philosopher to a student, she was doing an admirable job. Thankfully, the mystery of the dispatches intrigued him enough to continue, despite her irritating game of making him investigate what she already knew. If she'd been one of his men, he would have demanded a brief summary of the information, not this long, drawn-out affair. But this was the empress, and he needed to play her game if he wanted to regain any of the respect he'd lost.

The last few letters pointed to Hostilius Pacilus, the provincial governor of Lucrilla, as someone of interest in this plot. Not that it was very surprising. Any man who would offer his own daughter to the imperial harem in order to gain the emperor's favor was despicable at best. Rumors spoke of how he'd risen to power by eliminating rivals and burning down sections of Tivola, buying them cheaply from the ashes and rebuilding fancy villas on them to become the wealthiest man in the province. Combined with the recent insult of Emperor Sergius choosing to wed an Alpirion over a purebred Deizian, and he could see Hostilius as a prime suspect for wanting to overthrow the emperor.

"If the clues all point to Hostilius, why doesn't the emperor arrest him?"

"You're not thinking of the potential consequences, Galerius." Azurha rose from her chair and took the most recent letter from his hand. "If Titus went around arresting every Deizian who could possibly be a threat to him, we'd have an uprising on our hands faster than you could draw your sword."

He mulled over her words and agreed. One provincial governor had already tried to kill him, and he suspected the emperor's choice in a wife had gained him more enemies among the ruling class than friends. And yet, for all the harsh criticisms he'd heard whispered during the wedding festivities, he'd come to begrudgingly respect the new empress. She was sharp, courageous, and had more than once shown her love and loyalty to the emperor.

"Where do I come in to this?" he asked, hoping to get to the essence of his mission so he knew what was expected of him. He was a man of action, not thought. A soldier, not a philosopher. And right now, his muscles twitched as though he were about to order a charge on the battlefield.

"Your mission is twofold. First, we need to know what Hostilius is plotting and why he's having so much ore shipped to

Tivola. Second, we would like to know who the informant is, if only to protect the person when we go in to stop Hostilius."

"It's not like he's going to invite me into his home with open arms. I am the former Captain of the Legion, after all."

Azurha answered him by narrowing her eyes. "That's where you're wrong. Outside of those in the throne room yesterday, no one knows the real reason you resigned from the Legion."

His jaw fell slack. "I thought it would be common knowledge after I cost one emperor his life and almost failed his son."

She laughed, a mixture of mirth and mocking that rankled him. "You are far more critical of yourself than anyone else will ever be."

Not as critical as my father was.

"As far the public knows, you could have resigned over opposition to me," she continued, speaking slowly so he wouldn't miss the implication of her words.

"Surely you don't think—"

"No, I have no reason to doubt your loyalty." The lethalness of a seasoned assassin glittered in her eyes, and Galerius knew that if she did have doubts about him, he wouldn't leave the room alive. She probably still carried multiple concealed weapons on her. "But my husband was clever enough to keep your reason a secret, both to protect your reputation and in case a situation like this arose."

It was so perfectly planned, it could have been a scripted play. Anyone who had doubts about Emperor Sergius's ability to rule the empire obviously didn't know how well the analytical emperor's mind worked. And just like how he'd kept quiet on the resignation, Emperor Sergius probably used his reputation as a lover of books to keep his enemies from suspecting too much from him.

"So, I propagate this lie to gain the trust of Hostilius?"

"I would recommend that." She moved to the scrolls and started unrolling one of them. "Once you gain access to his

19

home, you need to familiarize yourself with the layout. I've taken the liberty of drawing you a map of the different levels of the home, including the two secret passages inside the villa."

He took a step back, studying her carefully. "How do you know so much about his villa?"

She met his gaze wearing the same predatory expression he'd seen more times than he'd cared to witness in his empress. "Do you really expect me to answer that question?"

Of course I don't. The last governor of Lucrilla had supposedly died in his sleep, but that didn't mean he hadn't had a little help entering the afterlife. Any suspicion, though, had been cast on Claudia, the daughter of Hostilius and wife of the late governor. And there was no rabbit's foot found near the body. "You didn't leave your usual marker."

Her eyes widened in feigned innocence. "Surely, you don't think I had anything to do with his death."

"Your string of victims is legendary."

She chuckled and returned to her maps. "I've only broken the assassin's code once in my life, and that was to save Titus's life. I will never do it again."

The unexpected softness in her voice caused something to tighten in his chest. She'd risked her life to save the man she loved, almost dying in the process. He'd never felt a fraction of the emotion for someone that she carried for her husband, and he doubted he ever would. The life of a soldier was not conducive to long-term attachments.

A wave of melancholy washed over him, and he changed the subject before he let it consume him. "Since you know so much about Hostilius's villa, why doesn't the Rabbit silence him before he has a chance to carry out his plan?"

Her lips pressed together in a thin line, hinting that she would gladly do it if allowed, but something held her back. Or rather someone. "Titus doesn't want me to leave the palace."

Before he could ask why, her hand brushed against the gentle swelling of her stomach.

"You're with child?" How had he not noticed it before?

20

"Yes, and I trust you will keep quiet on the matter. Titus has gained enough enemies for marrying me. If they learn that I'm carrying his child…" Her voice broke with an uncharacteristic display of vulnerability. She swallowed and regained her composure. "Tell me, how many citizens do you think will accept a half-Alpirion as the heir to the throne?"

"I think you underestimate how well you are loved by the people."

"The slaves, perhaps," she replied with a healthy dose of bitterness. "Maybe the Elymanians, but the Deizians have made their displeasure well known."

"And yet they dare not openly oppose the Rabbit."

"I *was* the Rabbit, but now I'm the empress, and I've found it to be far more dangerous than any job I've ever taken." She rolled up the map and placed it on top of the chest of letters. "These are yours to take. If we receive any more dispatches from the informant, we'll send it to you."

As she moved away from the table, the high-waisted gown easily concealed her pregnancy now, but how much longer could she keep it a secret? It made the urgency of his mission all the more apparent. Whatever Hostilius was planning, he needed to stop it before the news of the empress's pregnancy leaked outside the palace.

He gathered the chest of letters and scrolls under his arm. "I appreciate you taking to time to provide me with so much information, Your Majesty."

"I only gave you a map. You deduced most of the information yourself." She paused by the door leading to her private chambers and added, "Titus and Marcus came to the same conclusion that you did about the informant—that it's a member of household or a scribe."

If this meeting had proven anything to him, it was that the empress knew more than she let on, and this was no exception. Her silence on the matter hinted that she did not agree with her husband's suspect. "Who do you think it is?"

A smile lit her face like a soldier who'd been promoted.

21

"Hostilius's daughter, Claudia."

Her suspect surprised him. Why would a daughter betray her own father? But before he could ask why, Azurha slipped through the door to her chambers, leaving him alone with his thoughts.

Galerius turned to find a grinning Varro standing in the doorway to the throne room, his hands clasped behind his back. "The empress is quite an extraordinary woman, isn't she?"

"You've always known that, though, haven't you, Varro?" From the moment Azurha had arrived in the palace posing as concubine, the old steward had told them she was more than she seemed.

"Perhaps I have," he replied with a smug grin.

"Do you think there are any grounds for her suspicions?"

"From my limited interaction with Lady Claudia, I would say she is a woman who should not be underestimated."

Yes, no woman becomes known as the Black Widow of the Empire without a good reason. Hostilius's rise to power was closely linked to his daughter's three brief marriages. "But why would Hostilius's most valuable ally turn against him?"

"Why indeed?"

The steward's cryptic reply irritated him, but he tucked away that piece of information for future reference. If he ever found himself in the company of Claudia Pacilus, he would have to test the empress's theory. Hopefully, he wouldn't end up like her three husbands.

"One more thing, Galerius." Varro pulled a scabbard out from behind his back and offered it to him. Inside was a captain's sword.

As he drew closer, Galerius recognized it as his sword, the one he had surrendered when he resigned from the Legion. He grabbed it with his free hand, but the steward held on to it for a moment.

As Varro released the sword, he rotated his wrist so his tattoo was visible. Like Galerius's, the two boughs of laurel leaves framed the insignia of the Legion, marking him as a former captain. "Remember, once a member of the Legion, always a member of the Legion."

4

Claudia crossed the courtyard of the villa just in time to see a man exiting her father's study. She paused, hoping to catch a glimpse of his face and add him to the list conspirators she was forming. Once she had all of them, she would send the list to Emona and stop her father once and for all.

But instead of the Deizian nobleman she expected to see, it was Captain Galerius Metellus. He stopped and locked eyes with her. *Has he come to investigate my letters? Did he tell my father?* Her mouth turned to sand, and her knees shook underneath her gown.

But following the initial shock and fear of finding him here came a flush of warmth that spread from the pit of her stomach to her cheeks. It was the first time she'd even see him out of uniform. The muscles of his broad chest rippled against the fabric of his tunic as he walked. His brown hair was short, as most men wore it, but his grey eyes never left her as he came closer. The heat under her skin intensified when she realized he looked upon her as though he were imagining what she looked like with her clothes off.

"Lady Claudia, how good it is to see you again," he said as he took her hand. The brief contact of his lips against her fingers sent a shockwave up her arm more powerful than any magic she'd ever cast.

She jerked her hand away, unable to hurl the insult that sat poised on the tip of her tongue. Normally, she would have berated an Elymanian such as him for daring to touch her without permission, but her mouth refused to work properly. No man had even left her speechless like that.

What was even more annoying was that he grinned and gave her a wink as if he knew exactly what kind of effect he had on her.

By the time she gained control of her senses, he'd already left the courtyard. Rage quickly overcame any fear or desire that had consumed her. She balled her hands into fists and went straight to her father's study. "What was the Captain of the Legion doing here?"

Her father didn't glance up from his papers, completely unconcerned about his recent visitor. "You mean, the former Captain of the Legion. Apparently, he resigned shortly after the emperor married that slave girl."

The blood rushed from her head, forcing her to sink into the chair across from his desk. *If Galerius had resigned, who was receiving my letters?* "Did he give a reason why?"

"It seems he doesn't approve of the new empress and had some hesitation about giving up his life to protect her." Hostilius finally raised his eyes from his papers. "Or so he claims, anyway."

Her pulse jumped. *What if he's here to follow up on my letters? If Father suspects Galerius's motives, how much longer do I have before he finds out about me?* "You don't believe him?" she asked, hoping her voice sounded innocent.

"Once a member of the Legion, always a member of the Legion." He straightened a stack of papers and set them aside. "He's staying at Pontus's old villa in town. He came here today to pay his respects to me as governor and ask for permission to search some of the cliffs to the south for sapphires. I told him if there were any left, he could claim them, less his taxes to the province, of course."

Tivola had once been famed for its sapphires, but greedy

miners generations ago had all but stripped the region of any that could be found. The only legacy left behind was a delicate lacework of tunnels crisscrossing the ground under the city all the way to sea, creating large sinkholes when they finally collapsed.

"Do you think that's his real reason for being here?" A new wave of heat rushed through her when she remembered the almost predatory way Galerius had looked at her moments ago.

"That remains to be seen." Which meant her father would probably send a couple of men to tail him for the next few weeks to see if his story was true.

"Perhaps Claudia should find out for us," Asinius said as he strolled into the study.

"What are you suggesting?" She hoped the higher tone her voice would be mistaken for indignation at the prospect of having to keep the company of an Elymanian rather than her panic of what her body would do if he ever touched her again.

"I saw the way he looked at you during your little interlude in the courtyard." His sly smile made her stomach clench. "What's even more interesting is that you made no move to stop him."

"I was too stunned to react. He came up to me and kissed my hand as if he were my equal."

"And that flush that filled your cheeks?"

"Anger, dear brother, nothing more."

He laughed like he didn't believe her.

Her father rested his chin on his hands, his elbows propped up on the top of the desk. "Very interesting. You didn't tell me that, Claudia."

"You didn't ask, Father."

Asinius stole behind her, dragging his finger across the top of her back and sending cold shivers of warning through her body. "I'll bet we could get answers about Galerius's motives much faster if Claudia gave him a taste of what he obviously wanted."

Her spine stiffened. "How dare you suggest such a thing!

26

I'm a Pacilus, a member of one the purest Deizian families in the empire, and you want me to seduce an Elymanian?"

"Come now, don't tell me you wouldn't enjoy it," her brother taunted. "Besides, you've never had any problems spreading your legs before when Father asked you to do so."

His reminder of how many times she'd played her father's whore left her wanting to rush to the baths and scrub away the guilt that clung to her from her part in his plots. "This is different, and you know it. It's one thing to lay with a man who's of my class. It's another to lay with a man who's beneath me."

"Actually, you'd probably be beneath him if he fucked you."

Anger shot through her system, and she bolted from the chair and into her brother's face. "I can't believe you're insulting me, your own sister, like this. Father, I demand you make him apologize for his insults."

Instead of coming to her defense, her father replied, "He has a point."

Her muscles went lax as the outrage that had coiled them up vanished. "What was that?"

She wanted to smack the smug expression off Asinius's face as he took his place beside their father. "Don't pretend you didn't hear him, Claudia. He agrees that my idea has merit."

She gripped the edge of the desk to steady herself. *By the gods, I can't believe I'm hearing this. One minute, they think I'm washed up, and now they're ready to bring me back into their schemes, but only if I play the same role I'm always delegated to perform.*

"If you managed to capture Galerius's attention like Asinius suggests, it should be simple for you to discover his real reason for being here."

It was too much. Part of her wanted to march up to her room and write the most damning letter she could to the emperor, spilling all her family's secrets. But that would include damning herself for her part in her father's schemes. *No, there has to be a way around this. Think.*

She released the desk and leaned her hip against it, trying to appear calm and collected. If they were involving her in this, then maybe they'd be willing to include her in their plot to bring down the barrier, thus giving her the final information she needed to pass on to the emperor, or perhaps Galerius, and stop them. But in order to convince them of that, she had to play the part of the self-absorbed daughter. "And what would I get in return? Obviously, he's not marriage material."

Her father raised a brow at her question. "What would you suggest?"

"The villa in Padero."

Asinius's face turned a mottled shade of red. "But that's supposed to be my estate."

"On the contrary, dear brother, it belonged to my first husband." Pleasure, soothing as a warm bath, washed over her at seeing her brother's annoyance. "If I remember correctly, it came to our family when he died."

Now she had control of the conversation. If she was forced to lower herself like that, she'd get what she wanted in return—freedom from her father. Once she had that, then she would continue her plan to bring him down without fear of repercussions, without the constant worry of wondering when she'd be tossed off the cliffs for his pleasure, without being present when the emperor finally brought him down.

Hostilius ignored her brother, keeping his attention focused completely on her. "And what would you do in Padero if I gave you the villa?"

"I haven't decided. Maybe raise chickens. Live out the rest of my days in comfort. After all, didn't you say I'd outlived my usefulness to you?" She chose her last words with care, flinging the insult he'd given her months ago back in his face.

He frowned and leaned back in his chair. "It seems I was a bit hasty in my judgment."

It was the closest thing she'd ever get to an apology from him. She lifted her chin like the proud Deizian she was. "So, do we have a deal?"

Seconds ticked by as Hostilius weighed her demands. "If you manage to discover Galerius's true purpose for being here in Tivola before I do, I agree to give you the villa in Padero."

"Thank you," she said as a cry of outrage broke free from her spoiled younger brother's lips. This battle had been won, and she would revel in the glory of it later. "Just one concern, Father. How should I arrange a meeting with him? After all, it would not be fitting for me to call on him at his lodgings." Not to mention unsafe, considering her body's reaction to him.

"Leave that to me. When you see him, you know what to do."

She smiled and curtsied before she left the study. Her brother's protests echoed through the house, but she didn't care. She'd struck a deal with her father, and she was one step closer to gaining her freedom and perhaps unraveling his plan to bring down the barrier. But first, she had to figure out what to do with the riddle of Galerius Metellus.

5

Galerius looked at the address on the invitation one more time to make sure he was in the right place. Then he glanced back at the vast villa on the cliffs overlooking the sea. Yes, this was the right place, and that made his gut tighten in warning. He was walking into a trap, and he'd made the mistake of leaving all his favorite weapons at home. Instead of riding into battle in full armor with a gladius at his side, he was reduced to the small blade concealed in his bracer.

To any normal person, gaining an invitation to a dinner party at the home of a wealthy Deizian should be something celebrated, not feared. But Galerius was not a normal person. He'd witnessed too many intrigues during his time in the Legion. Deizians didn't mingle with people like him unless they wanted something. The fact that the invitation had arrived mere hours after his meeting with Hostilius didn't help matters. His gut urged him to leave before he fell into their clutches, but his mind resisted. Running away would only raise their suspicions.

He folded the invitation back up, smoothed his crisp linen tunic, and drove his chariot up the long driveway to the front door. A slave stationed up front dropped his jaw at the sight of a horseless chariot under the command of what appeared to be a normal Elymanian, as only Deizians had the magic to control such machines. But the taint of his Deizian blood was well hidden by his darker features. Only his eyes, which varied from grey to pale blue, betrayed the anomaly in his ancestry.

His eyes flickered along the torch-lit façade of the home, looking for any archers concealed in the shadows. The tension in his muscles refused to ease, despite the fact everything appeared to be as expected. He'd stood guard over the emperor at hundreds of these parties, and nothing seemed out of the ordinary. But this was the first time he'd been invited into the viper's den.

The invitation served as his ticket to be admitted into the party, and the privately hired guard at the door let him pass without question. A slave led him through the main atrium of the house with its marble columns and brightly painted frescos into a large room. Soft music drifted from the corner, barely audible from the din of dozens of conversations. The room was packed with mostly golden-haired Deizians, but the occasional darker head of a wealthy Elymanian dotted the scene like the black spots he saw when he stared at the sun too long. The party spilled out into the garden behind the room so the guests could enjoy the mild spring evening and perhaps escape the cloying scent of perfume that filled the air.

Galerius took a deep breath, never feeling more like an imposter than he did at the moment. As soon as he entered the room, another slave offered him a gold cup filled with wine. He took it to match the others in the room, but didn't drink the contents. He'd learned too much about poisons over the last few years and how easy they were to slip into food and drink.

"Ah, Galerius, there you are," Hostilius called from across the room like they were old friends. "Come over here. There are some people I'd like you meet."

The governor looked flawless dressed all in white. A purple stripe ran along the edge of the toga, signifying his rank as an imperial official. He stroked it with his fingers as Galerius wove his way through the crowd, as though he wanted to remind everyone around him of his ties to the emperor, but the effect was lost on Galerius. A snake was still a snake, no matter what he was dressed in, and if there was even a hint of truth to the mysterious dispatches, he needed to be on guard around Hostilius.

One by one, the governor introduced him to the other men in the circle. A Deizian lord, Decius, who was visiting from the next province. Galero, a retired general. Minius, an Elymanian who'd made his fortune in the shipping business. Nothing seemed to draw them all together other than their acquaintance with Hostilius.

"Weren't you the Captain of the Legion?" Galero asked.

"I was, but I resigned for personal reasons." He'd been practicing the story over and over again since he left Emona, hoping it sounded convincing.

"It seems he has issues with the emperor's choice in a wife." Hostilius took a sip of his wine and waited for the others to catch the meaning of his words.

Galerius took the opening and ran with it. If he was to gain the trust of the governor, he needed to play the part of a dissenter, no matter how much he admired the current empress. "I think he should have chosen a wife more fitting for his station."

Decius nodded. "You're not alone. He had his choice of any of our daughters, yet he chose an Alpirion to be his wife." He wrinkled his nose as he mentioned the empress's race.

"Even someone with the taint of Elymanian blood would have been more acceptable than a former slave." The general drank deeply from his cup as though it would wash the taste of having to call an Alpirion "empress" from his mouth.

"You have no idea how much trouble it's caused my business," Minius added. "My slaves have the ludicrous idea that they'll be set free soon. Getting them to do anything requires twice as many whips as before."

Galerius inwardly flinched as he listened to them, even as he outwardly tried to match their expressions of disgust. No one would dare speak of such matters in Emona, where word could reach the emperor's ears within minutes. But here, in another part of the empire, these men believed they could insult the empress freely. *What were they saying in other parts of the realm?* Suddenly, Azurha's fears became all too real. No wonder she and the emperor wished to keep her pregnancy secret. Once the heir was born, there was little that could be done to dispute his claim to the throne.

As if Hostilius were reading his thoughts, he said, "Let's pray to the gods that the empress never produces an heir. The taint of her blood in the child would doom all our children."

The general nodded like a puppet on the governor's strings. "Imagine if the child became emperor. Who would maintain the barriers?"

"Precisely." Decius exchanged his empty cup for a full one as a slave passed by them. "Only a Deizian can wield the magic that maintains the barrier. The purer the blood, the stronger the barrier. We can't afford anything less than a pure Deizian heir."

Galerius wanted to say they were wrong, that he'd witnessed the empress wield a power that was stronger than any Deizian magic, but he kept his mouth shut.

The conversation went in circles, but he drowned it out as he studied each of the men. Each of them had a reason to hate the emperor. Decius was from Gracchero, which was one of the places in the empire where the ore was mined. The Elymanian could transport the ore to Hostilius. The general, although retired, probably still had friends in the army and could control battalions of men, if needed. They all could conceivably fit into the plot, but they seemed more full of bluster than action. Only Hostilius seemed calculating enough to carry out a plan to see that a half-Alpirion child never had a claim to the throne.

Someone bumped against his shoulder, pulling him away from the conversation. Claudia paused mere inches from him, looking back at him over her shoulder. His mouth went dry as he soaked in her appearance.

She'd been beautiful yesterday morning in her simple gown, but tonight she was dressed as a temptress. Her sheer red silk gown hung loosely off her shoulders, exposing a wide expanse of the creamy skin along her back before it pooled above the swell of her buttocks. Her lips, painted a matching shade of red, called to him like a siren's song. And the open invitation in her eyes screamed pure sex. The corner of her mouth curled up into a smile before she turned and continued on her way through the crowd.

The blood rushed from his head straight to his cock. *Surely, that invitation wasn't meant for me?* He looked back at Hostilius and the other men in the group, but they seemed too engrossed in their conversation to have noticed her. *How could they have missed her, looking the way she did?* But he had been the one she bumped, not the others.

He scanned the room for her again and found her at the doorway to the gardens. She caught his gaze, her smile widening, erasing any doubt that she had set her sights on him and him alone. Then, even so subtly, she crooked her finger, beckoning him to follow her.

The ache in his cock intensified to the point where he ignored the nagging feeling his gut. He had to follow her and find out why she targeted him out of all the men in the room. "Excuse me, gentlemen. I need a breath of fresh air."

He placed his still-full cup on a table as he followed Claudia into the dimly lit garden, hoping he wouldn't lose her in the shadows. The sea breeze cooled his desire enough for him to realize his odds. Claudia was Hostilius's daughter and possible accomplice. Most likely, she was trying to seduce him away from the conversation before he put the pieces of the plot together. However, she also could possibly be the informant, and the invitation was her way of drawing him alone so she could feed him the key information he needed to stop her father.

A flutter of red caught his attention, and he went deeper into the gardens where the only illumination was the light of the full moon. The waves crashed below, mingling with the now-distant sounds of the party. He strained in the dim light for any sign of Claudia, but saw nothing. His stomach tightened.

"Looking for someone?" a rich female voice asked from his left. There, leaning against the wall of a small mausoleum, stood Claudia.

Galerius swallowed past the lump forming in his throat and approached her. "Possibly."

Her chuckle mocked him. "For a soldier, I expected a far different answer from you."

"Meaning?"

"Usually, you would know your target before pursuing it." The tip of her tongue darted out between her red lips, drawing slowly across as if she were licking honey off of them.

A groan formed deep inside his chest as he watched her, wishing he were the one licking her lips instead. He'd been around plenty of beautiful women. In the last few months, he'd visited the most renowned brothels in Emona. But no woman had had this effect on him. It took every inch of his self-control to keep from tasting those lips for himself. "Perhaps, but sometimes the discovery of a new target can be just as rewarding."

Her blue eyes searched him from head to toe, lingering on the ridge forming under his tunic. He couldn't hide his desire for her. He was a fly trapped in the Black Widow's web, but he could still resist her charms if he needed to. And yet she stayed cool, distant, continuing to lean on the marble wall rather than ensnaring him in her embrace the way an experienced whore would.

At last, she sighed. "What are you doing here, Galerius?"

The tension eased from his shoulders. He took a step toward her, his confidence growing. Whatever she was, she wasn't a threat.

Yet.

"You tell me, or was your invitation directed toward someone else?"

"Are you really so inexperienced with women that you would have to ask that?" She shifted so her dress strained against her breasts, making him want to cup them in his hands and run his thumbs over the stiff peaks of her nipples.

"Not inexperienced." His voice dropped to a low growl. If she only knew how much he wanted to show her the realm of his experience. "Just trying to figure out the best way to approach the situation."

"Always the soldier. What is it they say? Once a member of the Legion, always a member of the Legion?"

He froze when she mentioned his former affiliation with the Legion. This game of seduction was turning into cat and mouse, and he wondered what kind of claws she had hidden beneath that flimsy excuse for a dress. "So they say, but as you can see, I'm not a member of the Legion now."

That got her moving. She pushed off the wall and came toward him, her head slightly cocked to the side. She was testing him as much as he was testing her, inching closer but still ready to flee should he threaten her. She reached for his right hand, turning it palm side up, and traced the tattoo on the inside of his wrist with her cool fingers. "And yet you will always bear the mark of the Legion."

"Is that why you had me follow you? To ask me about my tattoo?" *To find out if I was still working for the Emperor?* He dared not speak the final question.

She raised her eyes, so very blue in the moonlight, and watched him. "What are you doing here?"

Her fingers still lay over his wrist, and he suspected she probably felt the jump in his pulse caused by her question. She was trying to pry the truth from him, but she wouldn't get it. "I'm here because I followed you."

Claudia shook her head, causing a stray lock of her golden hair to slide down her check. "That's not what I meant, and you know it."

She was close enough now for him to feel the heat of her skin and inhale the clean scent of lemons and lavender that rose from it. He brushed a stray lock of hair behind her ears, not missing the way her body trembled at his touch. "Then perhaps you should phrase your question differently."

Annoyance flashed across her face before she could regain her seductress's mask. She trailed her fingers down his arm, pausing to massage tiny circles into his palm. Her breasts grazed his chest as she asked, "What do you want with me, Galerius?"

"I think that's quite obvious." He wrapped his arm across her waist, pulling her against him so that his erection pressed into the softness of her stomach. "Unless you're so inexperienced with men that you would have to ask that."

Her lips parted, either from surprise or outage, but that was all he saw of them before he covered them with his own. She stiffened, resisted for moment, and then finally yielded to his kiss. His tongue delved into her mouth. He tasted the sweetness of the fresh berries she had used to stain her lips, followed by the rich wine she'd drank at dinner.

He'd wanted to scare her with the kiss, to throw her off balance and perhaps even earn a slap in the face for his impudence. Instead, Claudia clung to him, grinding against him to the same intoxicating rhythm of her tongue until he became lost under her spell. They stumbled backward until they slammed against the cold marble wall of the mausoleum, but that didn't quell the fierceness of her kiss, the way her fingers dug into his shoulders as if he were the only thing keeping from falling down onto the rocks below.

Galerius would never question Claudia's experience with men again. She knew how to touch him, kiss him, tease him until he was ready to beg on his knees for sex. But he didn't. When he finally broke away from her lips, he continued along her smooth cheek, nibbling on her earlobe. She inhaled sharply before releasing her breath in a throaty moan that made his cock long to be buried deep inside her.

While he planted a trail of kisses along her neck, his hands fought with the low neckline of her dress, tearing the thin silk and finally freeing one the breasts he'd longed to hold minutes ago. Just like he'd imagined, it fit perfectly in his hand. A flick of his thumbs across her nipple produced another one of her moans. A shiver of desire rippled down his spine. He kept waiting for her to tell him to stop, to shove him away even as he raked his teeth along the taut peak. Instead, she threaded her fingers through this hair, holding him prisoner, wordlessly begging him to continue.

He drew her breast into his mouth, swirling his tongue around the center and listening to her breath hitch when he sucked harder on it. A new scent overwhelmed the clean citrus notes he noted before. Something raw and primitive. Something he'd smelled and tasted before, but never as strong as this. Desire.

But what troubled him was that he wasn't certain if it was coming from him or her.

He pulled his attention away from her breasts, seeking her lips once again. The same hunger greeted him as before. The Barbarians could have broken through the barrier and started killing everyone around them, and he would not have cared less. The only thing he cared about was soothing the aching need building up inside him.

"What do you want, Claudia?" he asked, his lips less a breath apart from hers. He pressed against her so she could feel how hard she made him. "This?"

She answered him with a kiss, catching his lower lip between her teeth. He was used to being the aggressor. He was usually the one driving the sexual encounter with women. And yet her mouth plundered his, her leg wrapped around his thigh, her pelvis arched to tease his cock with the place it longed to go. Every time he fought to regain control, she answered him back with her own attack. But the soldier in him refused to be dominated.

He tugged up the skirt of her dress, caressing the silky skin of her thighs. With one finger, he grazed the opening of her sex.

She broke away from the kiss, struggling for air, wrapping her leg more tightly around him.

At last he was in control again. He ventured deeper into

the warm, wet folds. "Is this what you want, Claudia?"

When she didn't reply, he added another finger and pressed deeper. A hiss escaped her lips, but still, she said nothing. While his fingers stroked her in a way his cock envied, his thumb massaged the tiny nub above it. She whimpered, digging her nails into his shoulders, but still refused to answer him.

As much as he wanted her, as much as he wanted to fuck her until they both collapsed with exhaustion, he refused to enter her until she conceded that she wanted him as much as he wanted her. "Tell what you want, Claudia."

"Can't tell by now?"

"Yes, you're all wet and hungry for me. You want me inside you. You want me to make come harder than you've ever come in your life. And I'll give it to you. But first, I need to hear it from your lips."

She caught him in another searing kiss that nearly stole his breath away. If this continued, he'd come before he had a chance to enter her. She challenged him, refusing to surrender, but he wasn't as easily broken as some of her earlier conquests had been.

She tugged his tunic up and blindly searched for his cock, her lips still toying with his. Her fingers traced the throbbing length of it, from the base to the tip, smearing the drop of pre-cum over the head. Now, it was his turn to moan. *By the gods, which of us will break first?*

A deep, throaty laugh vibrated from her throat. "No, you want me. You want to be inside me. You want me to make you come harder than you've ever come in your life."

He no longer cared about who won this battle. He just needed release from the pent-up desire raging inside him. He pulled her up into his arms, holding her by her buttocks so the tip of his cock brushed against the opening of her sex. "Then say yes."

Claudia wrapped her legs around his waist to pull him deeper into her, but he refused to budge. First she had to admit she wanted him.

"Stop teasing me." Her voice cracked under the weight of her desire. Her hips bucked in his hands, coating the head of his cock with her wetness, but he resisted the temptation to enter her. Her breath quickened, her lips tore at his, but he remained as still as a statue until she finally whispered, "I need you now."

Once she'd given her permission, he plunged into her with one swift stroke. For a moment, he forgot to breathe. She was so wet, so hot, so tight, he could have sworn he'd died and gone to the paradise of the afterlife.

***

After all the buildup, all the teasing, all the foreplay, Claudia's body demanded release. Yet her sex betrayed her. It tightened around Galerius's cock, embracing it like a familiar lover. She had expected a moment of sharp pain from the way he filled her completely, but instead, another low moan of longing rose from her throat.

His warm breath tickled the edge of her collarbone, followed by a kiss. "My sentiments exactly."

"Shut up and fuck me, damn it."

Her cheeks burned red when she realized what she'd just said. She was a Deizian, a noblewoman of the purest blood, and all she wanted was to have this Elymanian thrust into her over and over again like she was some common whore on the street. Thankfully, she'd chosen a place far away from prying eyes and listening ears.

He chuckled and withdrew his cock until only the tip rested inside her, leaving her feeling empty. "Is that what you want, Claudia?"

By the gods, the way he said her name, so hoarse with desire, almost had her coming right then and there. She wiggled her hips, impatient with desire. "Yes."

He caught her lips and kissed her as he plowed into her again. She gasped from the sheer pleasure-pain of it, the sound lost under his primitive growl. She dug her nails into his back, holding on for dear life as he slid into her again.

Her husbands had never been like this. They had been

older men closer to her father's age, wealthy and well established politically. She'd coyly resisted, as was expected of a woman of her standing, before submitting to them. She'd pretended to be pleasured as they pounded into her over and over, secretly praying the whole time they'd finish soon so she could push them off of her and be done with her wifely duties.

Galerius was different. He was all strength and muscle, a solider set out to conquer her. He held her against the wall with ease while he continued his powerful thrusts, reaching into the deepest recesses of her sex. His teeth nipped along the sensitive areas of her neck, shoulders, and breasts. Every aspect of his actions was rough and crude. Every motion was meant to show his dominance over her.

And she loved every second of it.

She savored the exquisite friction of his cock against her inner walls. She relished the way his strong fingers massaged her buttocks. She delighted in the way her flesh stung from his kisses, wanting his lips back to that spot as soon as they left to explore another part of her body. It all came to together like the music of master musicians, with each stroke sending out waves of pleasure that rolled through her body.

She wanted to shout orders to reestablish her authority over him. *More. Harder. Faster.* But her lungs burned for air, and her breath came as sharp and quick as his thrusts. She barely felt the cold marble of the wall against her back compared to the heat between them. Her lower belly grew tighter and tighter, aching, begging for release. Her body was stretched to the point of breaking. She was close—so close to crossing into the unknown. Only fear kept her from giving into it.

"Don't fight it, Claudia."

He had controlled her like an archer did a crossbow, and his command acted like a trigger. Something inside her snapped. A cry broke free from her lips, but she barely heard it from the throbbing of the blood in her ears. Her body refused to follow her commands, clenching and releasing of its own accord. A shudder formed deep within her sex, growing stronger and stronger, pulsating ecstasy with each throb of her heart.

"Yes," he said, his thrusts growing harder and more erratic. "Yes, y—" His voice broke, and his body grew stone still except for the rhythmic twitching of his cock inside her. Several seconds passed before he released his breath in a groan and fell against her. They slid down against the wall until she sat in his lap, with him still fully sheathed inside her.

Claudia had no idea how much time passed as they struggled to catch their breath. It could have been seconds or hours, but she didn't care. She pressed her cheek against his and closed her eyes, completely drained from the new sensations he had awakened in her. None of her prior lovers had ever made her come like that.

Galerius ran his fingers up and down her bare back, delicately tracing swirls along her flesh. *Such a contrast with the way he fucked me.*

That thought, which should have matched the bliss that enveloped her body, jerked her back to reality. She'd just been fucked by an Elymanian in the middle of a garden. She'd allowed him to take her in a half-clothed, rushed, crude manner.

And what was worse, she had enjoyed it.

Her chin trembled, matching the staccato movements of her muscles as she tried to move them. She planted her palms against the hard muscles of his chest and shoved him away. The chill of disgust replaced the warmth of fulfillment that had had hummed through her veins moments before. *What have I become?*

She wanted to hurl insults to answer the look of bewilderment on his face. She wanted to lie and tell him he was only mediocre, a mere shadow of her former lovers. She wanted to tell him this would never happen again, but she feared her tongue would betray her and beg him to take her once more.

So she gave him only silence as she stood and fled the scene.

Her dress barely covered her breasts as she ran through the garden, the torn silk rubbing against her sensitive nipples and reminding her of how his tongue had teased them. Her hair tumbled free from the remaining pins, grazing her shoulder and the places where his kisses had left her skin raw. Her cheeks burned at her disheveled appearance, and she paused when she came within view of the house. She couldn't let anyone see her like this.

She stayed in the shadows, holding her dress closed while she hugged the side of the house, and searched for her father's litter when she reached the front. She would send it back once she got home, once she washed away the evidence of how far she'd fallen.

Someone grabbed her from behind and twirled her around. "Going somewhere?" Asinius asked.

Claudia wrenched her arm free. "Yes, I'm going home."

"My, you work quickly." Her brother closed the space between them, leaning his nose near her bare shoulder and sniffing. "You even smell like him."

A shiver coursed down her spine, and she stepped back, eager to put some space between them.

"So, how was it, being fucked by an Elymanian? To spread your legs for someone as low as him? Did you enjoy it?"

She slapped his face, earning a scowl in return. "I did what Father asked of me."

"Don't pretend it was all done in dutiful sacrifice for our family." He circled her, sliding his fingers through her fallen hair. "I watched everything."

Nausea rolled through her stomach, and her fingers went numb.

"I saw the way you coaxed him into following you into the garden, the way you trapped him with your feminine wiles. I watched how he violated you over and over again. And I heard how much you enjoyed it." He chuckled. "I'm surprised the whole party didn't hear how much you enjoyed being fucked by Galerius."

Revulsion clawed at her skin, making her feel even more unclean than before. She fought the urge to scrub her arms right there. "I never realized what a sick pervert you were."

43

"And you're not?" Asinius taunted. "Come now, this is all business. We both want the villa in Padero. I'm just making sure you earn it."

She waited until he stood in front of her again before saying, "Make no mistake. That villa will be mine."

"And I will never let you forget what you did to get it." He retreated a few feet, fading into the shadows. "Sleep well, Claudia."

She waited until she knew she was alone before resting her flushed forehead against the cool walls of the house. Tonight had not gone according to plan. She'd expected have Galerius wrapped around her finger and spilling his guts by the time she kissed him. She'd always been able to keep her wits about her, even in the middle of sex. She'd never lost control of herself like that. She'd never let her desire override her control.

And yet, from the moment his lips touched hers, everything had shattered. What she'd thought had been desire seemed like the flicker of a candle compared to the raging inferno that had engulfed her. He'd practically had her begging him to fuck her.

Maybe I need to come up with a different plan. One that doesn't involve me falling into the same trap again.

But all she could think about was how much she wanted him inside her again. She clenched her teeth together in frustration. She needed to leave before she sought him out again. Or worse, before he found her.

The litter carriers seemed to move slower than usual, and she wished for the swiftness of a horse, or better yet, a Deizian chariot to whisk her far away from the party. When she entered the house, it seemed the eyes of every slave were fixed on her. She ignored them, marching up the stairs to her room with her chin held high. The last thing she needed was to show them any sign of weakness.

Even after she closed the doors to her bedroom, she didn't falter from her act. "Draw me a bath right now, Zavi."

Her personal slave nodded, her dark eyes wider than

usual, but leapt into action as though this was a common request. From the other side of the door, Zavi ordered several slaves to bring up buckets of water. When she returned, she kept her gaze on the floor. "The bath will be cold, my lady."

"The tub is made from ore. I can heat it."

Claudia retreated to her dressing room, preferring to hide from any more prying eyes. She sat in front of her mirror and soaked in her appearance. Her golden hair fell in loose waves over her shoulders, barely disguising the red welts along her neck and collarbone that would undoubtedly form bruises by the morning. Her lips were full and swollen, and the red color she'd carefully applied to them this evening left faint smears around her mouth. Her dress was torn beyond repair. But even if the evidence of tonight's liaison would fade, the memory of it would be burned into her mind forever.

"My lady," Zavi said timidly from the doorway, "your bath is ready."

Claudia left the red silk dress in a puddle on the floor before she entered her bedchamber. A stream of magic flowed from her fingers when she touched the side of the tub, sending a current of liquid fire through the water. Steam rose from the placid surface within seconds, and she eased into the warm water.

"Can I get you anything else, my lady?"

Claudia remembered how he came inside her, and a new fear stole over her. She may have played his whore tonight, but she refused to conceive Galerius's child. "Bring me a cup of pomrutin tea."

Her slave left to fetch it, leaving Claudia alone with her thoughts. The warm water cleansed away his scent, but the evidence of his touch lingered, no matter how much she scrubbed with the sponge. Her sex remained sore and swollen, still longing for the thick cock that had filled it earlier. She ran her finger over the tender nub inside. Her body shivered in response just as it had when he'd touched her there.

She closed her eyes and leaned back in the tub, slowly

increasing the pressure as she stroked it. She tried to picture another man—any man—but all her imagination could conjure was a man with dark brown hair and slate-grey eyes. A man with a soldier's build. A man with strong hands and a tattoo etched on the inside of his wrist.

She rubbed harder, faster, until her body jerked to a climax. "Galerius," she moaned as came, her fingers still stroking her clitoris as though he were the one bringing her pleasure. She could almost see the fire in his eyes as he watched her come. The flames of his desire licked at her skin, searing it, and her mind passed into a void where she all she was conscious of was him. Her body felt weightless in the water, and she soared on the ecstasy of her orgasm.

Eventually, the cold water of the tub pulled her back to reality. Her arms and legs hung heavy and useless from exhaustion. She refused to open her eyes for fear she'd find him absent from her room. Or worse, that her slave had witnessed her moment of weakness. When she cracked open one eye, she was alone.

A soft knock echoed through the stillness of her room a moment before her slave came in with a steaming cup. "Your tea, my lady."

Claudia scarfed it down, ignoring how it singed her tongue and throat. The sooner she erased any memory of tonight, the better. Lingering on Galerius would only destroy her from the inside out, creating weakness where she needed strength.

She stood and allowed her slave to dry her off and rub her favorite scented oil over her skin. The lemon and lavender soothed her frazzled mind and eased her tension. She could finally replay the events of her meeting with Galerius without letting her emotions distract her. He kept asking her what she wanted, echoing her question. *Does he suspect me of working for my father? Or has he discovered I'm the writer of the dispatches, despite my best effort to keep my identity hidden?*

By the time she crawled into bed, she knew what she had

to do. She could still find out Galerius's motives and discover if he was her ally. If not, then she could send a letter to the emperor himself and retreat to the villa in Padero before the emperor's true servants arrived to stop her father's plot. She needed to make sure she avoided him in the process, though. One more interlude could prove fatal to them both, especially if he managed to wrench a confession from her.

6

Galerius groaned as the sunlight poured into his bedroom. Sleep had eluded him all night, and when he did manage to drift away, his dreams were haunted by a woman with golden hair and piercing blue eyes. *By the gods, what kind of spell did Claudia cast over me?*

He threw his arm over his face to block out the light. The scent of lemon and lavender tickled his nose, and a new wave of desire washed over him. He remembered how tight and wet she felt around him. His cock hardened, reminding him how much he had enjoyed fucking the arrogant Deizian princess last night. She wanted him as much as he wanted her, was more responsive than any woman he'd been with before, and had made him come so hard his balls still ached from it.

Then his memory flashed to the look of horror on her face before she shoved him away, and he knew he'd crossed the line somewhere last night. He racked his brain, searching for what he'd done wrong. He hadn't forced himself on her. He'd made sure she gave her permission before he entered her. He hadn't revealed his true purpose for being in Tivola. He hadn't murmured something foolish in the heat of the moment.

His lips curled up into a smirk. Maybe she was horrified to learn an Elymanian like him could satisfy her better than any of her purebred Deizian lovers.

He forced her out of his mind as he crawled out of bed and got dressed. He wasn't here to indulge in the pleasures of the flesh. He needed to find out what Hostilius was planning, and trying to get information from Claudia had proven to be a dead end. A fun one, but still a dead end. He wouldn't be surprised if her father had sent her to distract him so he wouldn't overhear what his plan was. One thing was for certain—the emperor had plenty of enemies here.

Or to be more accurate, the empress did.

He lifted the loose floorboard where he'd hidden the letters and the maps Azurha had given him, and reviewed them once again. The most logical place to start would be to find the secret entrance to the governor's villa. If he could find unrestricted access to it, he could find the clues he needed.

What is Hostilius planning on doing with all that ore? Creating a fleet of airships to attack the palace in Emona? But there was no place to hide such a giant fleet along the coast without it being seen. His ties with the general meant he could possibly have the army at his command, but most of the soldiers in the empire were Elymanian and had no use for the ore.

Galerius rubbed his hands along the stubble on his cheeks. Nothing about this made sense, and the only person who seemed willing to share anything with him was the mysterious author of the letters. If the gods smiled upon him, the author would magically appear at his doorstep and reveal everything. But the gods rarely took any pity on him.

The sun was almost at its zenith in the sky by the time Galerius stepped outside onto the crowded streets of Tivola. A ripple of warning wormed up his spine, making the hair on the back of his neck stand on end. He searched the crowd for any hostile expressions, any threats, but saw nothing. He adjusted his pack to allow him easy access to his knife if needed, and headed south on foot.

Today, he dressed like a simple tradesman, hoping to blend in with everyday citizens of the city, but feeling of unease grew stronger with every step he took. Despite his efforts not to stand out, he was being watched. He pulled up to a produce cart and pretended to inspect the apples for sale, scanning the streets. The faces blurred together into an unfamiliar blob. He moved further down the street and repeated his inspection at a baker's stand, but again, saw nothing. Whoever was following him was almost as experienced at concealment as he was.

As he haggled over the price of a loaf with the baker, he ran through his options. He could try to elude his tail, but that would only alert whoever was having him followed that he was on to them. Or he could hold off on exploring the mine shaft that led to the villa for a few more days and hope his tail would grow bored and move on. He fished a coin out of his pocket to exchange for the warm bread in his hand and decided the price losing a few days would be worth it if he didn't blow his cover.

Today, instead of investigating Hostilius, he would play along with his story of looking for a new sapphire mine.

***

Claudia let the wind from the sea tousle her hair and cool her skin as she stood in the gardens, avoiding the edge of the cliffs. Despite her best efforts, her thoughts kept returning to Galerius. She pulled her palla tighter around her arms to erase the memory of his strong hands against her skin. He was here in Tivola for a reason, and she hoped it was to stop her father. She just needed to summon her courage and take the next step to find out.

Bestius was leaving her father's study when she entered the villa. Instead of heading to her room like she'd planned, she changed her course to find out why. "Who are you having followed now, Father?" she asked as she entered the room her father rarely vacated these days.

"What makes you think that?" he replied, never looking up from his desk.

"Come now, you only have one use for Bestius." She settled into the chair across from him and twirled a loose strand of hair while she discreetly scanned the papers scattered across his desk. Every time she managed to sneak into the study when her father was absent, all the papers had been secured, but any information she gleaned would only work to her advantage.

"Very well, if you must know, I sent Bestius to follow Galerius." He finally lifted his eyes and drilled his accusing gaze into her. "I had been hoping you would be able to discover his motives for me."

Resentment curled in her muscles, creating knots in her shoulders. "Who says I haven't?"

That sparked her father's interest. "Yes, Asinius told me you were successful in seducing him. But since you failed to tell me anything this morning, I assumed you had learned nothing more than the size of his cock."

She winced at his crude accusation and fought to keep the redness from creeping up into her cheeks. Thankfully, her voice remained calm and steady as she said, "Patience, Father. You of all people know there's an art to what I do."

"And what are your plans for Galerius?"

"I've given him a taste of ecstasy. Now that he knows what I can give, he'll be back for more. He'll practically be begging to be with me again." Desire pounded through her veins, tempered by only the slightest taint of doubt. Would he want her again after last night? "And once I have him on his knees, I'll use my most charming form of interrogation to get answers from him."

"Meaning you'll tease him until he tells you what I need to know."

If I don't give into him first again. "Naturally."

Hostilius clasped his hands on his chest and leaned back in his chair, his piercing blue eyes focused on her.

Claudia forced her emotions deeper inside and gave him a confident grin. She needed her father to believe she was his ally, not secretly trying to undermine his plot to destroy the emperor. Soon, she would be free of him. She just hoped it wouldn't involve surrendering to the unsettling power Galerius wielded over her.

"When do you plan to engage him again?"

She shrugged. "I haven't decided. I figured I'd give him a day or two to ruminate over our little interlude, let his desire for me reach the breaking point."

"And then?"

She let her fingers trail along cheek, reminding her father she wasn't a withered crone. Her beauty had won her three husbands, after all. "He'll come to me, and I'll have him in the palm of my hand."

To his credit, her father chuckled. "That sure of yourself, eh?"

"Have I ever failed you?"

The mirth faded from his face. "Yes, you have."

Panic swelled in her throat. She was so close winning him over. "Just once, and that's only because that Alpirion had usurped my place by bewitching the emperor."

"I need to know why Galerius Metellus is here, and if you want that villa, then you need to make sure you find out soon. I've already suffered enough setbacks." He turned his attention back to his papers, a sharp dismissal.

She stood and walked out of the office with her shoulders squared, never giving him a clue as to how rattled she was on the inside. Yes, she needed to know why Galerius was here, to know if he was friend of foe. And she needed to outsmart her father in the process.

"Zavi, send Kafi to me," she said as soon as she entered the secure confines of her room. Her slave had dashed out of the door before Claudia sat at her desk.

She pulled a sheet of paper from her drawer and wrote in the same non-descript block letters she'd used in her prior messages.

You're being followed. Be on guard for a large Elymanian man with burn scars on his left hand.

Kafi arrived as she was sealing the letter with a bit of hot wax. The young Alpirion boy was just shy of thirteen summers, but she'd come to value his speed and cunning. He knelt before her. "You sent for me, my lady?"

"Are you familiar with the villa that belonged to Pontus?"

The boy's dark eyes lit up. "The one a block from the Via Lupas?"

Claudia wrinkled her nose. She'd forgotten that it was so close to the road lined with brothels. Perhaps Galerius would be satisfying his sexual needs there instead of coming to her. Her jaw involuntarily tightened at the thought of him sharing another woman's bed, much to her distress. "Yes, that's the one."

She stood and handed him the letter. "I want you to deliver this to the man staying there, but I need absolute discretion from you. Do not be seen."

He nodded, hiding the letter under his rough tunic. "Will there be anything else, my lady?"

She hesitated, checking the room to make sure they were alone before adding, "Perhaps."

Kafi grinned, his white teeth a stark contrast to his coppery brown skin. He jumped at any chance she gave him to leave the house. Not that she blamed him. Her errands were considerably kinder than any task her father's steward would assign him. But he was her slave, not her father's, a part of the small inheritance she'd managed to retain after the death of her first husband, and she'd always felt an urge to protect him.

"Do you think you could follow the man staying there? He's a tall Elymanian, built like a soldier, with grey eyes."

He nodded again, his smile widening. "The man who came to visit your father the other day?"

"Yes, the very one." She reached into her purse and retrieved a few coins. "I need to know where he goes, what he does, every day. Here is some money to buy some food from the street vendors." She paused, pressing the coins into his outstretched palm and waiting until his gaze met hers. "Again, I cannot tell you how important it is that you are not seen."

"I understand."

"Good." She released him and backed away. "I expect a full report of his activities tomorrow evening. In the meantime, deliver that letter."

He bowed as he stood, keeping his head low until he reached the door.

Claudia exhaled. This was the best plan. She could find out what Galerius's true purpose was without risking another loss of self-control. She'd discover the truth with falling into his arms and feeling his lips crushing hers, drawing out the longing she'd kept buried for so long.

But when she glanced at her reflection in the mirror, her flushed cheeks betrayed her. Despite what her mind cautioned, her body still craved Galerius.

7

Galerius stepped outside his villa, pretending to adjust his pack while he scanned the streets. The crawling sensation on his neck was more intense today than yesterday, and it all had to do with the letter that had been slipped under his front door last night. Everything matched the previous letters—the paper, the ink, the writing. And the warning.

He didn't know what bothered him more, the fact he was being followed or the fact his mysterious informant knew he was here in Tivola. He'd tried to keep his arrival quiet, choosing to stay in a villa in town instead of one of the more ostentatious manors along the coast. Therefore, his informant would have noticed him in only two places—Hostilius's home or the party the other night. If it was the latter, then his list of suspects was multiplied by at least a score.

Nothing seemed out of the ordinary, so he ventured south again, hoping he could shake his tail long enough to explore the shaft that led to Hostilius's villa. Like yesterday, he pretended to inspect the wares of the various vendors in his neighborhood market. Every few booths, he'd pause and look for the man described in the letter. It wasn't until he reached the end of the square that he caught a glimpse of a man ducking between booths a few feet behind him.

The sense of unease doubled, spreading from Galerius's

neck into his shoulders. He didn't need to see the burns on the man's hand to confirm that this was the man he'd been warned about. Years of following suspects in Emona had taught him to recognize a tail.

He moved out of the market and toward the shafts on the edge of town. Although the man tried to match his footsteps, Galerius heard the subtle off-time slap of leather sandals on the cobblestone street. He wrapped his hand around the hilt of the dagger sheathed in the shoulder strap of his pack, his muscles tightening and the rest of his senses on high alert. The letter said he was being followed, but that didn't mean the tail wouldn't attack if they were caught alone.

The winding maze of city streets led to an open field. The warm spring breeze ruffled the tall grass, parting it from time to time to reveal the stout wooden beams that announced the openings to the abandoned sapphire mines. A century ago, these fields would have been as crowded as the market by miners, both slave and free. Now, only the occasional orange striped bird seemed to call this place home.

He stopped and leaned against the one of the frames of the shafts. The sound of loose pebbles scattering came from behind him, followed by the rustling of the grass. But when he looked in that direction, he saw nothing.

Galerius dropped his sack and drew in a deep breath. Another day lost. At least he could get a feel for these mines before exploring the one leading to Hostilius. And if he found his tail tomorrow, he'd confront him.

***

"Tell me what happened today," Claudia commanded as soon as Kafi reported to her room. A stern glance at her maid implied she would decide which dress to wear after this conversation, and Zavi backed away, closing the doors behind her.

"I'm pretty sure he spotted Bestius at the market."

She narrowed her eyes. "Pretty sure, or certain?"

"Almost certain." But the way the boy's dark brows

bunched together told her he was hiding something else.

"Anything else you wish to tell me?" She leaned forward, dangling her purse from her fingers. This was the third day she'd had Kafi follow Galerius, and the reports had always been the same. Lots of indications that Galerius knew he was being followed. Lots of days spent exploring abandoned mine shafts. The only thing that gave her a glimmer of hope was that the shafts he'd explored all seemed to cluster around the one shaft that led here. Of course, the earthquake last summer had closed it off, making it no longer an escape route from the villa in a time of siege. It also meant that no one could sneak in that way anymore. If Galerius was looking for it, he was going to be sorely disappointed.

"He managed to shake Bestius."

Claudia sucked in a breath. How long would he keep that bit of news from her father? "He didn't discover you, did he?"

Kafi laughed. "I'm smarter than Bestius."

"And smaller, too." The wiry youth was perfect as her messenger and spy. She reached into her purse and pulled out another coin. "For your cleverness."

He took the coin, his wide eyes already calculating how much more he would need to save for his freedom. Some Alpirions were able to buy their freedom if their masters agreed to it. Others gained their freedom when their masters died and bequeathed pieces of jewelry to them in their wills. But all freed slaves needed the required gold jewelry that proclaimed their status and kept them off the auction block.

She studied him. If he proved useful in helping her be rid of her father, she might just reward him with his freedom. "Continue the good work, Kafi, and I look forward to your report tomorrow."

He bowed his head at her dismissal and crossed paths with his mother as she came into Claudia's room. "Be careful with him, my lady. He's too smart for his own good."

Claudia laughed. Zavi didn't know how spot on she was. "Did I hear correctly that Father will be entertaining a guest for dinner tonight?"

"You did indeed, my lady. Atius Cotta will be dining with you."

A groan rolled up her throat. The man became insufferable when he had arranged a marriage between his daughter and the future emperor several years ago, constantly gloating how he'd succeeded where her father had failed. Of course, Lucia had been stupid enough to be caught in the arms of her another man, prompting Sergius to divorce her. In true Deizian fashion, she'd chosen to drown herself rather than face the stigma of the divorce. Since then, Cotta griped how Sergius practically killed his daughter, and now that the emperor had married an Alpirion, Claudia was certain a majority of the dinner conversation would revolve around that.

"I'll wear my pale green dress tonight," she decided.

Zavi wrinkled her nose. "But it's so plain, my lady. Your father would want you to wear something finer with a guest for dinner tonight."

"That's precisely the idea. I have no wish to offend Cotta when he is still grieving for his daughter." Or attract his attention. The last thing she needed was for her father to marry her off to one of his decrepit friends.

The memory of how strong and virile Galerius was in the garden last week flashed through her mind, sending a flush from her core to her face. If she were married to a man like him, she'd have no need for a lover.

"Are you too warm, my lady?" Zavi opened one of the windows, bathing the room in the cool sea breeze and dousing Claudia's momentary passion. "Is this better?"

"Yes, thank you." She stood still as Zavi removed her day dress and draped silk the color of new spring grass over her shoulders. Why did Galerius keep ambushing her thoughts that way?

Maybe I should arrange another meeting with him. She closed her eyes and imagined how it would feel to sneak him into her bed, to be caught between the cool silk sheets and the warm weight of his body as he made love to her until the first sun broke above the horizon, and drowned out the purple glow of the distant supernova that lit the night sky. His stubbled cheek against hers would provide a rough contrast to the way his cock would slide in and out of her sex, slowly building to the climax that would leave her shaking and breathless.

"Are you sure you're well, my lady?"

Zavi jerked her from her reverie like a splash of cold water. Claudia rubbed her arms as if it would erase the memory of his touch. "What makes you ask that?"

"You've been acting different since the night you asked for that bath. I wouldn't wonder if you caught an ague from bathing so late."

She'd caught something that night, all right. But she needed to purge Galerius Metellus from her system if she wanted her plan to succeed. "I'll be fine."

Her reflection argued otherwise. The bright spots in her cheeks still lingered, giving her a fevered look. She drew in a slow, steady breath. If she wanted to glean any information from her father, she needed to appear calm and bored. Then they wouldn't notice how she hung on every word they said, hoping to find the final piece of evidence that would condemn her father.

"Is my harp in the dining room?" she asked, smoothing her dress.

"I don't think so, my lady, but I can see that it's brought in for you." Zavi added a comb to Claudia's hair. "Planning on playing tonight?"

"Yes, I think our guest will enjoy some soothing music." And it will give me the perfect excuse to linger in the room after dinner.

***

Claudia stifled a yawn as she descended the stairs. Last night had been a long, drawn-out affair, but at least it was fruitful. Whatever her father was planning, Atius Cotta was involved with it. Other than that, she knew little more than she

59

did when she went down to dinner. And judging by the way her father kept his voice low so it blended in with the harmony with her harp, he wanted to keep her from learning anything.

She frowned and paused, clutching the banister until her fingers blanched. *Please don't let him suspect me.*

She managed to swallow her fears before Asinius saw her. "Ah, there you are. I thought you would sleep well past midday."

"I was told Father wanted me at breakfast," Claudia replied as she continued down the stairs.

"Yes, he did." In an uncharacteristic show of manners, he offered her his arm. "Let's not keep him waiting."

It took her a moment to realize that Asinius was steering her outside rather than toward the dining room. Her pulse doubled. "Are we dining on the terrace today?"

"Yes. Father thought Cotta might like a little entertainment with breakfast."

Her throat constricted. She knew what kind of entertainment her father enjoyed while dining on the terrace. She only hoped she wasn't the final act.

Thankfully, Asinius led her to one of the couches surrounding a table laid with fruits and sweetbreads rather than continuing down the stairs to the edge of the cliffs. She sat on the edge of the cushion and wondered who would die today.

Cotta gave her a smile devoid of any warmth. "Good morning, Claudia. I would like to personally thank you for your exquisite music last night."

She forced herself to appear pleased with his compliment. "Thank you. I'm glad to know my years of practice have elevated my abilities to be worthy of your praise."

"As they should be for a woman of her station," Hostilius added. "I spared no expense making sure she had the finest tutors in the empire."

She sighed and leaned against the edge of the reclining sofa. Once again, she was back to being a prized possession for her father to parade in front of his peers. A lap dog who was only useful for performing tricks to entertain his guests and nothing more.

A slave appeared next to her, holding a silver plate with some of the food from the table. She plucked a fig and nibbled on it while the men discussed the recent seizure of yet another ore shipment by the emperor. They groused, but she found nothing useful in the context that she could relay to Galerius.

That is, if that was why he was here in Tivola in the first place. She hesitated to tell him anything of value until she knew his motives. Part of her wanted to know who the new Captain of the Legion was so she had a person she could trust with the content of her letters.

"Ah, there he is," her father announced, pulling her back to the scene around her.

Three of her father's largest bodyguards led a battered and bruised Bestius to edge of the cliff. Her gut clenched as she met his gaze. They both knew what awaited him.

Hostilius leaned toward his guest. "The art to this is that you have to time it before the tide goes out. Otherwise, the body begins to stink by midday, and you have flocks of those annoying gulls swarming outside your window."

Ever since her father had been named governor of Lucrilla, he'd made a sport of tossing his enemies off the cliffs onto the rocks below. When he ran out of rivals, he turned to his slaves or any member of the household who'd displeased him. This morning, it was Bestius.

"What did he do to annoy you, Father?" she asked, turning her gaze away from the victim.

"He let himself be caught."

Nausea rolled through her stomach, mingling with guilt that made the sweet fig in her mouth taste bitter. Bestius was condemned because of something she'd done. Inside, she wanted to scream for mercy, to apologize to the man whose face already appeared as pale as death while he counted the last minutes of his life. But she remained silent and kept her eyes fixed on the rippling linen of her dress. If she opened her mouth, she'd be standing next to him.

Agonizing silence filled the garden while Hostilius mentally tortured his victim. Below, the waves crashed against the sharp rocks. The breeze ruffled his hair. Sometimes, the condemned would cry out, pleading with her father for his life. Usually, Bestius was the one who pushed them over the edge when her father refused to show mercy. He knew none would be granted for him his morning.

Claudia's pulse pounded in her ears. How she hated this. But to excuse herself would be a sign of weakness, especially in front of Cotta. If she proved herself to be anything less than what was expected of her, her father's punishment would be swift and harsh.

Her father's arm stretched out, his thumb pointing toward the sky. Bestius stiffened. A cruel grin played on Hostilius's lips. Then his wrist twisted, turning his thumb down.

Instead of having to be shoved to his death like the victims of every other execution she'd witnessed, Bestius raised his chin, took a step back, and disappeared over the edge in silence. No screams. No grunts. Just a quiet thud, followed by the roar of the tide.

Tears burned Claudia's eyes, but she dared not let them fall. The weight of his death pulled at her soul. What had she done?

Cotta laughed and applauded. "Very clever, Hostilius. I must try this the next time I'm at my villa in Pisarino."

Bile filled her mouth as she listened to the men laugh about death as though it were the bawdy song of some minstrel poet. All the more reason to stop the heartless man who had sired her. If he became emperor, how many people who suffer the same fate as Bestius?

"Claudia, any updates on your plans for Galerius?" Her father turned to her with the same stern expression she'd seen him wear when issuing orders to his servants.

She pushed her grief aside and fixed her mask of calm composure in place. "I'm still contemplating the best location to engage him."

"And I'm still waiting for him to come begging for you like you implied he would."

She sat up. "Are you suggesting I'm something less than desirable for an Elymanian like him?"

"I'm suggesting you stop playing around and find out what I need to know. Tonight, if possible."

She smoothed her hair as though the wind had disrupted it, even though Zavi had pinned it so well that it would take a storm to move a strand. "I'm terribly sorry, Father, but I'm already occupied this evening."

Hostilius crossed his arms, his expression darkening. "Doing what?"

"Attending the opening performance of the new play the emperor commissioned. I mentioned it to you three weeks ago, but since you showed no interest in attending, I thought it only proper I attend in your stead so at least our family shows some semblance of compliance to emperor's support for the arts." She paused to let her words sink in.

His shoulders dropped. "Very good. Yes, it would be unseemly if our family did not make an appearance."

"Precisely." She stood, relieved he didn't argue with her. "You seem so wrapped up in your plans that you forget we are being watched closely. The actions of a provincial governor like yourself do not go unnoticed, and I'm making sure we stay in the emperor's good graces."

Her stomach still churned from Bestius's death, making breakfast unappetizing. A clammy sweat prickled along her neck. She needed to leave before her father forced the issue with Galerius further. "Now, if you'll excuse me, I have an appointment with the dressmaker this morning."

She retreated back into the cool shadows of the villa, never letting her fear show until she was safely behind the locked doors of her room.

8

Galerius broke a piece of bread off the loaf and reread the latest letter from his informant again. *You may have lost your tail, but what you seek is not what you hope to find.*

He crumpled the paper in his fist. Of all the cryptic nonsense. What the hell did he mean, he wouldn't find what he sought? He needed to get into Hostilius's villa through that shaft, and since he'd confronted the man who'd been following him, he had awoken this morning with every intention of finding it.

That is until Carbo, the freed slave who had come with him from Emona, handed him this letter.

He threw it across the room and raked his fingers through his hair. He'd been here a week and found nothing, spending all his hours pretending to hunt for sapphires to continue his ruse. The only thing he'd learned was the informant knew he was here in Tivola and wanted to tease him with nonsensical comments that never told him what he needed to know. If he ever found out who was behind these blasted letters, he'd wring his neck.

Galerius stood and paced the room, reviewing everything he knew so far. Hostilius was up to something that involved massive amounts of ore. He had an army of powerful allies on his side who either had a grudge against the emperor or the empress, or both. And based on his rise to power, he wasn't above shedding blood to get what he wanted.

The only problem lay in how to get close to Hostilius without getting his throat slit in the process. Or worse, telling a score of lies that he'd not only have to remember, but would also eat away at his conscience as they formed on his lips. He absentmindedly rubbed the tattoo on his wrist. Once a member of the Legion, always a member of the Legion. His oath was as much a part of him as the Deizian blood that flowed through his veins.

What he needed now was a new strategy. Unfortunately, the only one he could think of was trying to pull information from the one person he knew he should avoid at all costs.

Claudia.

A knock sounded at his door. "Enter."

Carbo entered with a folded letter. "This just arrived for you, sir."

"Do you know who delivered it?"

"Yes, sir. The messenger said he was from the household of Hostilius Pacilus."

Suspicion coiled along the base of his neck. Galerius took the letter as though it were on fire and waited until he was alone again before he examined it closely. The paper bore the same weight and consistency of the letters sent from his informant, but the color was stark white compared to the rich cream color of the previous ones. A red wax seal embossed with the crest of the Pacilus family was stamped on the back. His hopes sank. It wasn't the same.

He ran his finger under the wax, pulling it from the folded sheet and opening the contents. His brows bunched together as he read the hastily scribbled message that was so different from the neat block letters of the other notes.

Please join me in the governor's box at the theater tonight. Take care to be discreet.

No signature. No indication who had sent it. Nothing. For all he knew, it could be an invitation for an assassin to plunge a dagger into his heart during the climax of the performance.

He ran his thumb over the last sentence. *Take care to be discreet.* Whoever sent it wanted their meeting to be secret. He only prayed it was because it involved Hostilius's plot against the emperor.

Of course, if this was Claudia's way of inviting him for another interlude, would he be wise to refuse?

***

Claudia rolled her eyes. It might be her civic duty to attend this play, but the rose-colored idealism the emperor was trying to promote with it needed to be tempered with a good dose of reality. Glancing around at the faces of the other Deizians in the boxes around her, they shared her sentiment. If he wanted change, Emperor Sergius would be met with considerable resistance.

The subtle scuffle of leather against the marble floor sounded above the actor's overly dramatic pause on stage. Claudia stiffened. What if her father had sent an assassin to finish her off? What if Bestius had seen Kafi delivering her messages to Galerius? Her heart fluttered in her chest, but she dared not move, dared not give the person behind her any acknowledgement. She only had a few seconds to catch her attacker off guard, and as long as he thought she was enraptured by the play, he wouldn't expect a fight from her.

Of course, he'd be wrong.

She tightened the muscles in her thighs, ready to pounce. Her fingers wrapped around the arms of her chair so she could use it as both a weapon and a shield. Then she waited for him to take the next step toward her.

"I didn't expect to find you here alone, Lady Claudia," a rich, masculine voice said behind her.

Her pulse jumped into her throat. She'd rather face a whole army of assassins than the one man standing behind her.

Galerius's hands encased her shoulders, holding her in place while his warm breath tickled the nape her of her neck. "I'm surprised your father isn't here."

Her voice trembled, although not necessarily with fear, as she replied, "He had other business to attend to tonight."

"Lucky me." He pressed his lips to her bare skin, his hands sliding down her arms.

She wanted to bolt for the corridor on the other side of the curtain. Galerius was dangerous, and for all the right reasons. Her mind ordered her to shout for help, but her body surrendered to him like wax to a flame. His touch molded her movements. Her head fell to the side, allowing him greater access to her neck as he trailed a string of light kisses from her shoulder to her ear. Tonight, he was being soft, gentle, treating her like a treasure rather than a conquest. So unlike their previous encounter, and yet wielding the same power over her.

"What are you doing here in my father's private box?" she finally whispered once she gathered control of herself.

He jerked to a stop, and warning bells went off in her head. Something was wrong here, and she'd bet her life that either her father or her brother was behind it.

Several long seconds passed. "Do you want me to leave?"

Her chin trembled. *Tell him yes.* But her mouth refused to form the word. He'd already awakened the desire that now hummed through her veins. It was as strong as the magic in her Deizian blood, and ten times more intoxicating. She wanted him to continue to kiss her, caress her, make her come as hard as he had the other night.

When she didn't answer, he moved in front of her on his hands and knees. "Perhaps I can make this evening a bit more enjoyable for you, then."

She didn't dare lower her eyes to him. If she did, he'd know how much control he had over her. She kept her gaze fixed on the players as they strutted across the stage while Galerius massaged his hands up her legs, along her thighs, inching agonizingly closer to the place that craved his touch. The pounding in her heart drowned out the long soliloquy below. She was too enraptured with imagining what he'd do next.

By now, he'd worked her legs apart and hiked her skirts up around her waist. She wanted to blame the cool night air for the shiver that coursed through her body, not the man whose lips pressed against her inner thighs. Whatever game he was playing needed to stop before she had the entire audience focused on her for the evening's entertainment.

"You shouldn't touch me in such a manner," she hissed. "What if someone sees you?"

The vibration of his quiet laughter heightened her arousal instead of dousing it. "I'm well hidden behind the railing. The only way anyone would know what I'm doing is if you scream out in pleasure."

The arrogance of him. Perhaps she should scream out, but in something other than pleasure. Then someone would come to her rescue and drag him out of her box before she completely embarrassed herself.

But her scream faded into a mere gasp as he cupped her bare buttocks in his hands and drew her hips closer to his mouth. His tongue lapped the outside of her sex, and her breath caught. She gripped the arms of her chair for dear life, unsure if she should stop this outrageous behavior now or let him continue.

His tongue pressed deeper this time, flicking across the aching nub inside, and forcing a whimper to rise from her throat. Another wave of his quiet laughter followed. "What's wrong, Claudia? Never had a man pleasure you like this before?"

She weighed the consequences of her response. A Deizian man would never dream of humbling himself like this, but if she told him that, then he'd probably stop. And for some insane reason, she wanted him to continue. She wanted to know how he intended to pleasure her with only his mouth. She wanted him to ease the ache that had been building up inside her since she had heard the timbre of his voice moments ago.

So she sat there quietly, fighting the moans that longed to break free with every slip of his tongue. She refused to let him know how much she enjoyed the contrasting rhythms he played along her sex, delving deep inside her one moment and then lightly grazing the edges the next. It was no different than what he'd do if he were kissing her mouth, yet her response was stronger.

Onward he played, teasing her. He knew what she liked, what made her breath quicken, because he'd slowly build her to the brink only to retreat when she came near to coming. She dug her fingers into his short hair to hold him in place, to keep him focused on the areas that caused her sex to clench. "Please," she begged, her voice a mere whisper.

His actions changed, becoming more aggressive and hungry. It was like the night in the garden all over again, only this time, she wouldn't fight him. Her eyes closed, and her body tightened, sliding further down the chair and closer to him. His teeth grazed her clit. She jumped from the intensity of the sensation and fell further under his control.

Please, please don't stop. Please don't back off. Not now. Not when I need this so badly.

He obeyed as if he heard the thoughts rushing through her fevered mind. The thrashing of his tongue became as frantic as the pitch of her hips. His fingers dug into the soft flesh of her buttocks in an almost bruising manner, but she ignored it. She was too close to coming, too far gone to care. He drew her clit into his mouth, sucking on it harder and harder until she finally shattered.

Warm waves of ecstasy throbbed through her body, started from where his lips touched her, and never losing momentum until they reached the tips of her fingers and toes. Her vision blurred, and her head swam as though she'd drunk too much wine. She could've been making a complete spectacle of herself in the middle of the theater, but she didn't care. She was already lost.

Her muscles refused to work, and she continued to slide further out of the chair until she was on the floor with him, her legs straddling his lap. The stubble of his cheek scratched her forehead and let her know she hadn't died. It wasn't some dream she'd conjured up in her bed.

Something seemed wrong about all this. He said he wanted to give her pleasure. Men never gave freely when it came to sex. They only took.

If he gave, it was because he wanted something in return. She'd just fallen into the one trap she had sworn she would avoid. She'd allowed herself to surrender to Galerius. But that didn't mean she had to accept that.

***

Galerius wrapped his arms around Claudia, willing his breath to slow. He'd only intended to tease her to the point where he might be able to loosen her tongue and find out where her father was tonight. But she'd been so warm, so vibrant, so responsive, that he'd gone much further than he'd planned. He managed to make her come, and now his body demanded its own release.

Yet despite the aching in his cock, he remained still. A trickle of fear formed at the base of his neck, tempering his desire again. As much as he wanted her, he couldn't trust her. Not completely. Not enough to let his guard down and enjoy the pleasures of her flesh. This was Claudia Pacilus, after all, the woman who'd sent all three of her husbands to a funeral pyre within months of their taking her as their wife. For all he knew, her orgasm could be part of a complicated ruse to falsely reassure him right before she plunged a knife into his heart.

His chest burned as if she'd already done so, even though his skin remained intact. By the gods, what was she doing to him?

Her lips brushed against his in the softest of kisses. "That was…interesting."

Interesting? Was that all she had to say after he'd made her come?

"Of course, now I have to ask what you want in return, right?"

He was about to ask her what her father was doing tonight, but she'd already found what he wanted. Her fingers lightly traced the length of his shaft through the linen of his tunic. He gritted his teeth keep from moaning.

"That's the wonderful thing about men. Your desires are always so blatant."

Sweat beaded along his forehead as she pulled back his clothes. His muscles remained locked. He closed his eyes, unwilling to watch her game of seduction and be lured into it. How could he tell her to stop when every fiber of his being wanted her to continue?

"You only gave me pleasure because you thought I'd let you fuck me again. You wanted to be inside me again, didn't you?"

"No, Claudia." Resistance strained his voice, making it sound like he was receiving a hundred lashes instead her gentle caresses.

Her touch became more purposeful, encasing his length in her hands and stroking upward. He dug his fingers into his palms in the hopes that the pain would distract him. If she continued this much longer, he wouldn't be able to resist. He'd come in her hands like an inexperienced youth.

A drop of liquid pooled at his tip. She caught it with her thumb and smeared it across his head in a set of spiraling circles. "You're lying."

Galerius opened his eyes and found her watching him with a sly grin. She was the cat, and he'd just become her mouse.

"What if I gave you what you wanted?" She shifted her hips so that the entrance of her sex hovered over his cock. "What if I said I wanted this, too?"

He licked his lips, even though his mouth had gone dry. What kind of game was she playing? His mind still yelled for him to practice caution even as his hands moved toward her hips.

She lowered herself onto him so that her tight wetness encased just his tip. "But remember this, if I let you fuck me, it's not because I want to give you pleasure. It's because I want to take my own."

As if to prove her point, she impaled herself on him in one quick movement. The groan he'd been fighting broke free.

She was everything he remembered and more.

"Yes, Galerius, I know you want to feel me sliding up and down around you." She raised her hips and lowered them, enacting her words within a torturous rhythm. "I know you want to feel me squeeze you tightly as I ride you."

He tightened his hold on her hips in a futile effort to direct her movements, to quicken her strokes and bring him closer to the edge. She caught his lips with her hers, allowing him to take control. The kiss started out submissive, passionate, until her teeth grabbed his bottom lip. Her fingers coiled in his hair and jerked his head back. She raised her hips, withdrawing his cock from her inner heat. All motioned stopped as she glared at him.

"No, I'm in control here." Her face was hard, stern, commanding. "You only exist for my pleasure. If you fight me, we end this right here."

He nodded, unable to think of anything else to do. Sex was her weapon, and she was as skilled as any gladiator in the ring at wielding it in combat. He'd been defeated in this round.

Claudia grinned and lowered herself onto him again. "I knew we could come to an understanding."

He allowed her to find her own rhythm, massaging her buttocks as she moved up and down on him. He'd never actually watched a woman during sex before tonight. His previous sexual encounters had always been about him, about what he wanted, about making him come. He had never realized how arousing it could be to witness a woman finding her own pleasure.

Every little detail mesmerized him. The way her fingers moved down his neck and dug into his shoulders. The way her eyes barely closed. The way her lips parted. The way her breath came quick, hitching just so when his cock hit a sensitive area. The way little mews of satisfaction rose from her throat with every stroke.

Claudia was a beautiful woman in her own right, but seeing her completely enraptured like this elevated her to an entirely new level. He couldn't take his eyes off her.

His body responded with the familiar ache deep inside his stomach. His balls tightened. He was close to coming, and yet he fought it. He didn't want her performance to end.

He buried his face in the hollow of her neck, hoping it would give him the time needed to let her finish before he lost control. The scents of lemon and lavender filled his nose. The salt of her skin made his mouth water as he laved his tongue across her flesh. Everything about her turned him on.

The ache in his cock intensified threefold. He stood on the brink, and every second he resisted became agonizing. "Claudia, please," he begged, echoing her plea from earlier that night.

"I'm close." Her words were sharp, punctuated with the quick stabs of her hips. Her movements became erratic. Her eyes tightened in sync with her inner walls. "So close. So very, very—" She managed to catch his lips and smother her squeal of delight as she came.

As soon as her sex clenched around him, the white-hot heat building inside broke free. He came so hard, his body shook from the intensity of it. He pulled her closer to him, drawing out the kiss as though it would keep him grounded on earth while the seismic aftershocks of his orgasm threatened to dislodge the very core of his being.

As the remnants of his pleasure faded, he became conscious that she was kissing him back. But something had changed in those brief moments after they came. Her manner became lighter, gentler. Her fingers now caressed the edge of his jaw, barely touching him. Her tongue danced slowly around his in an intimate fashion as though they were lovers and not just two people using sex to manipulate each other.

And his heart lurched when he realized how much he was enjoying it.

She broke off the kiss with a few notes of shy laughter, her eyes softening, and leaned her forehead against his.

Galerius couldn't explain want he was witnessing. He was seeing Claudia in a whole new light. He ran his hands up and down her back, savoring the warm flesh under the dampened silk that clung to it. He allowed his breath to flow in time with hers. He drew in the scent of her arousal that mingled with the perfumed oil she always wore. He soaked in her radiant grin.

The woman he held in his arms right now wasn't the haughty Deizian he'd always perceived her to be. This woman was uncertain, vulnerable, and yet so deliciously sated that he didn't want to let her go. "I'm so glad you invited me to join you tonight."

She stiffened and pushed him back, her eyes wide. "I didn't invite you."

A stone dropped into his stomach, sending chills over his skin that chased away any contentment he'd had moments before. "Are you saying you didn't send me the letter asking me to join you tonight?"

Her lips thinned, and she nodded. "Leave now."

Galerius reached for the letter tucked inside the pocket of his tunic. "But here it—"

"Didn't you hear me?" Her expression wavered between fear and anger. "I said leave now."

He scrambled to his knees, still hidden behind the railing, only to see her retreat to her chair. He would have accused her of being fickle, for teasing him until she satisfied her needs and then orchestrating his death so no one would dare know how much she enjoyed fucking him. But something in the way she sat cooled the anger brewing inside him. Her knees, which had moments ago braced his hips, now curled up to her chest, and her arms stretched out in front of her as though she were about to shield herself from a blow.

"If you don't get out of here now, I'll scream," she threatened, her voice quivering.

She didn't have to say more. The laws protected pure-blooded Deizians like her. All she had to do was tell someone he'd touched her without permission, and he'd hang before he had a chance to tell his side of the story. He tightened his jaw and stood, not caring anymore if someone saw him as he left the box.

Once he was outside the theater, he opened his mouth and drew in a cleansing breath. A growl of frustration rose from his throat when he exhaled. His thoughts tossed inside his mind like an airship caught in the gales of a hurricane, trying to make sense of the evening's events. His pride stung at how she once again had hid behind her rank rather than lingering in his arms. And his neck tingled from the growing feeling of uncertainty.

But one thing was certain. If Claudia was telling the truth and didn't invite him, then who did?

9

Claudia's eyes felt dry and gritty as she loaded her plate with the fresh sweetbreads and fruit from the tray offered to her by a slave. She wished could blame the bright morning sun for the urge to rub her eyes, or the pink sand that sparkled on the beaches along the coast, but the morning was cloudy, and the winds were mild. The blame all belonged to one person— Galerius Metellus.

She cursed her cowardice last night. She should have broken down and told him the truth about her father, about his plans, about everything, but the words had refused to form on her tongue. Instead, she'd hidden behind a hollow threat. She spent the remaining half of the play trying to straighten out her clothes and hair, wishing she had her perfumed oils to cover up his scent. She could only imagine what the gossips would say if they knew what had happened in her box last night.

But she knew why she drove him away. She didn't want to admit that she'd been her father's pawn once again. Who else would've written a letter telling Galerius to join her at the play, especially after her father had been encouraging her to set up another liaison with him? Who else would've known far enough in advance that she'd be there alone?

Looking back, she should have told him from the onset he wasn't welcome in her box, but the touch of his lips had overwhelmed her common sense. Her desire had gotten the better of her, and she was all the more a coward for refusing to acknowledge the power his touch had over her. Even this morning, the pleasant soreness between her legs served as a reminder of how hard she'd ridden him, of how hard he had made her come, of how much she had wanted him inside her again.

Voices filtered in from the hallway, and she turned with her plate to eat her breakfast outdoors in solitude. But her father was faster than her.

"How was the play last night, Claudia?"

She froze, trying to decide the best way to reply. She could keep Galerius's visit to herself, but what if her father had sent someone new to follow the former captain? Besides, if she lied and said he didn't appear, her father would lose faith in her ability to garner information from Galerius and shut her out of his plans to bring down the barrier.

"It was interesting," she replied, hoping he'd be happy with her vague answer while she kept her back to him.

Her father came closer. "I have it on good authority that you had a guest in your box."

Something tripped inside her, and she spun around to confront him so quickly, several berries rolled off her plate. "Spying on me, Father?"

His grin carried no warmth. "I sent Verres to follow you. After all, I worry about the safety of my only daughter."

Liar. He was only worried about someone disrupting his plans to take over the empire. Someone like Galerius. "Then you already know what happened."

He grabbed her arm as she tried to leave, jerking her so forcefully that her silver plate clattered to the floor. "Any more disrespect from you, and I'll have you standing on the edge of the cliffs."

Her heart flew up into her throat, fear replacing her anger. How much did he already know? "But if you have so little trust in me, then why should I repeat everything Verres already told you?"

His fingers loosened enough for her to pull her arm free. The blanched skin quickly turned red, outlining the mark each of his fingers left. "Verres has enough discretion to have stayed behind when he saw Galerius enter your box. Now, tell me what transpired between you. Did you learn why he's here?"

"He was probably too busy fucking her to say much," Asinius said behind them. "Isn't that right, Claudia?"

Shame washed over her. Even her family saw her as nothing more than a whore. She weighed her words carefully, wondering if they would be her last. How could she twist this in her favor? "He did come, and yes, he tried to seduce me again, but not before I managed to get some information from him."

"Are you going to tell me what he said?" Her father stared at her as though he were questioning a criminal instead of his child.

Her mouth went dry as she searched for a way to appease him. What lie could she spin? "He was very curious as to where you were, Father."

"Go on," he commanded.

She prayed to the gods that he wouldn't catch on that she was stalling. "He thought it strange that a provincial governor was absent at the premier of the emperor's play, almost as though he were questioning your loyalty to the empire."

As soon as the words slipped from her tongue, she worried that she'd said too much. As much as she wanted to be free of her father, she didn't want to cause the death of another innocent man, especially when she had no idea where Galerius stood in the web of deceit her father was spinning.

"And what did you tell him?"

"I told him your duties as governor demanded your attention at the last minute and that you would attend a performance soon." Another lie, but one she hoped he would believe. "After all, if he is working for the emperor, I didn't want to give him any cause to doubt your loyalties."

"It's not my loyalty that is in question—it's his." He

closed the space between them, forcing her to lock every muscle in place to keep from flinching and revealing her deception. "Did you learn his real reason for coming to Tivola?"

Her gaze flickered to the smug expression on her brother's face. He'd called her a whore since she'd seduced her first husband. Her father had showed no interest in her until she was of a marriageable age, and hence, useful for his plots. Neither of them had ever treated her with respect. Perhaps a whore was all she'd ever be to them, but last night taught her she was more than that. She could be in control of her body, of her desires. She didn't allow Galerius to fuck her because her father ordered it. She'd used him to satisfy her needs, and nothing more. Never mind the tender way he'd held her in his arms afterward. Never mind the way she foolishly believed he could actually care about her. Never mind the secret urge to arrange another meeting with him so she could decide if it was all for real or nothing more than a ruse.

She leveled her gaze with her father and kept her voice cold and heartless to match his. "It was as Asinius said. I distracted him to keep him from asking any more questions. By the time we finished, he was too tired to say much and left."

"Very resourceful." Her father chose his words as carefully as she did. "At this rate, I'll be an old man before you manage to screw the truth out of him."

"He's testing you as much as you're testing him, Father." And testing her in the process. How many lies would she have to keep straight so she wouldn't end up on the rocks below? "I'm trying to keep your secrets safe while learning his."

Her father ran his finger along her cheek, but it could have been the blade of a knife for all she cared. The gesture carried more menace than comfort. "Such a loyal daughter."

He walked past her, followed by Asinius, who whispered, "Such a generous slut."

Each barb hit its intended target—her soul. She managed to hold off her shivers until they were out of the room. She raised her fist to her mouth to block the sob that wanted to break free. If she didn't find a way out of this soon, she'd lose herself.

That is, if she hadn't already done so.

***

Galerius rubbed the remnants of his overindulgence of wine out of his eyes, grateful for the low clouds that blocked the sun. He still couldn't believe he'd been stupid enough to fall into Claudia's snare once again. But not even a jug of fortified wine could erase the memories of how sweet she had tasted when he'd teased her, how tightly her sex clenched around his cock when she came, how softly she had lain in his arms before he stupidly opened his mouth and ruined everything.

But in his drunken haze, one thing became very clear. Claudia was telling him the truth when she said she didn't send the letter.

"Either that, or she's the best damned actress in the whole empire," he muttered.

But that spurred more questions than he cared to answer. If she didn't invite him to join her, who did? And more importantly, why? Every time he tried to come up with an answer, it all pointed back to Hostilius. But what did the governor hope to gain by arranging a discreet meeting between him and Claudia?

Maybe he's hoping her rapid mood swings will drive me insane. Hot and passionate one minute, cold and distant the next. Always teasing him, only to push him away. Is that how Deizian women were taught to treat men? No wonder his real father had carried on with his mother for years, even though they were both married to someone else. And if she ever decided to cry rape when she tired of him, he would be dangling before sunset.

All the more reason to be on guard around her.

And yet, he couldn't help but wonder if the glimpse of the vulnerable side of Claudia was the real woman buried underneath that haughty façade. Would that woman stoop to such a thing? And would catching another glimpse of that woman be worth the risk of seducing her once again?

A sharp knock sounded at the door, vibrating through his skull, followed by the screeching of a door that needed a good oiling. Carbo poked his head in. "Good morning, sir. Sorry to disturb you, but another one of those letters just arrived."

Galerius snatched it and broke the seal. "What do you mean, just arrived? Did you happen to get a glimpse of who delivered it?"

"No, sir. There was nothing there this morning when I awoke, but when I returned from the market with your breakfast, it was waiting for me."

Galerius frowned as he opened the letter. The time of delivery may have changed, but everything else remained the same. Same paper. Same handwriting. Same sort of cryptic message that teased him worse than Claudia's kisses. *Do not become a pawn in Hostilius's game. He is still watching you.*

"Tell me something I didn't know." As much as he appreciated the warning, he would've been happier with information he could use, such as the identity of his informant. Or better yet, the details of Hostilius's plan.

Carbo glanced down at the empty clay wine jug. "Will you be in the mood for breakfast this morning?"

Galerius tested his stomach with a sip of water and nodded when it didn't hurl in protest. At least his tolerance hadn't completely faded from his brief absence of drinking.

He glanced down at the letter once again. *A pawn, hmm? Did that explain last night? And if so, what would Hostilius's next move be?*

***

Galerius emerged from the mine shaft and let the cool drizzle wash away both the grime that coated his skin, and his frustration. The little voice inside his mind nagged at him for wasting the day, but he had to know if the informant was correct. Sure enough, about two miles into the shaft where he'd expected to find the secret entrance to Hostilius's villa, he'd run into an unstable wall of fallen rock. His groan earned him a shower of pebbles, and he'd retreated back to the opening of the shaft before he triggered another rock fall.

Whatever had caused the cascade had to have been recent, or the empress wouldn't have wasted her time telling him about the secret entrance. That meant he had to gain access to Hostilius the old fashioned way—face to face. And that meant he had to earn the governor's trust by convincing him he hated the emperor.

He ran his fingers through his hair, shaking the dust from it. Somehow, he never thought he'd have to resort to lying to regain his honor.

Of course, there was still another route to try, but that one seemed far more dangerous that taking on Hostilius himself. Claudia. As if on cue, a breeze stirred up the grass, blowing petals from a nearby grove of lemon trees into his face. Their faint scent triggered his memories of her, of the way she always smelled. He closed his eyes and allowed himself to indulge in it for a moment. His cock stiffened. Damn! How could one woman trigger such a reaction in him? After all, it was just sex. She wasn't any different than any of the whores on Via Lupas, right?

Disgust rolled through him for letting her get under his skin like that. The letter this morning cautioned him from becoming Hostilius's pawn, and that included becoming Claudia's pawn. Why else would someone try to get them alone together last night?

Worse, what if she was part of this scheme and was playing him as well as she had her prior lovers?

This called for a new distraction, something stronger than wine so he could forget about her and focus on his mission. After a quick trip to the city baths, he found himself in front of one of the many brothels on Via Lupas.

Named after the girls who sold their services, the street was home to anything a man could desire. He browsed the various *lupanars* where woman of various ages, and a few young men, advertised their wares for the passing customers. The light of the setting sun peeked out from the clouds, gilding the street in a bronze glow to cover up the harsh reality that endured for many of the workers. Almost all of them were Alpirions. Some were freed, some were still slaves, but their dark eyes all stared at him with the same flat expression that betrayed their inviting smiles.

The street began filling up with men willing to part with a few of their coins for a moment's gratification in a whore's arms. Galerius leaned against the side of a corner building, watching them come and go while asking himself what he was trying to prove by coming here tonight. By the time night fell, the odors sex and smoke filled the air. The moans of lovers sang out like the chorus of a play. But none of it had any effect on him.

That is, until he got a whiff of lemon oil from behind him.

Desire stirred deep within him, warming his blood. He turned around, half expecting to see Claudia behind him, only to stare into the black eyes of an Alpirion *lupa.*

She pressed her barely concealed breasts against his chest. "Can I help you with anything?"

He drew in a deep breath and realized he missed the calming notes of lavender that always accompanied the clean citrus scent Claudia always wore. "Perhaps."

Her grin widened, and he could almost hear her calculating how much gold she could collect from him. She flicked her long black hair over her shoulder, but not quickly enough for him miss the tangles already in it. Although the night was young, he wouldn't be her first client. "What are you looking for?"

A way to forget about the woman who has me by the balls every time I get near her. But instead, he said, "Depends on what your specialty is."

"It's whatever you want." She turned her head so the light of a passing airship caught her profile and the way her golden earrings danced when she gave playful giggle. "Why don't you come to my room, and we can discuss this further."

He followed her into the building, watching the way her

short tunic wriggled around her bare, copper-colored legs with the sway of her hips. She was trying her best to seduce him, but somehow, it fell short. Every motion the *lupa* made seemed part of an elaborate act. He'd seen real passion last night, seen the hunger in Claudia's eyes as she sank onto his cock over and over again, and found it missing in the woman who invited him into her room.

As far as a prostitute's room went, it was decent. A straw-filled mattress lay on top of the concrete slab that served as her bed. The flickering oil lamp on the table across the room provided the strong lemon scent that covered up the presence of her former clients. A pile of dirty sheets in the corner showed that she at least took pride in maintaining a clean appearance to her workspace.

She sat on her bed and beckoned him to join her. "So, how would you like to fuck me? In the mouth? In the ass?" She spread her legs so he could the deep pink of her sex. "Here?"

Any other man would have been hard and shedding his clothes at such a display, but Galerius lingered at thin curtain that served as her door.

She cocked her head to the side and grinned. "Is this your first time?" she teased.

Pride stiffened his spine. "Do I look like an untried youth to you?"

"No, you look every inch a man." She threaded her fingers through his and pulled him closer. "A man whose cock I can't wait to have inside me."

Her invitation was meant to break him under the weight of his desire, but it had the opposite effect. Instead, all he remembered was how a certain Deizian woman told him that he existed only for her pleasure. Her command, so direct, so forceful, echoed in his mind and warmed his blood.

"Ah, that's better." The *lupa* released his hands and worked her way under his tunic, her calloused hands massaging his thighs. "You still haven't told me what you want."

All I want is to forget about the one woman who haunts my

dreams. If he could prove to himself his attraction to her was purely physical, then perhaps he could move past her and focus on his mission again. He swallowed hard. "I want you to..."

The words died in his mouth. He didn't want to admit his weakness for Claudia, nor did he want to insult the whore who seemed so eager and willing to make him forget his worries.

She chuckled. "I think I understand. You just want to come, right?"

He looked down at her. Her face was still young, but her eyes shone with a dull light that revealed too many weary years of serving her clients. She was pretty for an Alpirion. Not as striking as the empress, but still pleasant to look upon. He brushed a stray lock of her black hair out of her face, letting his fingers trail along her cheek. "Yes," he replied, his voice hoarse.

"Then don't think about her. Let me help you forget her."

The *lupa*'s words startled him. Was it that obvious that he was thinking about another woman while in her arms?

"Shhh," she whispered, unclasping her tunic and leaving it in a puddle around her feet. "Don't speak. Just feel."

Any man in his right mind would do just what she ordered, but he couldn't stop wishing her skin was pale ivory rather than rich copper, her hair shiny gold rather than black as a raven's wing, her body thin and graceful rather than short and curvy. She unfastened his belt and lifted his tunic above his head, pressing her naked body against his, but he felt no comfort in the contact. If anything, her touch repulsed him.

She tilted his head down. "Look at me. See how much I want you."

Her face was a mask of desire, but he couldn't see any emotion in her eyes.

"Touch me," she continued, guiding his other hand to her sex. "Feel how much I need you."

She was warm and wet, but not like Claudia. He craved the Deizian's silken heat. His mouth longed to taste her flesh again, to feel her fingers digging into his shoulders as she tried to

85

contain her ecstasy. Whatever this whore could do to him, it would be a poor shadow to what he had experienced last night.

He backed away, disgusted with himself. "I'm sorry," he mumbled as he reached for his clothes and pulled enough coins from his pouch to pay her three times her normal fee.

Her bottom lip trembled. "Don't you find me attractive?"

The plea in her voice struck a deep chord inside him. He'd heard his mother ask her lover that question hours before she took her own life. The last thing he wanted was for this young woman to suffer because of him. He pressed the coins into her hand and gave her a reassuring smile, wishing she had some other means to earn a living besides this. "Yes, I find you very attractive, but I can't get her out of my mind tonight."

She nodded as though she understood all too well what he meant. "She is very lucky to have your heart, then."

His heart? He wouldn't go as far as to say that, but as he left the *lupanar*, he wondered what kind of hold Claudia *did* have on him. Was it purely physical, or was it something more?

The warning of this morning's missive flashed in his mind. *Do not become a pawn in Hostilius's game.* He didn't worry about that. He was more worried about becoming Claudia's pawn.

10

Claudia crept out onto her balcony and crouched behind the railing. A visitor had arrived just as she was about to retire, and her father had instructed the slave to bring him to the gardens. This was the first place she thought of to overhear his meeting without being seen.

A wave crashed against the cliffs, and a knot balled in the pit of her stomach. What if the visitor was Galerius?

The purple glow of the supernova pulsated high in the sky above her from its zenith. Sunrise was hours away, but the conversation continued in earnest below.

"We should have no problem getting the shipment in tomorrow night," an unfamiliar man said, his voice low with intrigue. "I've already taken care of bribing the customs officials, and I'll make sure the wine is drugged when the guards receive their evening meals."

"Very good," her father replied, using the same tone as his guest. "Once I get this ore, I'll have everything in place."

"I hope you will remember my service to you once you succeed."

Her father spared a few jabbing notes of laughter, and Claudia's blood ran cold, chasing away the warm relief she'd felt when she realized it wasn't Galerius. Her father's accomplice would likely become the next man tossed off the cliff once her father no longer found him useful. "We shall see. First, I need things to go smoothly tomorrow night."

"They shall, my lord. Have your men ready at the warehouse this time tomorrow, and I'll have a ship full of ore ready to be unloaded for you."

Claudia held her breath, hoping one of them would tell her which warehouse the ore would be delivered to, but her father dismissed the man before she could learn that information. She waited several long moments until she knew the garden was empty before she stretched the cramps from her legs. The gods were cruel to tease her with what she'd overheard. If only she had all the details.

But a clue was a clue, and if she had a chance to thwart her father's plans, she'd take it.

***

"Sir, you've received another letter."

Galerius was beginning to hate those words. He snatched the paper from Carbo's hands and contemplated crumpling it up and tossing it into the kitchen fire instead of reading it. He already knew the contents. Nothing more than a teasing riddle. Nothing that would help him stop Hostilius and complete his mission.

"Do you need anything else?"

He raised his bleary eyes to the naively calm servant. "Yes. I need to know who's sending these damned letters," he growled. "Then maybe I can get some real answers."

"I cannot tell you what I do not know, sir. All I can say is that they arrive before dawn."

"Then maybe we need to post someone at the door all night."

Not missing a beat, the servant replied, "Then perhaps you should hire someone to do so." He turned and left before he was volunteered for the job.

That was the problem with having a freeman for a servant instead of a slave. He couldn't make him do anything. Galerius was almost tempted to do the job himself, but the letters had no definite pattern to them, which could equate to many long, sleepless nights.

He tossed the letter on his bed and went to the basin to splash some cold water on his face. Whatever tidbit of information it contained could wait until he finished getting ready for the morning. He had more important things to clear from his head before he dealt with it—like how to get his mind off of Claudia. His skin burned from the memory of last night. Normally, he had no problems enjoying the entertainment of a skilled *lupa*.

The whore's words still troubled him more than he cared to admit. She accused Claudia of having his heart. Nonsense. She was nothing more than a quick fuck, a woman to be used for his enjoyment. No different than the *lupa* he ran across last night. But whenever he closed his eyes, he couldn't shake the image of her seductive smile as she rode him to her climax.

Damn it! He punched the cool plaster walls, welcoming the pain in his knuckles. At least that distracted him long enough to finish dressing and get to his desk.

He'd forgotten about the letter until it arrived on his breakfast tray. The wrinkles had been smoothed out as much as possible. It leaned against his cup, mocking him.

He paused from going over his notes and studied it. This time, the letters weren't as straight and uniform. Whoever his informant had still taken care to disguise the handwriting, but this seemed to be written in haste. He broke the familiar wax seal and scanned the contents.

A shipment of ore will be smuggled into the warehouses tonight. A cart will be sent to retrieve it during the fifth hour of the night. Do not let it leave the docks.

Galerius's breath caught. Finally, something he could use. A clue. A chance to intervene.

Unfortunately, it remained as vague as the previous clues. There had to be dozens of warehouses along the docks. He had the time, but he no clue what the cart would look like or how big the shipment would be.

But he did know a merchant who was friendly with Hostilius.

He pushed back his desk and loosened the floorboard under it, his pulse pounding. This would be his chance to stop the plot against the emperor and regain his honor. He reached into the small space for the smooth crystal orb hidden there. A spark of magic tingled along his fingertips as they brushed against it. He pulled it out by its bronze ore frame and focused his mind on the palace in Emona.

The clear glass clouded for a moment. He doubled his efforts and was rewarded by the hazy image of a Deizian man's face. "Do you have a message for the emperor?" the man asked, the nasal twang in his voice revealing his annoyance as he came into focus.

"I have an urgent message for the emperor himself and no one else."

The man's eyes narrowed before his face faded from view, and Galerius was left wondering if the messaging orb would be delivered to Emperor Sergius or if he'd be ignored. Several agonizing minutes passed before the crystal clouded again. This time, he found himself staring into the sharp blue of eyes of the emperor himself.

"You have news for me, Galerius?"

"Yes, Your Imperial Majesty. I received a notice that another shipment of ore is going to be delivered into Tivola tonight."

"I know nothing of that." The image blurred for a moment, followed by the hazy outline of another man in the distance. "Marcus, have you heard anything about this?"

"Nothing at all," Marcus replied. "They had to be pretty sneaky to get it past me."

"Or knew you'd tattle on them to the emperor," Galerius replied, enjoying a chance to tease the emperor's best friend like he'd done when he was still the Captain of the Legion. "Anyway you could intercept it?"

"I have no idea where it's coming from, and even if I

did, I couldn't get there fast enough, even if I had the speed of *The Seventh Wind* at my command." Marcus turned his head to Sergius. "And I do love captaining your ship, by the way."

"Should I increase the guard around it?" Sergius grinned. "I'd hate for it to go missing one night."

"I'd only borrow it for a few hours to impress Sexta."

Galerius cleared his throat. If left to their devices, the two friends would go on forever, and he needed to come up with a plan before Hostilius got the ore. "I need to make sure that ore doesn't fall into the wrong hands, but I have a feeling it will be well-guarded—far more than what I can handle on my own."

He hated to admit that, but he wasn't going to commit suicide, either.

Sergius nodded, his face serious once again. "I agree. I cannot send any reinforcements from Emona, but I can spare you a few men from the detachment I have stationed there. I'll contact General Pansa and let him know."

The hairs on the back of his neck prickled. Hostilius already had most of the influential people in the province under his thumb. Would that include the current general, too? "If you don't object, I'd like to keep him out of this. I still have a few contacts left in the army, and they're men I can trust."

A hint of worry washed over the emperor's face. "Are you saying the general is part of the plot?"

"I have no proof that he is, but I know Hostilius has plenty of contacts in the army, too. He seemed to be very friendly with General Galeo at a party a couple of weeks ago."

The emperor's lips thinned. "That doesn't sound promising. Anyone else?"

Galerius rattled off the names of the men he'd met at the party, including the name of the Elymanian merchant, Minius Culleo. "If anyone is smuggling in the ore, that's who it would be."

Emperor Sergius turned back to Marcus. "Have you heard of him?"

Marcus gave an undignified snort. "Yeah, I have. I

wouldn't put it past him to try something underhanded like that, especially if enough money were involved."

The chill persisted along the back of Galerius's neck. "Neither would I. His warehouses are going to be the first ones I investigate."

Emperor Sergius drew in a long breath and took his time exhaling. Surely, the man knew how many enemies he had. "Sounds like a good plan. If you run into any trouble recruiting men from the detachment—"

"I won't, Emperor Sergius," Galerius interrupted. "If they're here, I can trust them to help me out. They owe me."

"The Brotherhood of the Army?"

Galerius shook his head and grinned. "More like a lost bet."

***

Hours later, Galerius tapped his fingers on the table while he waited for Rufius and his men to arrive. The bar close to the docks provided the perfect meeting spot, and the late hour meant most of the occupants were so deep in their cups that they wouldn't notice the meeting. He rubbed the back of his neck, relieved for once to be free of the sensation that he was being constantly watched.

An Elymanian man strolled into the bar a few minutes later, dressed in civilian clothes, his face little changed from their years growing up in the shadow of the army. He weaved through the tables to join Galerius and extended his hand. "Good to see you again, Captain."

Galerius inwardly cringed at the use of his old title. "I'm not a captain anymore, Rufius."

"Bullshit. Once a mem—"

"Keep your voice down," Galerius hissed. He glanced around the bar, but so far, no seemed to be taking any notice of them. "I thought I asked you to come armed."

Rufius poured a cup of wine from the bottle on the table. "You also said to dress where I'd blend in to the surroundings. No offense, but carrying a weapon in these parts is an open invitation to a fight."

"I assume you have something hidden that you can use?"

Rufius nodded and took a long drink. His nose wrinkled as he gulped the bitter wine. "Can't you afford something better than this shit?"

"I can, but I purposely ordered this so you wouldn't be falling down drunk later." Galerius pointed to his own cup, which remained full.

"Fine." Rufius pushed the cup away. "Let's talk about why you asked me and a few of my men to join you tonight. Your letter was vague, at best."

He surveyed the room again, waiting for that trickle of warning, but felt nothing. "I need your help stopping some smugglers."

"Sounds like something the customs officials should be looking into, not us. Why the secrecy?"

"Why the questions? You had no problem doing what I asked before."

"You outranked me before. Then you left us poor army guys for the Legion, la-di-da." He danced his finger in the air as though he were conducting an orchestra. "If I didn't know better, I'd say this involved something with the emperor himself."

Galerius clasped his hands together and leaned forward. "If you can keep your bloody mouth shut, I might be able to spare a few details."

"That's the Galerius I know." Rufius reached for his cup again, only to set it back down on the table after catching a whiff of the sour contents. "I have six of my best men waiting down the street with all the weapons we need, but first, I need to know why you want us to risk our necks in the middle of the night."

He grinned. "Besides the fact you owe me?"

"I can't believe you're still holding on to the bet we made as kids. Damn, I wish my father had been as hard on me as yours was on you. Maybe then, I'd be the one sporting a laurel wreath on my wrist."

Galerius rubbed the leather bracelet covering his Legion tattoo. His father's words echoed in his mind. *You'll never be anything more than a disappointment to me.* "Too bad the son of a bitch didn't live long enough to see me make Captain."

"Despite what you think, he was proud of you. You rose through the ranks quicker than any of us, and you should have seen the pride in his eyes when you were chosen for the Legion."

"Funny, he never let me know that." Resentment coiled in his stomach, threatening to break free if they continued to talk about his father. "The point is, I won our bet when I became Captain, so now I'm coming to collect."

Rufius cocked one brow. "And this is what you're asking of me?"

Galerius nodded. "I can't do it alone, and I need someone I can trust, old friend."

"Are you sure we're not walking into a trap?"

He hesitated, checking his gut before he replied. So far, his informant hadn't led him astray. "No, which is why I wanted you armed."

Rufius leveled his gaze and seemed to be searching for any hint of doubt or fear. Galerius tightened his jaw, never blinking, until his friend nodded. "Then lead the way."

Galerius threw a few coins on the table and went straight for the door. Once outside, he let Rufius lead him to where the rest of the men waited. He sized them up. They all appeared to be well-disciplined soldiers capable of handling what he needed.

Rufius slid the scabbard for his gladius into his belt and buckled it around his waist. "Satisfied?"

"We'll see." For the first time that evening, a trickle of doubt wormed into his mind. What if he guessed wrong about the warehouse? What if he missed stopping the ore delivery, and Hostilius used it to overthrow the emperor? But every time he checked his gut, it told him Minius Culleo was the merchant smuggling the ore in tonight. And once he stopped him, he'd be able to get the proof he needed to arrest Hostilius before the plot wreaked havoc on the empire.

He went through and checked off the gear they'd brought. Ropes. Grappling hooks. Swords. One bow with a quiver of arrows. And a small burlap sack that was securely fastened. "What's in there?"

Rufius looked to his men and laughed. "You'll see. If we need it, I'll open it up."

Galerius tested the weight of the sack and frowned. "It's heavy. Are you absolutely sure we need it?"

"It depends on what you want tonight. If you want us to rush in and kill everyone, then probably not. If you want survivors to pump for information, then I say we take it."

"Why the secrecy?"

He crossed his arms. "I could ask you the same thing, Galerius. Let's just say I put my nuts on the line to get that, and if we don't need it, then I'd prefer to return it so no one would ever know it was missing in the first place."

His friend's loyalty eased some of his doubt. "It sounds like I might owe you something if we have to use it."

"Just use your imperial connections to get General Pansa off my ass for taking it."

"I will." He removed the toga he'd loosely draped around his torso to hide his weapons and faced the seven men before him. "In less than an hour, someone will be smuggling in an illegal shipment of ore. We need to stop it. More importantly, we need to know who ordered it. From my understanding, they aren't expecting trouble, so I don't expect them to be heavily armed. However, if they are, we will not rush in and attack. Understood?"

One by one, the men nodded. They were all here without orders, and he doubted any of them were willing to die tonight.

"Good. Then follow me."

He led them through the dark, deserted streets toward Minius's warehouse at the end of the docks. A thick fog was rolling in from the sea, almost obscuring the pulsating purple glow of the supernova above. Thankfully, he'd scouted out the area during daylight hours and knew all he possibly could about the location. If anything, the fog was a small blessing from the gods—it would hide their approach from any guards stationed in the area.

Rufius stopped and crouched over a slumped figure along the side of the street. He lifted the man's arm and let it flop back down to the motionless body. "Now we know why the guards sent to the patrol the area wouldn't notice a cart full of ore passing through the area."

"Is he dead?"

His friend leaned closer to the body. "Nope. Just passed out drunk." He straightened and grinned. "Maybe we need to start offering the men that piss you had on the table tonight."

One of the men chuckled. "You take away our wine, and you'll have a mutiny on your hands, sir."

Rufius rolled his eyes. "You see how spoiled these new recruits are?"

Galerius was tempted to laugh with them, but his mission drove any mirth from his system. If Minius had ensured the guards patrolling the docks were drugged, then there was a chance he might have been expecting trouble. "Let's keep moving."

When they reached the area of the warehouse, Galerius motioned all of them to be silent. He leaned his ear against the warped wooden wall. The doors remained closed, but he could still hear the muffled sound of voices inside. As usual, his gut instinct had been right.

He signaled the two men with the ropes and grappling hooks to set up. A flash of silver metal shone through the fog as they whirled them around before letting them fly to the retractable roof. A faint clunk indicated they'd hit their target, and each men tested the ropes before turning back to him.

Galerius and Rufius scurried up the ropes to the thin rim of metal that formed the fixed portion of the roof. Most of the warehouses along the docks had retractable roofs to allow the airships to land inside and unload their goods quickly and securely. It also made smuggling easy, especially on nights like this when the fog was thick enough to obscure the glow from the ship's engines.

Rufius peeled back the canvas awning and drew in a sharp breath. "You weren't kidding."

Galerius peered into the warehouse below and ground his teeth. Although the ship was already gone, the goods filled the warehouse. This wasn't a small shipment of ore like he'd first suspected. This was enough ore to line a dozen airships. What in the world was Hostilius planning on doing with it?

He counted the men inside. A dozen slaves worked silently, carrying bars of ore to the long wagon bobbing patiently under the weight of its load. Like Deizian chariots, it required neither wheels nor draft animals to move. Its driver, a half-Deizian, chatted comfortably with Minius as they supervised the activity.

"I'm not seeing any muscle down there," Rufius whispered. "Are you?"

He shook his head.

"Good. That means we get to use my toy." His friend turned around on the narrow ledge and jerked on the rope. A few seconds later, the rope twitched, and Rufius began pulling something up from below. "I've already discussed my plan of action with the men. I told them that if we used this goody, they were to run and subdue those inside as quickly as possible."

They were outnumbered two to one, but Galerius doubted any of the slaves would put up much of a fight. "I'm mostly interested in Minius and the driver."

"You and me, both. What the hell is going on here?"

"I wish I knew."

The burlap sack appeared at the end of the rope, and Rufius unfastened it with a grin. "Ever play with a flash bomb before?"

His friend's giddiness was infectious. "You have one in there?"

"At your service." Rufius held out a golden sphere the size of his palm.

Galerius took care when he picked it up. Flash bombs were designed more to stun the enemy than do any actual damage, but he didn't want to take any chances. One errant surge of magic, and they'd be the ones blinded, not the men working below. A thin coat of ore surrounded a clay jar with compressed oil inside. He rolled it around and found the indentations for his fingers. "You want the honors?"

Rufius pointed to his brown eyes. "No Deizian blood, remember? It's all yours."

He pressed his fingers against the cool metal and focused his magic on the six needles of ore that pierced the clay and sank into the oil inside. He started with a trickle, careful not to make the bomb explode in his hands, and slowly increased his concentration. The ore glowed golden and grew warm to the touch. The oil inside started swirling, becoming violent with each pulsation of magic until it reached the critical point where the bomb was fully armed. Then Galerius released it into the warehouse below, and covered his eyes.

Even through the thickness of flesh and bone, the brightness of the explosion seeped through his eyelids and left him blinking afterward. Pandemonium reigned below. The slaves frantically ran with their hands stretched out, running into each other. The soldiers outside rammed the doors and splintered the weathered wood with one blow.

Galerius tossed his rope inside and rappelled down into the room. He needed to capture Minius before he got away. The Elymanian merchant stood less than twenty feet away from him, rubbing his eyes. It was almost too perfect.

The hiss of metal sliding out of a scabbard came from his left, and Galerius turned to see the driver running toward him with his sword drawn. He stepped to the side at the last minute and rolled. The whoosh of the missed blow rippled his tunic, but he managed to draw his own gladius before he made it fully around.

The driver lunged for him again, his blue eyes blazing, his face twisted in fury. The smell of stale ale and sweat clung to

98

his skin as he drew nearer.

Galerius raised his sword and deflected the blow. He followed with a short jab, nicking his opponent's bicep.

The shallow wound only infuriated the driver more. He swiped his sword through the air, catching Galerius's tunic and exposing his abdomen through the torn fabric.

Galerius rocked back on his feet. The extra foot of distance gave him a moment to think. He needed survivors to answer his questions. He needed to know where the driver was taking the ore next. Unfortunately, that meant Galerius had to incapacitate him without killing him. And based on the bloodlust in the man's eyes, that wouldn't be a small task.

He danced around the warehouse, dodging the driver's blade. The perfect moment would have to appear soon. All he needed was for the driver to become tired enough to open himself up to attack. Behind him, he saw Rufius had already captured Minius. The other soldiers had confined the slaves. Everything was left up to him now.

A whistle of wind ruffled his hair as the driver's sword fanned by, coming uncomfortably close to his ear. Galerius took advantage of the blade being off-center and made another quick jab. This time, a circle of red appeared on the driver's shoulder.

The driver took a step back and pressed his free hand against his new wound.

Galerius moved in and leveled his gladius at his opponent's chest. "If you surrender, I'll see your wounds are properly tended to. I have no desire to kill you."

The man grinned, revealing a missing front tooth. "You think you're showing me mercy?"

"Mercy in exchange for what you know."

The driver's laugher was low and bitter. His gaze flickered to Minius, who nodded. He dropped his hand and stood straighter.

At what seemed to be an act of surrender from his opponent, Galerius lowered his weapon. "I need to know where you are taking the ore."

"I know." A strange light replaced the bloodlust in the driver's eyes. Chills rippled through Galerius's veins. It was the look of a man wrapped up in both fear and desperation. "Too bad that information will die with me."

The word "no" sat frozen on Galerius's lips as the driver lifted his sword and plunged into the left side of his chest.

Galerius caught him, hoping to catch some clue on the man's dying breath. Warm blood coated his hands. "Tell me where you were taking it."

A gurgle of red-tinged bubbles from the driver's mouth answered him.

Galerius let him fall to the ground in a heap. His skin crawled with the sense of failure. What information would prompt a man to take his own life to keep it a secret?

A cry from Rufius ripped him from his thoughts. Galerius whirled around to see Minius sink to his knees. White foam poured from the corners of his mouth. "What happened?"

"I tried to stop him—" Rufius began, but then clamped his mouth shut. No soldier wanted to admit failure.

"What did he do?" Galerius grabbed his friend by the tunic, his fingers itching to wring the information from him by force. "Tell me."

"He must have had the vial hidden on him," Rufius said in a rush of words. "It happened so quickly, I—"

Galerius released him, turning his attention to the merchant who had maybe a minute of life left in him. The foam was now pink and turning a deeper hue of red with each passing second. He knelt in front of him, steadying him with an outstretched arm. "What is Hostilius planning?"

Minius cackled, spraying Galerius's tunic with the red liquid. "Death would be kinder than what he has in store for me."

"And you'd let him win? You'd die being his cowering fool?"

The merchant's breath grew ragged. "You have no idea."

Galerius shoved him back, letting Minius surrender to

the last of his death throes. He wiped his hand on a clean corner of his clothes and wished he could wash away his sense of failure as easily. He had them. He had them in the palm of his hand, and he had failed to get the one thing he needed.

You'll never be anything more than a disappointment to me. Only this time, he heard Emperor Sergius saying those words instead of his father.

He fled outside and let the cool mist of the fog bathe over him. Two questions plagued his mind. One, how would he explain tonight's events to the emperor? And two, what was Hostilius doing that would cause two men to commit suicide rather than fall into enemy hands? Suddenly, the scale of the provincial governor's plot seemed far larger than any of them had suspected.

Slow, plodding steps came from behind him. He glanced over his shoulder at Rufius. "I'm sorry I failed you, sir," the soldier said quietly, his face drawn.

"There was no way you could have known Minius had a vial of poison on him." Why was it so much easier to comfort his friend than himself?

Rufius shook his head. "No, I should have suspected it the minute I saw the driver fall on his sword."

Galerius turned back to the desolate streets. His throat tightened as he admitted, "I should have, too."

"We still have the slaves. Maybe they could tell us something."

A single note of bitter laughter worked its way out of his chest. "You know as well as I do that a Deizian elitist like Hostilius wouldn't reveal that kind of information to an Alpirion."

"I'll still question them. Sometimes slaves know more than they let on."

"Maybe." Just like his informant knew more than he let on. It would be ironic if the informant was a household slave who happened to be educated enough to write those missives. But the chances of that were slim to none. The strict laws passed against the Alpirions after their enslavement forbade such education, and he didn't picture Hostilius as the type to try to advance his slaves.

"At least we captured the ore. That's the important thing, right?"

A rueful grin teased the corners of his mouth. "Always the optimist, huh?"

"Just like you've always been the pessimist." Rufius clasped him on the shoulder. "I know what you're thinking, Galerius. You've always been your own toughest critic. You set out to stop the shipment from falling into the wrong hands, and you did it."

"But whose hands was it going to fall into?" He turned his attention back to the half-loaded cart. The bright bronze sheen of the ore mocked him. "That's the riddle I need to solve. And soon."

11

Angry shouts burst into Claudia's room when Zavi opened the door. "What's going on downstairs?"

Her maid's pinched face spoke volumes. "Your father is in a dreadful mood this morning. I'd suggest you stay up here until he calms down, my lady. There's no telling who he'll throw over cliffs when he's like this."

She stood and allowed Zavi to remove her nightgown. Her heart fluttered in her chest. Had Galerius succeeded in stopping the shipment of ore? "Do you know what set him off?"

"No, my lady, although I did overhear him say something about delaying his plans."

Claudia grinned. It had worked. Now if only Galerius could gather enough information to convict her father. "Such a shame his plans were ruined. I suspect he'll pout all day."

"I suspect he'll be doing more than pouting." Zavi selected a pale pink dress and pulled it over Claudia's head. "I've never seen such a flurry of messengers leaving the house."

Which would provide the perfect cover for sending another message to Galerius. "Has Kafi left for the morning?"

Zavi stiffened while adjusting the folds of the dress. The wary look on her face spoke volumes. "Why do you ask, my lady?"

The insolent slave! Claudia narrowed her eyes and

103

yanked her arm free from her maid. "Do not challenge me like that. Answer my question."

Zavi lowered her gaze to the floor. "No, my lady, he hasn't."

"Then send him up to my room immediately."

The slave woman backed away slowly, her bottom lip trembling. "My lady, I do not wish to offend you, but he is my son. Please do not involve him in anything dangerous."

An uncharacteristic lump formed in Claudia's throat. How strange it was to hear a parent plead for the safety of her child. She doubted her own father would do something like that. And if her father caught her, Kafi would be punished alongside her. Now she regretted involving the youth in her plans and offered a prayer to the gods for his safety. "Do not worry, Zavi. I am quite fond of Kafi and do not wish any harm to come to him. I'll do my best to protect him."

"Thank you, my lady." She opened her mouth as if to say more, but seemed to think better of it. "I'll send him up immediately."

The sound of her father's wrath filled the room once again when Zavi opened the door. Claudia couldn't help but smile as she sat down at her desk and pulled out a sheet of paper. So far, her plans to thwart her father were working. Now if only they would lead him away in chains. Then she'd finally be free of him and sleep better at night, knowing the barrier was safe.

***

The mid-afternoon sun poured in through the windows of his house by the time Galerius rubbed the sleep from his eyes. The heat of the day drove him from his bed, and now he sought the cool shadows of the tiny courtyard. He dipped his hands in the stream of water that poured out of a stone man's mouth into the small cistern, and bathed the back of his neck.

A sense of foreboding clung to his soul. He still hadn't reported what had happened last night to the emperor. What if his failure was enough to have him removed from the mission? What if he never regained his honor? He closed his eyes and leaned on the cistern, wishing he could erase the doubts from his mind.

For as long as he could remember, he'd always felt the need to prove himself. Yes, his father had been hard on him, but no harder than he was on himself. It had driven him to excel in his training in the army, to quickly rise through the ranks and to apply for the Legion, to become the youngest Captain in the history of the Legion. And yet, it all meant nothing. All he had to his name was a hollow feeling in his chest and a hunger to prove himself yet again.

"Good afternoon, sir," Carbo said in his crisp tone. "Considering the late hour at which you returned this morning, I decided it best to let you sleep as long as possible."

"I appreciate that." Galerius splashed water on his arms and face, shivering slightly from its icy temperature. He was awake now. After he dried off, he turned and saw Carbo holding another letter from his informant. "When did that arrive?"

"Around mid-morning."

What kind of trouble awaited him with this letter? Maybe he'd get something solid this time, a real clue to his informant or Hostilius's plan. He snatched the letter and ripped open the wax seal.

Congratulations on stopping the shipment of ore last night. Well done. But you are in more danger now than before. He's watching you closer than ever, and you'd best do something to appease him.

Galerius crumpled the paper in his fist and cursed. One step forward, but another step back. And if Hostilius was watching him, then he needed to divert his attention long enough to solve the riddle of this plot to harm the empire. But more than ever, he needed to find the identity of his informant. If he was in danger, he could only image what lay in store for the person who had betrayed the governor.

He returned to his room and retrieved the hidden messenger orb. While staring at his reflection in the crystal, he drew a deep breath and released it with a hiss between his clenched teeth. It was time to report to the emperor.

A trickle of magic flowed from his fingers to the halo of ore, and the crystal clouded. This time, however, instead of finding some snide Deizian on the other end, the face of the empress filled the orb.

"You have news for us, Galerius?" she asked.

His mouth went dry. It was one thing to confess his failure to the emperor. It was an entirely different matter to confess it to the Rabbit. "Yes, Your Imperial Majesty. I wish to report what happened last night."

"I'll send for Titus." She stood, and her round belly filled the image. There was no disguising her pregnancy now, and his pulse quickened. If Hostilius and his allies found out about it, they might act quicker than expected.

Azurha's face filled the orb once again. "Do you wish for me to have him contact you when he returns?"

"No." He blurted the word without thinking, and clamped his mouth shut. It took him several seconds to realize why he'd done so. "If you don't mind, Empress Azurha, I'd like to speak to you about your suspicions on the informant."

"You mean Claudia?"

As soon as she said her name, his senses were overwhelmed by the memory of the Deizian. He could feel Claudia's nails biting into his shoulders, smell her scent, see the passion in her eyes as plunged into her over and over again. He swallowed hard to clear those thoughts from his mind. "Yes," he replied, his voice cracking.

The empress raised a dark brow. "What did you wish to talk about?"

"I've started to follow up on your suspicions," he began, grateful his words seemed to be flowing normally once again, "but every time I get close to her…"

His tongue failed him as he was assaulted by memories of her once again.

"You get distracted?"

Azurha's knowing grin irked him, but he nodded.

"Do not be so hard on yourself, Galerius. Claudia's been

trained from birth on how to use her wiles to wrap a man around her finger. How do you think she married three of the most powerful men in the empire?"

"But if she is the informant, wouldn't you think she'd be working with me, not making me lose my focus whenever I'm within a few feet of her?"

Azurha laughed. The sound sent a dozen little jabs through his gut. "You have much to learn about women, Galerius, especially a complicated woman like Claudia."

His jaw tightened. "I think you're wrong about her. I think she's more her father's pawn than ever."

That wiped the mirth from her face. "I can see why you'd think that. But answer me this—who else in the household would be privy to Hostilius's plans?"

She had him there. "That's what I need to find out."

The empress nodded. "In the meantime, perhaps you should try a different approach with Claudia."

"Meaning?"

"Haven't you ever wooed a woman before?"

He ground his teeth. "Life as a soldier is not conducive to forming a long-term attachment to a woman." He'd seen what being a soldier's wife had done to his mother. His father's long deployments had driven her into the arms of another man, the wealthy Deizian who'd sired him and then abandoned his mother when he tired of her.

"Then I shall give you a piece of advice. Earn her trust."

"And how should I go about that?"

"You're a clever man, Galerius. You didn't rise to become the Captain of the Legion without earning the trust of the emperor and your men."

He rubbed his jaw. This conversation was growing more and more uncomfortable. "I'd hardly compare getting cozy with the Black Widow of the Empire to the Brotherhood of the Army."

"Just remember—the strange thing about trust is that you have to give it in order to receive it. If she is the informant, she's risking a great deal to betray her father, and she's not going to tell you anything without first knowing she can trust you."

"And if she isn't the informant?"

"Then it will still work to your advantage. After earning her trust, she might let something slip that you could use. Do not be fooled by her haughtiness. I've seen a glimpse of the real Claudia hiding beneath the surface. She's more frightened of her father than you think."

Yes, he'd seen a glimpse of the real Claudia, too. The one of soft sighs and gentle caresses. The one who intrigued him far more than he cared to admit. "I'll try to gain her trust."

"And the first step is to engage her in ways other than sex."

Azurha's blunt comment left him speechless. Her face vanished from view, but thankfully, he managed to regain his composure before the emperor appeared.

"How did last night go?"

His breath caught. "Not as well as I had hoped."

Emperor Sergius's face remained unreadable. "What happened?"

The orb threatened to slip from his sweaty fingers. "I managed to stop the ore before it left the warehouse, but have no clue where it was going or what it was intended for."

He recounted the events of the mission, from the size of the shipment to the dual suicides of the two men who could've answered his questions. "I apologize for failing you, Your Imperial Majesty."

"Failing me?" Sergius drew his brows together. "It doesn't sound like you failed to me. You stopped the ore from falling into the wrong hands, and that's what's important. You've created a major hitch in their plans, and now they'll either give up or begin scrambling for an alternative, which gives us more time to stop them."

The contents of this morning's letter flashed in his mind. *But you are in more danger now than before.* "Perhaps, but I would've liked to have wrapped this up by now."

"I understand, and I have no doubt you'll continue to work hard to uncover the conspirators and their plot."

The emperor's calm reassurance was so different than the harsh criticism he'd received from his father growing up. If Galerius had failed to do something perfectly, he earned at best a tirade that left his ears ringing, or at worst, a sound thrashing. A glimmer of confidence formed inside his chest and seeped into his limbs.

"In the meantime, I'll send Marcus to collect the ore you found. He should be there by tomorrow evening."

"That confident in my abilities, Emperor Sergius?"

"Of course. I trusted you with my life when you were Captain of the Legion, and although you've resigned, my trust in you hasn't wavered."

Sergius's words humbled him, and unease wormed its way around his chest, drowning out the faint confidence that had just bloomed. What if he proved unworthy of the emperor's trust? "I thank you for that, Your Imperial Majesty."

"Marcus will contact you after he's landed. Is there anything else, Galerius?"

The last line of the letter nagged at him. "Yes. Our informant suggested this morning that I do something to appease Hostilius."

"What do you have in mind?"

"Short of doing something to blatantly betray you and the empress?"

Sergius laughed at his sarcasm. "I know you are not a man of that nature."

Azurha's voice entered the conversation. "Hostilius is a man driven by power and money. If you can offer him either of those, you can use his greed to blind him."

"I've told him I'm here to look for sapphires," Galerius offered. "He laughed at me and wished me luck in finding them."

The emperor grinned. "Then let's prove him wrong. I'll stop by the Imperial Treasury and find a few raw sapphires to send with Marcus. Then you can present them to Hostilius as proof of your findings."

The plan seemed solid enough to buy him some time, but Galerius was already thinking three steps ahead. "And if he asks for more?"

"I'm sure you'll think of something."

Galerius nodded. Hopefully, he'd be able to stop Hostilius before it came to that. "I appreciate your generosity, Emperor Sergius."

"You're close, Galerius. I can feel it." But behind the emperor's words, Galerius saw a sense of unspoken worry. He wanted this plot stopped before the child arrived, and Galerius wouldn't fail him.

He lifted his chin. "So can I."

12

Claudia squinted in the bright midday sun as she emerged from the shadowed colonnade of the coliseum. The smell of dirt and sawdust tickled her nose, and sweat prickled the back of her neck. A blast of trumpets filled the air, announcing her father's arrival, followed by a melody of flutes, harps, and drums.

Four days had passed since Galerius had seized her father's shipment of ore, and his ire was just now beginning to abate at home. But today, in front of the large crowds who filled the rows to celebrate their governor's birthday, Hostilius appeared jolly and benevolent in the midst of the fanfare. She watched him wave to the crowd and carry out his masterful performance to those who watched him.

He's not the only actor in the family, though.

She forced a genteel smile to her face and sat to his left. The governor's box was filled with over a dozen high-ranking Deizians today. Some of them were merely sycophants trying to seize her father's favor. But most were his allies—men who held a grudge against the emperor. Men like Atius Cotta. She kept her ears open while pretending to watch the dancers below, hoping to catch a clue about the next step in her father's plan.

"It's a pity Labeo couldn't make it today," Cotta said. "I would have welcomed his insight into our little venture."

At the mention of another governor, she honed in on the conversation between her father and Cotta.

"Yes, he was delayed by provincial business and expressed his deepest regrets at missing today's celebrations, but he assured me he'll join us tomorrow."

Claudia's heart jumped. If she understood correctly, the governor of Pisarino was also part of her father's scheme. But more importantly, her father was planning on meeting with his allies, and she need to know where and when.

"But please, let's not talk about business today," her father continued, his voice wary. "I only wish to indulge in the merriment of the games."

Claudia bit her bottom lip and exhaled through her nose. So much for learning more today. She'd have to pay close attention to what was said when they returned to the sanctuary of their villa. If the gods were on her side, she'd learn something she could pass on to Galerius.

"Good day, Governor Hostilius, and many happy returns on this day to you," a rich voice said from behind her.

Claudia froze and kept her eyes focused on the dancers in the arena. *Speak of the man himself.*

"Good day to you, Galerius." Her father's greeting sound warm to the untrained ear, but she detected a strain of underlying hostility.

"I was honored to receive your invitation," Galerius continued.

No, no, no, no! She wiped her hands on her dress. This had "trap" written all over it. She wouldn't be surprised if her father was planning on having Galerius arrested in the middle of the games. Or worse, tossed over the balcony into the arena below when they brought out the lygers.

"Consider it thanks for finding a new sapphire mine in my province. The stones you sent me to me were some of the finest I've ever seen."

She resisted snapping her head around to see if they were jesting or telling the truth. Instead, she tilted an ear in their direction and watched from the corner or her eye.

Galerius stood next to her father, dressed in a fine steel-grey toga draped over a crisp white tunic. Everything about him, from the style of his hair to the way he carried himself, mimicked the wealthy Elymanians of the empire. Only the leather bracelet covering his right wrist betrayed his roots as a soldier.

"I'm so very glad you found them pleasing. I hope to extract more as I explore the vein further."

"And of course, you'll pay your proper duties to the province, I'm sure." Greed flashed in her father's eyes.

"Naturally." Galerius's smile appeared forced as he bowed, and Claudia stifled a smirk. They were all nothing more than actors.

"Please, take a seat next to my daughter, and enjoy the games."

Claudia's mouth became as dry as the Alpirion desserts. The games would be trying enough on their own. Now she had to endure them sitting beside the one man who drove her to distraction.

She lifted her eyes to her father, who sent her a discreet nod. The message was clear. She was to use her powers of seduction once again to extract information from Galerius.

A jolt raced up her thigh when his knee grazed hers. She shifted in her chair, sitting as far away from him as she could. If she wanted to dissect the truth, she needed to have a clear mind. One that wasn't revolving around ways to slip away with him and ease the ache that was already building deep within her sex.

"So, you were successful in finding sapphires here in Tivola?" she asked, keeping her tone light and bordering on disinterested.

He stared straight ahead, mirroring her posture. "Yes."

"That's strange. I thought the area had been stripped of any gems long ago." *Not to mention, Kafi hasn't reported you visiting any mine shafts in days.* But he didn't need to know that she was still having him followed.

"I fortunately stumbled across an undiscovered vein."

"Where?" If she was going to support his claims to her father, she had best make the best showing of questioning him. She only knew of one sapphire mine left in the area, and she prayed he hadn't found it.

He turned to her and raised the edge of his mouth in a cocky grin. "Trying to steal what I've rightfully found?"

Her lips longed to wipe that arrogant expression off of his face with a kiss that would have him begging at her feet once again. She turned away from him before she acted on her impulses. "Just curious. I know this city and its surroundings well, and if you've found some remaining sapphires, there might be more to claim."

"Your father and I have an agreement. I keep the location secret while exploring the depth of the vein, and he gets a very generous portion of the find. You don't need to try so hard to extract information from me."

Her cheeks burned. "Of all the absurd accusations. I should have you beaten for saying such a thing."

"Why should I be punished for speaking the truth?"

Claudia's jaw dropped. How dare he call her out in front of her father and his guests. "You are the most insufferable man I've ever met. But then, I should expect that from a low-born Elymanian soldier."

She'd hoped to inflict shame or anger in him with her insult, but he laughed it off. She waited for him to return with some equal retort, or better yet, whisper something seductive in her ear, but nothing came. Instead, he turned his attention to the slaves below as they set up for the chariot races.

Her blood chilled. Something was different about him. Normally, she could capture his attention with a smoldering glance or flash of her cleavage. The man sitting next to her, however, seemed immune to her charms. She chewed on her bottom lip and searched for reasons why.

By the time they'd led the first two racers into the ring, she'd come up with nothing. At least his cool demeanor wouldn't distract her from her favorite part of the games. She leaned her elbows on the railing and rested her chin on her hands.

"Eager for the races to begin?" Galerius asked.

"Yes."

He moved closer to her so his breath warmed her ear. "Care to make a wager on the outcome?"

Her breath hitched. He was so close, she could smell the leather and spice of his skin. But she dared not look at him. No doubt, he'd instantly notice her desire and try to use it to his advantage. She refused to give him the upper hand. She could play cool and distant as well as he could. "You'd lose."

"That sure of yourself?"

She grinned. "Absolutely. I'm an excellent judge of horseflesh."

"The race involves more than just the animals. What of the chariots themselves? Or the drivers?"

She shook her head. "In the end, it all comes down to the horses, and I'll prove it to you."

"So you do want to make a wager."

"Very well, Galerius, since you are so interested in being made a fool, I'll agree to make a wager with you." She studied him, trying to find something more proper than asking him to pleasure her with his tongue again. "If I win, I want one of those sapphires you've found."

"And if I win?" The heat she'd always seen had returned to his eyes, and she squirmed in her seat.

She licked her lips and angled her chest toward him so he had a clear view of her breasts. "I'm sure you could think of something."

Now it was his turn to shift in his seat. "Indeed, I could."

She knew he couldn't resist her for very long.

Now that she had Galerius back under her control, she shifted her attention to the horses. As tempting as it was to have him buried inside her again, she wanted to prove she knew far more about the races than him.

The first two racers paraded around the track. Behind

her, she overheard her father's guests making their own wagers, but she tuned them out and focused on the horses. The powerful, six-legged beasts native to this planet were magnificent to watch. Under the shiny coats, their muscles rippled with each step, and they tossed their manes proudly, testing the will of their Alpirion drivers.

By the time they'd reached the halfway point of their pre-race circle around the track, she'd picked the winner. "The green chariot will win."

Galerius craned his neck to take a closer look. "You must be joking. Look at how much trouble the driver is having with the horse. It's a crash waiting to happen."

As if on cue, the horse bucked, and the chariot teetered to one side before righting itself.

"Doubt me all you want, but in the end, you'll owe me a sapphire."

He laughed. "I'm looking forward to collecting my prize."

He practically looked ready to devour her. As well-behaved as he appeared to be on the surface, there was no hiding his lust when he met her gaze.

Now was the time to play coy. "Wait and see."

In the early days of the empire, the chariot races belonged solely to the Deizians. Their floating, ore-lined chariots would whip around the track without the need for horses, much to the thrill and awe of the crowds. But as the years went on and the number of pure Deizians dwindled due to intermingling with the native Elymanians, the races were deemed too dangerous and were replaced by the native horse-drawn, wheeled chariots that could be maneuvered by expendables.

The racers lined up at the starting line. Their colored banners rippled in the wind, the only perceptible movement from the frozen drivers and horses. Claudia held her breath and waited for blast of the trumpet.

When it blared, the horses jumped forward. Just as Galerius predicted, the driver of the green chariot struggled to control his horse, but that was what had convinced her it would win. They rounded the first curve with only the inner wheels touching the ground. By the time they came to the straightaway of the second lap, the driver had given up on restraining the beast, and the horse surged ahead.

As they came to the final turn, the green chariot skidded to the side, blocking the blue chariot and forcing its driver to pull up hard on the reins to avoid a crash. It was the final blow. The green chariot crossed the finish line nearly three lengths ahead of its opponent.

Claudia turned to Galerius and smirked. "You were saying?"

He crossed his arms, his lower lip jutting out in what appeared to be a pout. "I still say it was a crash waiting to happen. The gods must have smiled on you this time."

"Are you being a sore loser?" She risked ribbing him and waited to see his reaction. If he'd been any other man she knew, he would've probably retaliated by shouting at her, perhaps even striking her. Deizian women were expected to know their place and never do anything to challenge the authority of a Deizian man. But Galerius was an Elymanian, someone beneath her in society, and would allow her to test how far she could go with him.

Much to her surprise, he grinned and shook his head, the evidence of his wounded pride vanishing. "I will concede that you won this race."

She grazed her fingers along his arm, rewarding him with an inviting glance. "Wise decision."

Once again, he struggled to contain his desire for her. His muscles tightened under her fingertips, and his grey eyes gleamed with the same hunger she'd seen right before his lips had crushed hers.

The moment came to an abrupt end as General Galeo slapped his hand on Galerius's shoulder. "What did you think of the first race?"

Claudia jerked her hand back and looked away, her body

flushed with a mixture of lust and embarrassment. It was one thing to give in to her lust in privately, but it was an entirely different matter to do so in front of everyone in her father's box. She drew in a steadying breath. *Flirt with Galerius, but control yourself.*

"It was an exciting race, sir." Galerius, for his part, seemed unaffected by what had passed between them seconds ago. "I look forward to the next one."

The retired general sank into the seat next to him. "Care to make a little wager?"

Claudia rolled her eyes. All these men seemed to care about was who could steal the most money from the others.

"Perhaps. Of course, I'll let Lady Claudia choose which horse I'll be betting on."

She stared at him as if he'd lost his senses. Just a moment ago, he'd been accusing her of being lucky.

"You'd let a woman choose for you? What nonsense!" the general said with a dismissive wave of his hand. "The only thing they're good for is in the bedroom."

Claudia gnashed her teeth together, but held her tongue. She'd borne such insults her entire life. No one ever expected much from her, which had worked to her advantage so far.

"I beg to differ. I think Claudia can read these races far better than we give her credit for. She is a woman of high intelligence, and I'd be fool not to trust her judgment." He gave her a wink as he echoed their earlier conversation.

Claudia's mouth parted, and she almost forgot to breath. Something strange stirred deep within her chest as she listened to Galerius defend her. All her life, she'd had men value her only for her body or her family's political connections. She'd never had a man praise her intelligence before.

"More like you'd be a fool to trust her judgment." Galeo reached into his purse. "How does a thousand korins sound?"

Her eyes widened at the sum. She whispered in Galerius's ear, "You don't have that kind of money."

"Then don't let me lose."

Her heart flopped. "But what if I—"

He pressed his finger to her lips to shush her. "You've proven to me you know what you're doing, and I trust you to pick the winner."

Trust. Such an odd word to hear coming from someone she barely knew. Not even her father trusted her. And yet, Galerius was placing his faith in her. A wave of emotion like she'd never experienced before choked her. She nodded and studied the next two racers.

Unlike the first race, this one didn't seem to have a clear winner. Both horses seemed too tame, too well controlled, too evenly matched. Doubt clouded her thoughts. Had she been too arrogant? And even if she was, why did it matter? After all, it was Galerius who stood to lose a large amount of money, not her. And yet, the word trust kept echoing through her mind in time with the prancing horses on the track below. He'd thought her of worthy of earning it, and strangely enough, she didn't want to disappoint him.

Galerius nudged her gently with his elbow. "Claudia, have you made your choice? General Galeo and I are waiting."

She leaned closer, looking for a sign that would give one horse the advantage over the other. Then, as they were lining the horses up at the starting line, she saw one of them snort and paw impatiently at the ground. Her doubt lifted. "The red chariot."

"You heard that, General." Galerius took her hand in his. "Lady Claudia states the red chariot will win."

The retired general jingled the coins in his purse, but didn't reach for any of them. "I think I'm going to be a thousand korins richer in a few minutes."

"I wouldn't be so certain if I were you." Galerius squeezed her hand, making her heart flop.

The trumpets blared once again, and the horses took off. Just as she'd predicted, the horses ran neck and neck. Her gut clenched as the yellow chariot moved ahead at the end of the first lap. She offered a quick prayer to the gods she hadn't chosen the wrong horse.

119

The red chariot caught up in the straightaway, the wheel hubs of the chariots rubbing against each other and sending a shower of sparks into the arena. Claudia tightened her grip on Galerius's hand, noticing it felt as damp as hers. The drivers struggled to regain control of their spooked horses. The chariots wobbled from side to side going into the last turn. A scream went up from the crowd, followed by a crash. A cloud of dust rose from the track, concealing the chariots from view.

Please, please, please. She gripped Galerius's hand with both of her own, rocking it back and forth. Her heart raced. *Please let me be right.*

A horse emerged from the dust, limping forward. A second later, she glimpsed the red banner on his chariot. Behind it lay the shattered remnants of the yellow chariot. The driver urged the horse forward, cajoling it until it crossed the finish line.

Claudia threw her hands up the air and cheered with the crowd.

Galerius clapped beside her and turned to the general. "I think you owe me a thousand korins."

With much grumbling, Galeo fished the coins out of his purse. His faced burned red, and he practically threw the money at Galerius. "Lucky break," he muttered.

"More like having an excellent judge of horseflesh on my side."

Claudia stopped cheering and soaked in his compliment. Her cheeks ached from smiling. This was one moment she'd always remember.

After Galerius stowed the coins in his purse, she leaned close to him and said, "You now owe me a very large sapphire."

13

Galerius could hardly believe what he was witnessing. Claudia Pacilus could actually be quite charming once he saw her as something more than a source of information. As the races continued, she laughed, smiled, and seemed to become more relaxed with each exchange he had with her.

Of course, he didn't miss the way she flirted with him. She'd send him sidelong glances through her thick lashes. She'd lean forward so the neckline of her dress dropped. A subtle touch here, a casual lick of the lips there. All enough to keep his cock reasonably stiff the entire time he sat next to her. But it all came so naturally to her that he wondered if she was truly interested in him rather than trying to seduce him to distraction.

Could the empress have been right about her? Could this be another glimpse to the real Claudia?

He shook the thought from his mind before it embedded itself and kept him up all night. As much as he wanted to believe that he was seeing the true woman, he couldn't forget who her father was. He'd always heard that children didn't stray far from their parents—her brother, Asinius, was a prime example of that—and he wasn't ready to completely let his guard down around her.

As they cleared the arena after the last race, the charming woman vanished. Claudia's shoulders stiffened. Her face became an unreadable mask, her eyes fixed forward.

"Is something wrong, Claudia?"

"What makes you think that?" Her voice was sharp and condescending. The Deizian princess had returned.

Galerius glanced around the box at the others. By now, some of them had drunk enough wine to flush their faces and raise their voices. They continued to laugh and continue their boisterous conversations as though nothing was amiss. No one seemed to notice the change in her but him.

Hostilius reached around his daughter and jostled him. "Here comes the best part of the games, Galerius—the gladiators."

He grinned and nodded enthusiastically, all the while keeping his eyes on Claudia. She sat straighter in her chair, her spine not touching the back. Her fingers toyed with the loose threads of her embroidered palla. But her attention remained locked below, watching the first two men enter the arena.

Within minutes, the metal clang of swords against shields hovered over the hushed crowd. The dance between the well-trained combatants mesmerized him, but not completely. His gaze kept darting to the woman beside him. Her breath quickened. Her nostrils flared, and despite her objections, he knew something was bothering her.

The crowd cheered as the first blood was spilled, but Claudia remained silent. The wounded gladiator fell to the ground while his opponent continued to pommel him, seeking out the weak points in his armor. Within seconds, he downed man's sword was kicked away from him, rendering him defenseless. His opponent paused and looked to the governor's box for direction.

A cruel grin lit Hostilius's face. He held out his arm, his thumb level with the horizon. If he turned his thumb up, the man would live. But Galerius already knew the fate of the wounded gladiator, his gut tightening at inevitable outcome. Hostilius was not a man of mercy. With a twist of his arm, he condemned the man to death, and the crowd cheered as the gladiator's head rolled across the arena.

Claudia remained pale and silent. Moisture gathered in the corners of her eyes, but her face remained an unreadable mask. If she had been any other woman, he would've expected her to look away from the bloody scene below or let her tears fall. But she concealed any evidence of emotion from those around her.

It both piqued his curiosity and stirred something deeper inside him. He touched her arm, and she jumped. "Lady Claudia, sun is getting hotter. Would you like to step into the colonnade with me?"

She stared at him with wide eyes as though he'd spoken gibberish to her.

"I think you could use a moment to cool down," he continued, hoping she would accept his offer. It now quite clear that something from gladiators' combat troubled her, and she was trying her best to keep up a brave appearance in front of her father and his friends. "Perhaps catch some of the breeze."

She glanced at her father, who was already completely absorbed with the next two combatants, and nodded. At the touch of her clammy hand on his, he feared she might faint before they stepped behind the safety of the curtain that separated the hallways from the box. He leaned into her and whispered into her hair, "Take a deep breath and follow me. It will be all right in a few seconds."

She clung to him as he led her up the stairs and into the colonnade. A flicker of movement caught his attention after they passed the curtain, but her tight grip on his arm kept him from turning toward it. "We're being followed," she warned.

As the words left her lips, he saw the man disappear behind a column. "Does your father fear I'll do something scandalous to you?"

Her lips twitched. "You mean you haven't already?"

The tension eased from his muscles. The Claudia who intrigued him had returned.

She leaned against one of the columns and closed her

eyes. The wind tousled her sweat-dampened curls and swirled the skirts around her legs. A few deep breaths later, she opened her eyes and said, "Was it that obvious?"

"Only to me." He brushed a lock of hair out of her face.

She gazed out toward the sea. "It's a vipers' den in there. They're all looking for some flaw, some sign of weakness before they go in for the kill." Her gaze hardened as she turned it back to him. "I can't let them see anything they'd use against me."

"You're a woman. You're allowed to show softness."

She shook her head. "No, I'm a Deizian, the daughter of the governor and a member of one the oldest and purest families in the empire. I—" Her voice caught, and she swallowed hard. "I can't give my father a reason to find displeasure with me."

Her words tore at his conscience. "And if you did?"

"Do not pretend to understand me, Galerius." She stared at the mosaic floor and closed her eyes again.

But he wanted to understand her. He wanted to know what demons haunted her, what she wanted to say but couldn't. And even though it had little to do with his mission, he wanted her to trust him.

He lifted her chin. "What is it about the gladiators that bothers you?"

Her jaw tightened. But when she finally opened her eyes, he caught a glimpse of naked terror. "I don't like bloodshed."

Like a punch to his gut, it hit him. Claudia was none of the things the empire thought she was. Yes, she had her moments of pride, and she was a skilled seductress. But beneath the surface, she lived in fear.

"Why is that?" he asked, hoping to learn more.

Her breath hitched, and she grew pale again. She jerked from his grasp, her posture becoming defensive. "Why do you want to know?"

He could only imagine what must have happened when she discovered that her last husband, Helvinius, had been decapitated in his bed while he slept. Did she scream when she saw the pillows soaked with blood? Did she faint? Or did keep a brave face during the day while the images plagued her dreams at night? Whatever her reaction, he knew without a doubt she couldn't have murdered her husbands with her own hands. She didn't have the stomach for it.

But that didn't mean she couldn't hire someone to carry it out for her.

He remembered what the empress had told him. Trust had to be given before it could be received, and he was willing to take a gamble. "I don't like unnecessary bloodshed, either," he confessed.

Her brows furrowed, and she cocked her head to the side. "How can a soldier not like bloodshed? Are you a coward?"

Her question rankled him, sinking below his skin to attack his very soul. Had he been a coward by resigning from the Legion? "I said *unnecessary* bloodshed. As a soldier, I've killed more men than I care to count, but there was always a reason for it, something more than just providing entertainment for a governor's birthday."

She nodded, her expression softening as she reached for his right hand. Slowly, she unbuckled the strap of leather around his wrist and let it fall to her ground. Her fingers traced his tattoo. "Once a member of the Legion, always a member of the Legion," she said softly.

His throat tightened, making his words sound harsh and gravelly. "I'm not a member of the Legion anymore."

She continued to trace the laurel leaves around the symbol of the Legion, the ones that marked him as Captain. "Perhaps. But tell me this, Galerius Metellus, what would you kill for?"

Despite the bluntness of her question, she bore no malice in her eyes as she waited for his reply.

His mouth went dry. What would he risk his life to defend? "I'd draw blood to defend the empire."

Her lips curled into a small smile. "As every good citizen should."

"I'd defend my friends."

125

"But what of your family?"

"I have none to speak of."

"Oh." Her expression remained unreadable as she moved from his tattoo to lace her fingers through his, drawing him toward her. "Anything else?"

She was testing him, trying to delve into his motives. He hesitated. Claudia may not be a murderer, but she could still be her father's puppet. If he told her he was still loyal to the emperor, would she become his ally or his enemy?

Her blue eyes remained questioning as she waited for his answer. He breathed in the scent of lavender and lemon, wondering if he'd ever be able to smell it again without thinking of her. He drew closer to her so he could feel the warm curves of her body beneath the sheer silk of her dress. Desire pounded through his veins with each beat of his heart.

"Would you defend me?" she asked.

His mind wrestled with his gut—or to be more precise, his cock. He wanted to tell her no on the grounds that he couldn't defend someone he didn't trust, but everything about her at that moment called to him. Her vulnerability. The sweet curve of her lips. Her soft breath bathing his cheek. If she had been as forward and brazen as she'd been in the theater last week, he would have excused her behavior as nothing more than a ploy to use sex as her weapon. But she remained shy, expectant, as though she merely wanted him to place a gentle kiss on her mouth and tell her she'd be safe with him.

He may not have been able to answer her question right then, but that didn't stop him from indulging in the woman standing before him. He brushed his lips ever so slightly against hers. Her breath caught, and her fingers tightened around his. Through the sheer material of her gown, her heart pounded against his chest.

He waited for her to slap him for his insolence or proclaim her dominance by taking the kiss further, but she remain perfectly still in his arms. Her face became that of a blissful dreamer. It was too much to resist, and he found himself lowering his lips to hers again.

"Claudia," a man called from the colonnade.

She jumped and backed away from Galerius, her lips still parted and her eyes still wide. "Over here."

Her brother sauntered toward them from the shadows. "Father sent me to fetch you and let you know the slaves have raised a tarp over the box. The sunshine…" Asinius glanced at Galerius before continuing, making no effort to hide a sneer, "…shouldn't bother you anymore."

"Thank you." Her brother offered to escort her back, but she chose to link her hand around Galerius's forearm instead. "Shall we return to the games?"

He caught the flash of panic in her eyes. "Only if you feel up to it. Perhaps we should linger in the rear of the box in case you get too warm again."

She gifted him with a grateful smile. "I think that would be the best plan."

As they walked back, he couldn't ignore the way Asinius looked as though he wanted to run him through. The back of his neck tingled. Perhaps he should be more wary of Claudia's brother than her.

***

The sun was low on the horizon when the last gladiator match concluded, and Claudia breathed a sigh of relief. Galerius's suggestion had worked. They'd remained in the back of the box, shielded by the tarp and her father's guests from the gruesome violence below. Somehow during the course of the afternoon, he'd convinced a slave to bring up a set of tesserae, and they played until it was time to leave.

Galerius stood and kissed her hand. "It was a pleasure to enjoy your company, Lady Claudia." He turned and bowed to her father. "And yours, too, Governor Hostilius. Thank you again for your invitation."

Her father's smile remained fixed until Galerius disappeared behind the curtain. Then he turned his attention on her, her face stern. No doubt, he would scold her as soon as they were out of the public eye.

She sighed and followed the entourage out of the coliseum. Her brother sided up next to her as they reached her father's litter. "Did I interrupt something, dear sister?"

Warmth flooded her cheeks as she remembered the gentle way Galerius had kissed her. It was almost more arousing than any encounter she'd had previously with him. "Jealous?"

"Hardly."

"You obviously have a problem if you feel the need to spy on me whenever I'm alone with a man."

He gave her a hollow laugh, his eyes narrowing. "And you've developed a concerning taste for Elymanian soldiers."

"Leave your sister alone," their father barked, smacking Asinius on the back of his head. "Go tell Galeo that we'll be meeting in my private room at the baths tomorrow afternoon."

Asinius scowled. "Yes, Father."

Claudia climbed into the litter and adjusted her skirts around her legs. "Using the public baths tomorrow?"

"Yes. They're as much my baths are they are anyone else's in Tivola, considering I was the one who funded their building." He sat next to her and tapped on one of the beams, signaling the slaves to lift them and start moving.

"What about Asinius?"

"Your brother can find his own way home after he's done conducting my business." He turned his icy blue gaze on her. "Speaking of my business, what did you learn about Galerius today?"

Best play naïve with this. She flicked a flower petal off her dress. "Ah, so that's why you invited him to your box today."

"And made sure he was positioned next to you all afternoon. I had a bit of a chore convincing Cotta to leave you alone."

Her pulse skipped several beats. "What interest does he have in me?"

"His line died with his daughter, and he needs a new wife. Someone with good bloodlines."

She bunched her skirts up in her hands. "I'm your daughter, not a hunting dog or a horse."

"Yes, you are my daughter, and you will do as I command."

She stared out into the crowded streets before her anger got the better of her. Cotta was at least as old as her father. And no doubt, once the marriage contract had been filed, he'd meet the same untimely end as her three previous husbands. With no heirs, all his wealth would revert to her father. Such a pattern should be enough to scare of any suitors, and she wondered what her father had promised Cotta to convince him he wouldn't suffer the same fate. "And what if I have no desire to marry again?"

"You have no say in the matter."

It was time to deliver her own killing blow to this conversation. She turned back to her father. "And what does he think about the fact I've been fucking an Elymanian and loving every minute of it?"

Hostilius's stony continence didn't change, but the color rose into his face at an alarming rate. Normally, she would have cowered and begged him for forgiveness, but she felt bolder, more confident than she ever had. "You will never speak of such things again," he said in a low, even voice.

"But didn't you just say that you purposely seated Galerius next to me this afternoon? I thought you wanted me to continue my activities with him."

Her father grabbed her arm so swiftly, the litter rocked on the shoulders of the slaves carrying them. His fingers dug into her flesh. "Listen here, daughter. The only thing I want from you is for you to discover his motives. If that includes fucking him, then do so, but don't you dare proclaim your activities publically and sully my name. Do you understand?"

Tears pooled her in her eyes from the pain, but she blinked them back. Just as she couldn't afford to show weakness in front of her father's peers, so she couldn't show weakness in front of him. She focused her mind on how wonderful it would be when Galerius and the rest of the imperial forces arrested her father and carried him back to Emona in chains. "Yes, Father."

He released her with a shove and remained silent the rest of the way home.

As soon as the slave lowered the litter to the ground, Claudia sprang from it and ran up to her room. Her father was plotting something tomorrow, something that involved gathering all his allies at the baths, and she needed to let Galerius know about it.

"What happened, my lady?" Zavi stood a few feet away and pointed at the blue marks forming on Claudia's arm.

"Nothing to concern you." She pulled out a sheet of paper and dipped her pen in the inkwell. "Go fetch Kafi now."

"Yes, my lady." Her maid disappeared from her chambers, leaving her alone.

With the same practiced care as her previous letters, Claudia wrote:

He's meeting with his allies in his private rooms of the baths tomorrow afternoon. If you want to know what he's planning, listen closely, but do not be seen.

She'd sealed the letter for Galerius and was already finishing another letter arranging for her to get a massage the next afternoon when Kafi appeared. "Take this one to the baths so they'll have a slave waiting for me when I arrive tomorrow, and send this one to its usual location. And be careful not to be seen."

He grinned and bowed, silently slipping through the door as he always had.

Zavi started unfastening her dress. "Let's get you ready for dinner."

Claudia allowed her maid to strip her bare and sank into the waiting tub, eager to scrub the grime of the day from her skin.

"Perhaps we can cover those bruises up with this?" Zavi held up a golden arm cuff. "Between that and your palla, no one will even notice them."

But Claudia would. Anytime her courage faltered, she'd look at them as a reminder of what lay in store for her if she did nothing. If she wanted to succeed, she needed to stop her father soon, before the barrier fell and before she found herself in the clutches of husband number four.

14

Galerius stared at the public baths from the street and rubbed the back of his neck. He'd been there numerous times since coming to Tivola, but usually only to enjoy the pools. Now, he was having to look at it from a different perspective, and the task was daunting.

Somewhere in this massive complex, Hostilius had a set of private rooms. He needed to not only find them, but also find a way to eavesdrop on the meeting today without being seen. If his informant had been kind enough to give him a few clues on how to do that, it would have been appreciated. Instead, he was working from a few hints and a ticking clock.

Dawn was rising on the city, and the baths were opening for business. The workers were dousing the flame-lit torches that illuminated the richly detailed frescos on the walls. He slipped past them and entered the main atrium.

If I were a pompous ass, where would I place my private rooms?

He scanned the passageways, marking off the ones he'd already explored as a client. The three public pools—the caldarium, tepidarium, and frigidarium—were clearly marked, as were the corridors to the gymnasium and massage rooms. The only part of the baths without a sign was a small wing along the exercise fields. He followed the corridors to it, only to be met by a locked door.

"Excuse me," he said to one of the passing workers, "but what's behind those doors?"

The worker shooed him away. "Nothing of your concern, sir. Those rooms are private."

Galerius allowed himself to be escorted back to the atrium, but only after he caught a glimpse of the bronzed lock panel on the wall. "Tell me, how do you keep the waters so perfectly warm here?"

"We have slaves manning the fires below," the worker replied. "They've mastered the art of making sure the temperatures are right for each pool."

He doubted Hostilius would meet with his friends in the cold waters of the frigidarium. If he could find a way to the underground workings of the bath, then he might find a hidden way into the private rooms. "And how to do the slaves get down below the pools. Do you keep them there permanently?"

The worker laughed. "The governor had these baths designed so that guests like yourself would be able to enjoy them without having any awareness of the work that goes on to maintain them. Now, if you are here for a bath, please enjoy our complex."

Galerius nodded and went toward the tepidarium. He stripped off his clothes and took a quick dip, washing the sweat away from his skin. His mind wandered back to Claudia and her question. Would he defend her? His indecision still clawed at his gut, as did his response to her. It was one thing to see her as one of the vipers she described, someone who only sought to gain power and didn't mind manipulating people to get it. But something had been different about her yesterday, something that still nagged at him like a sore muscle in his chest.

Was she asking if she could trust him? Or was she merely trying to collect her own set of allies?

He combed his fingers through his hair, letter the water run down his face. Part of him wanted to trust her. He couldn't deny the protective vibe she stirred within him. She'd let him see a part of her she kept hidden from those around her. She'd opened herself up to attack by admitting her weakness. Why? What did she hope to gain?

Things would be much less complicated if he could just arrest her and force her to give him a straight answer. That was the way he'd always handled things as a soldier. The games he was required to play here wouldn't allow that, though. If he made one wrong move, everything he'd spent weeks building would crumbled beneath him. Too much was at stake.

And as much as he wanted to allow himself to feel something for Claudia, he couldn't risk becoming vulnerable.

Galerius climbed out of the pool and dried off. The corridors were still empty, as most of the citizens preferred to visit the pools in the heat of the afternoon. He went straight for the private rooms and pressed his hand against the bronze square beside the doors. Magic flowed from his palm, but the locks didn't click. Just like on the doors of the imperial chambers, Hostilius had set the locks to only allow certain people into his corner of the baths.

He pulled his hand back and cursed. He'd hoped to be able to explore the rooms and settle in behind a statue or a tapestry where he could hide and wait for the meeting to start. Now he was forced to find another way into the chambers.

He wandered back to the main atrium, mulling over what the worker had told him. The slaves manned the fires below. If he could find them, he might find a way below.

"Are these the extra slaves we requested?" a voice called from the other side of the atrium.

Galerius smiled. The gods were on his side for once.

He peered around a marble statue at the two well-dressed Elymanians and the line of four chained Alpirions in front of them.

"They don't look like much," the other Elymanian replied, "but they should meet your needs for the day."

"They'd better, or the governor will take it out on me. And if I end up on his cliff, I'll make sure you're there, too." The first man waved his arm. "Follow me."

Galerius lingered a few steps behind them, clinging to the shadows as they headed to the back of the baths. The first Elymanian, whom he assumed was one of the managers of the baths, stopped in front of a fresco and pulled out a key. A second later, a portion of the wall swung forward, and the line of slaves disappeared into the darkness on the other side.

He waited until the door closed before approaching it. The lock looked simple in nature, something he could easily pick with the right tools. The tough part would be sneaking into the underground chambers without being caught. But as his mind whirled on the way back to his home, he came up with a solution that just might work.

***

Galerius lounged in the main atrium, the sun shining down on him through the clear glass tiles of the ceiling. A fine linen toga covered up the coarse homespun tunic beneath. His skin prickled from the combination of the fabric and heat, but he remained fixed on the bench. Hostilius was due any minute now.

He wasn't the only one waiting. The manager from this morning paced in front of the door as though a lyger would snap him up if he stopped. Then he paused and tugged at the neck of his tunic before putting on a smile of false confidence. "Governor Hostilius, so good to see you again."

Hostilius entered the baths with an entourage of seven other men, all of them Deizians from the most powerful families in the empire. Galerius's stomach dropped. Whatever Hostilius was planning, it was big.

"Are my rooms ready?" the governor asked. His upper lip curled up at the excessive ministrations the manager was making before him.

"Just as you requested, my lord."

Hostilius and the others walked past the manager as if he were a beggar on the street and went toward the rooms behind the locked doors.

Galerius waited a few heartbeats before heading for the hidden panel. The toga fell from his shoulders, revealing a

135

costume more befitting a laborer. He pulled out his tools and set about picking the lock. Sweat beaded on his brow, but it evaporated the second he opened the door, and was greeted by the blast of the furnace below.

He gulped and peered down the dark staircase. The red glow of the fires illuminated the walls, providing a dim light as he descended. The sound of sandals shuffling along the dirt floor and the crackle of burning logs were the only sounds. The slaves stared at him with glazed eyes, but said nothing as he passed them. The day's work had already drained them of any excess energy for talking.

By the time he reached the fires warming the governor's private baths, the muscles in his thighs ached, and his mouth was parched. His tunic clung to him as though he'd just climbed out of the sea. Even during his days stationed in the Alpirion desserts, he'd never encountered heat like this. How did the slaves endure working in these conditions?

Muffled voices sounded above him, but couldn't find where they were coming from. He circled the caldarium, trying to find a place where he could hear better, but the floor appeared to be impenetrable. Frustration knotted his muscles, and he sank into a crouch. Once again, another dead end.

One of the slaves paused from tending the fires and stared at him as though he were trying to figure out why someone who wasn't a slave would invade this inferno. Galerius tensed. Would he sound the alarm and ruin everything?

Then the slave grabbed a crate from along the wall and dragged it to the edge of the pool. He held Galerius's gaze, pointed to the ceiling, and resumed working.

Galerius rose to his feet. His head swam from the motion, and he waited a moment before moving toward the crate. He climbed up and looked where the slave had pointed. There, hidden in the shadows, was a small metal grate.

Relief washed over him, only to be driven away as he burned his fingers sliding the grate open. He stuck them in his mouth to choke his yelp of pain and listened.

"Yes, the confiscation of yet another shipment of ore was a setback, but now I think we have enough to finish building the device," Hostilius said.

Device? What device? Galerius leaned as close as he dared to the opening, hoping to catch a clue as to what they were building.

"When do you think it will be operational?" another man asked. Galerius visually catalogued the men who'd entered the baths earlier and matched it with the governor of Pisarino, Labeo.

"Soon," Hostilius replied, his voice like silk. "Very soon. Now that we have the supplies we need, things are moving along at a much faster rate than I first anticipated."

"Found a way to properly motivate your slaves?" Labeo asked, laughing.

"We've waited long enough for this day to come. I do not wish to postpone it any longer than necessary."

"Will it be safe this time?" another man asked, one Galerius couldn't place. "I don't want to risk another explosion."

"I've spoken with my engineers, and we've taken precautions not to let that happen again. Whatever the blue spark of magic was, we'll be more than prepared for it."

"It sounds like you've thought of everything, Governor Hostilius," General Galeo said. "When you are ready to test the device, let me know so I can have my men ready.

"Your men?" Cotta laughed, followed by the sound of a hand smacking against skin. "I thought you'd retired years ago."

"I may no longer command men on the battlefield, but any man of notable rank in the army is there because of me."

Galerius frowned. Galeo implied he held some sway over the commanders, almost as though he could blackmail them into doing his bidding. He needed to check with Rufius to see if there was any truth to the general's boast. If there was, that meant the army could answer to Hostilius instead of the emperor.

"I think that covers everything of importance that I wanted to discuss." Hostilius paused, and water splashed. "Let's enjoy our afternoon in the baths."

A soothing melody played by a harp filled the chamber above, and Galerius leaned away from the grate. More hints, but nothing seemed to fit together. Just more riddles for him to solve. At least he'd learned the ore was being used to build some device and that Hostilius had tried something similar before. He offered a quick prayer to the gods that the governor's new device would suffer the same fate as the prior one.

The heat was taking its toll on him, and Galerius started to back away until he overheard Cotta say, "Now that we've finished that, let's talk about your daughter."

His chest tightened. What did Atius Cotta want with Claudia?

"I've mentioned your proposal to her," Hostilius replied, "but naturally, the poor girl is a bit hesitant to be married again."

"As am I, but you understand my need for an heir."

"Of course I do, and any child my daughter conceives will have the purest bloodlines in the empire."

A growl formed in the back of Galerius's throat. They were talking about Claudia as though she were nothing more than a breeder to them. Did they have any idea about the woman she was?

"Are you sure she's fertile?" A hint of irritation entered Cotta's voice

"Are you implying my daughter isn't?"

A new sense of dread worked its way up his spine. He'd taken no precautions with Claudia. What if she conceived his child? Would he be as irresponsible as the man who sired him?

"She never conceived with her prior marriages."

"She was married to old men who were less virile than you." The water splashed again. "Once the marriage contract is signed, you are more than welcome to try her out and see if she conceives before you actually marry her."

Cotta laughed. "I might just have to do that."

Galerius curled his hands into fists. He'd die before he let Cotta force himself on Claudia. The violence of his possessive urges rattled him to the point where he teetered off the crate he'd been standing on. *What is she doing to me?*

The slave who'd helped him before nudged him and offered a dipper of water. Galerius took it and slurped up the contents, hoping they'd soothe the fires burning inside him. Was this what she was talking about when she asked if he would defend her? Or were their interludes something planned and conducted by her father, who clearly had no problem whoring out his daughter to different men?

He wiped the water from his mouth and pulled a few coins from his pouch to thank the slave. He'd heard enough for now. It was time to leave the fires before he melted. He started to go in the direction he came, but the slave tapped him on the shoulder and pointed to another corridor. Galerius hesitated, wondering if he'd get lost and spend eternity trapped down here if he went another way, but so far the slave hadn't shown any malicious actions.

He took a few steps into the dark corridor and tripped over a stair, stumbling across a different way out.

***

Claudia stared at the erotic fresco adorning the wall in front of her, watching for any movement of the hidden door concealed behind it. She'd spotted Galerius the second she entered the baths, despite his odd dress, and smiled when he took off after her father. Reassurance settled over her like a warm blanket. She had the proof she needed. She finally knew why he was here—to follow up on her letters and stop her father.

Now if only she could find the courage to tell him she was the one behind the letters. Would he despise her for betraying her father? Would he defend her? Would he lose all interest in her?

She closed her eyes and pushed that problem from her mind, enjoying the gentle pressure the slave applied to her aching muscles. "You asked your husband to keep an eye out for the man I described?"

"Yes, my lady," she replied. "I told him what to do if he saw him."

"Good." She cracked open one eye and wondered what was taking him so long. "When he arrives, you are to leave the room if he wants to linger here. Understood?"

"Yes, my lady."

The slave said the words as though she'd been present for more than one secret liaison between lovers, although Claudia had never arranged one here before. Based on what she'd told the slave, the other woman probably thought Claudia had lost her mind. But Claudia had to have him one more time. She had to know the pleasure of his touch again before she revealed her secrets and ruined anything that could be forming between them.

The sound of scraping stone filled the room. Claudia jumped. He was coming. She buried her head against her arms and pretended to be enjoying her massage.

The slave stopped rubbing her shoulders, signaling that Galerius had entered the room.

Claudia lifted her gaze to him. Sweat coated his bronzed skin, making the thin tunic cling to his sculpted muscles. A fire burned in his grey eyes as he openly stared at her nakedness.

"Are you lost, Galerius?" she asked casually, trying to keep her excitement from rising into her voice. Her skin grew warm. She wanted him more than ever.

"Perhaps." His voice was harsh, strained, as though he were fighting his own desire. He licked his lips. "What are you doing here?"

"Isn't it obvious? I'm enjoying a massage." She turned to her head to the side and waited for him to make the next move.

But he said nothing. She heard footsteps, a few splashes of water, and the sound of a door opening and closing. She chewed on her bottom lip, resisting the urge to watch him leave. Had she read him wrong?

She flinched when a new pair of hands touched her bare back. A pair that was larger and more calloused than the slave who had been there. "What are you doing?"

"Giving you a massage," Galerius replied.

Her pulse raced. That's not all she hoped he'd do. "Very well," she said, keeping her voice light and haughty as though she were still speaking to the slave. "I expect a complete massage, from my scalp to my toes."

The purely masculine sound of his chuckle made sex clench. He didn't miss her innuendo. "I'll do my best to please you, Claudia."

Then the movement stopped. His fingers traced the bruises on her arm from the day before. "What happened here?"

Her mouth went dry. *Tell him the truth*, her mind screamed, but she was too ashamed to let him see how much control her father had over her. She refused to let him see proof of her weakness. "All these questions are not helping me relax."

He remained silent, his light touch on her arm lingering a few seconds longer before he returned to her shoulders. She didn't need to see his face to know the bruises bothered him, and something tightened in her chest.

His hands worked their way down her spine, fanned her hips, and massaged her buttocks. She squirmed on the table, wishing his hands would continue toward the vee between her legs and ease the ache building there.

Instead, he moved to her feet, pressing his thumbs into the soles in circular movements. Then he moved to her calves, then her thighs, inching up her legs at an agonizing pace. A whimper rose from her lips.

His breath tickled her ear. "Am I doing something wrong?"

Yes, damn it, you're not fucking me. She drew in a shaky breath. Why did she lose control of herself whenever he touched her? "You seem to missing a spot."

"Here?" His finger brushed the outer lips of her sex, and she couldn't smother her moan of pleasure. "Don't worry, Claudia, I'll come to that."

"Just as long as you make me come in the process."

"Is that what you want, Claudia?" He continued to rub his hands from her back to her thighs, carefully avoiding the one area she wanted him to touch. "Is that why you were waiting here for me, all naked and slick with oil?"

If he didn't stop teasing her, she'd knock him to the floor and pleasure herself like she had in the theater. But this time, she didn't want to be the dominant one. She wanted him to take her into his arms, to be the one who couldn't hold back any longer. She wanted him to need her as much as she needed him. "It quite normal to be naked for a massage."

"I suppose it is." His thumbs moved in dizzying circles just above her hips. "Lucky for me, I stumbled across you like this."

Lucky me is more like it. "Yes, you don't make a bad masseuse."

He laughed again, and lowest part of her stomach tightened in anticipation. "I'm not finished with you yet."

Her breath caught. "Oh?"

He grabbed her ankles and yanked her off the table until she was bent over the sheets, her legs spread wide and her sex open to him. His finger pressed against her clit. "Do you want me to massage you here?"

She bunched her hands in the sheets to keep from crying out. "Yes."

"What about here?" He slid one finger into her, followed by another, easily finding the sensitive area that made her knees quiver.

She squeezed her eyes as tightly as she could, enjoying his touch. "Yes, but please, I need more."

"More, Claudia?" His voice teased her as much as his fingers did. "You've never had any problem telling me what you've wanted."

She raised up on her toes, increasing his access to her. She didn't care if he took her from behind, so long as he didn't stop.

He leaned over her, his bare flesh scorching hot against

142

her own. The tip of his erection slid across the opening of her sex. "Tell me what you want."

"I want you inside me." She shifted her hips so he could enter her, but he clamped his body around hers, not allowing her to let him inside. She bit her lip in frustration. "I want you to make me come."

His lips kissed the nape of her neck. "I want you, too, but if I'm going to make you come, I'm going to do it on my terms."

Something changed in the tone of his voice when he said that, but before she could decipher its meaning, he flipped her over onto her back. His hands gripped her ankles once again, raising them up past his shoulders, and pulled her to the edge of the table.

Claudia's mouth gaped open. What was he planning on doing to her?

"I want to take you this way, Claudia." His cock eased into her with a slowness that opposed the aggression behind his demeanor.

Her heart threatened to fly out of her chest. He felt so wonderful, and yet he seemed to want more than just a simple fuck.

"I want you looking at me the whole time." He withdrew and then slammed into her with more force. "I want you to know that *I'm* the one giving you pleasure, not some other man."

His name sat lodged in her throat. No, she'd never be imagining another man when she was in his arms. No man compared to him.

"I want to watch myself sliding in and out of you, watching your face light up with pleasure with each stroke." His voice dropped to a low growl. "And in the end, I want you screaming my name when you come."

A shiver coursed down her spine that had nothing to do with the increasing tension in the pit of her stomach. Men had always wanted to possess her, to claim her as their own. If Galerius had been any other man, she would've tried to wrestle her way free from him. But there was something different about his desire to be the only man in her mind. Somewhere behind his aggression was a hint of desperation.

She realized with a start that she'd never cried out his name when they were together. She'd always been so careful to keep her voice quiet, the nature of their liaisons secret. Did he crave the reassurance that she wanted him? Was he just as unsure about the nature of her desire as she was about his?

She held his gaze and nodded. She wouldn't be afraid to hold back now. "Yes, Galerius," she rasped.

He closed his eyes and seemed to savor the way she said his name. Yes, that was all he wanted. She would gladly give him that and more, and for once in her life, it wouldn't be a lie. With Galerius, there was no need to pretend she enjoyed his touch. There was no need to fake her climax as she'd had to do with her husbands. He knew exactly what she wanted, how she needed to be touched. He'd pushed to her open herself up to new experiences and the pleasure they offered. How could she even fathom another man doing that?

He continued to move inside her, bringing her closer and closer to the edge. Her murmured words of encouragement heightened each stroke. Her body bucked, her hips rising to meet him and allow him deeper inside. Her breath came in desperate pants. She was on verge of coming, and yet she fought it.

His grin grew wider. "Ah, Claudia, do you have any idea how beautiful you are, lost in your own pleasure? Do you know how much pleasure it gives me to see you like this?"

Sweat beaded along her forehead, and the sheets had long since become a tangled mess in her hands, but still she refused to surrender. She didn't want this to end. She didn't want him to know how her feelings for him were changing from something more than just the physical.

His face tensed. "Please, Claudia, don't fight this." His strokes become faster, more frantic. He sat on the brink of his own orgasm, but he was waiting for her. "Please, please, say it."

His pleading tore through her defenses. She let herself

fall into ecstasy, his name pouring forth from her lips as she came.

***

The world turned into a foggy haze as Galerius found his release. The only thing he was aware of was the sound of Claudia calling out his name. His muscles tensed. The blood throbbed through both his head and his cock. Pleasure rippled through his body. His own guttural cry echoed off the walls of the room.

And then everything seemed to crash around him. He pitched forward, collapsing on top of her. His ear pressed against the thin wall of her chest, his head buried between her breasts. The pounding of her heart became the sweetest melody he'd ever heard during those first few moments of consciousness. He closed his eyes and breathed in her scent while he tried to make sense of it all.

This afternoon almost seemed too easy, too perfect. What were the odds of him stumbling across Claudia naked today? As soon as he saw her, he knew he was done for. He'd been craving her too long. He needed to quench his desire for her.

But even when presented with the opportunity to do so, his needs changed. If he simply wanted to come, he could have eased that need with the *lupa* last week. Instead, he wanted to know that this attraction between them was real. He needed to know Claudia wanted him with every fiber of her being. He had to see the desire in her eyes as he was inside her. He had to hear her scream his name when she came so there was no question in left in his mind.

Now that he had, though, his found himself at a loss for what to do next. His emotions warred with his new knowledge, and uncertainty plagued the brief peace he found in her arms. His gut tensed. His feelings for her were changing, deepening, and that frightened him more than facing a swarm of Barbarians.

A purr of satisfaction vibrated through Claudia's chest, and her fingers combed through his damp hair. "That was nice."

Whether it was due fear or sheer exhaustion, his body

refused to move.

She lifted his head and slid along him until her lips captured his. The kiss was slow and easy, meant more to soothe him than arouse him, and yet his body responded eagerly to it. He pulled her into his arms, enjoying her soft curves as they pressed against him, ignoring the warning bells that urged him to stop before this went too far.

He lost track of time until she finally freed him from her embrace. "Oh, Galerius," she sighed, "we're so good together and yet so bad for each other."

Her words pulled him from his dream-like bliss faster than a bucket of cold water. The back of his neck prickled in warning. He pulled back, managing to stand without wavering. "What do you mean, Claudia?"

She sat up and pulled the sheet across her body, her eyes refusing to meet his. She chewed on her bottom lip, but said nothing.

He repeated his question, the growing sense of unease smothering him. "Answer me."

She took a deep breath before lifting her face. The grave seriousness of her expression made his gut coil into knots. "Be careful, Galerius. Don't let him catch you here."

He took a step back, his pulse racing. She knew. She knew why he'd been here in the baths in the first place, perhaps why he'd been here in Tivola all along. "I don't know what you're talking about."

"Yes, you do." She pulled the sheet over her shoulders, concealing the bruises on her arm.

A wave of anger washed over his fear. Did Hostilius harm her because of him?

Her voice shook as she continued, "Now leave, before he finds you."

As if on cue, the sound of men's voice grew louder on the other side of a gold door. Panic flashed in her eyes, and she jerked her head to the door he'd seen the slave exit from. He moved toward it, staring at the door that led to the bathing pools the entire time. When he reached the bronze plate, the locks clicked, and the door opened.

He cast one more glance at Claudia before he left, trying to understand her motives. Her solemn blue eyes met his once again, and a sudden calm filled him. Whatever she knew about him, he doubted she'd tell her father. But that didn't mean he was finished with her. The empress's suspicion that Claudia was the one behind the letters seemed more likely than ever.

"Go," she mouthed.

He slipped through the door, his mind itching with more questions than he had started the day with. Hostilius was building some sort of device that would threaten the empire.

And Claudia knew enough to hold his life in her hands.

15

"Ah, Claudia, you are looking particularly lovely this morning."

Claudia's skin crawled at Cotta's complement, but she fixed a smile on her face when he kissed her hand. How much longer would he be guest of her father's? She couldn't wait to be rid of him.

"I was just telling Cotta how well you run the household," her father interjected, and her blood ran cold.

"Yes, a fine quality to have in a wife." Cotta looked at her as though he were more interested in what she had to offer in the bedroom than how well she could run a villa.

"Hopefully you'll find a woman who meets your expectations." She searched the table for the decanter of chilled wine. Even though the sun hadn't reached its zenith, she needed a drink.

Cotta came beside her and ran his finger along her cheek. "Do you not think you're such a woman?"

Even inch of her body protested his touch, but one quick glance to her father confirmed he was watching the interaction between them. If she offended Cotta, she'd probably end up on the cliffs. "I have my shortcomings, as evidenced by my three prior marriages."

That seemed to cool his advances. Cotta stepped back.

"Yes, but you are still young. Perhaps you just need the right husband to help you overcome those shortcomings."

She wanted to blurt out that she was barren, even though she'd faithfully consumed pomrutin tea every day she was married to prevent conceiving a child. The last thing she wanted was a child from a man she despised. "Perhaps, but perhaps not. Sometimes shortcomings are so deeply ingrained that they can't be overcome."

Her father's eyes narrowed, and his lips pressed into a thin line. "Be patient with Claudia, Cotta. She might need to some coaxing to see things differently, but ultimately, she's always been an obedient daughter."

Anger stiffened her spine. There seemed no way around it. Her father would have her married off to Cotta in a matter of days at this rate unless she did something to stop it.

"Come along, Cotta. General Galeo is expecting us." Hostilius ushered his friend out of the room, but he lingered at the doorway. "Do not defy me, Claudia."

She held her chin up high until he left the room. In days past, his threat would have turned her into a blubbering mass of fear, but she was different now. She'd already defied him over and over again, and she wouldn't stop until she was free.

From the balcony, she watched Asinius join her father and Cotta in the Deizian carriage outside. Her brother took the helm, and they moved down the drive at a leisurely pace, fueled only by their magic.

She was alone. Now was the perfect opportunity to search her father's study for some clue as to what he was planning. He'd remained silent during meals, not even dropping a hint as to why his group of Deizian nobles lingered in Tivola after his birthday celebration. Her gut told he was going to strike soon. And if Galerius wasn't going to stop him, she would.

She closed the door to her father's study, approaching his desk with caution. The fact she'd neither seen nor heard anything from Galerius since meeting him at the baths three days ago bothered her on multiple levels. First, had he overheard anything useful from her father's meeting? If so, then why was it taking him so long to act? Then there was their meeting.

She'd cursed herself more than once for being so stupid. Every time she replayed the moments after they'd come, she wished she'd kept her mouth shut. She couldn't erase the memory of this mistrust in his eyes as he backed away from her. All she'd wanted to do was warn him, to protect him, to reassure him that she was his ally and not his enemy. But it didn't matter. He looked at her as if she were nothing more than a tool her father used to throw him off course.

"He still owes me a sapphire, though," she muttered as she looked over the papers strewn across the desk.

As usual, the contents of his desk held no clues to anything sinister. Official correspondence. Ledgers from the port. A plan to resurface the road to Emona for those who didn't travel by airship. Nothing that seemed out of place on a provincial governor's desk.

He had to be hiding something somewhere. Why else would he seclude himself in here with her brother and friends every night after dinner? What else would explain the hushed murmurs she heard when she pressed her ear against the door or listened outside from the garden?

Why did she keep coming so close only to be held back? She kicked the desk in frustration. Something rattled deep inside it. She paused, shaking the desk once again to recreate the sound. The gods were smiling on her once again.

Claudia crawled under the desk, knocking on the wooden bottom of what appeared to be a hidden drawer. She searched for way to open it and view its contents, but after nearly ten minutes of searching, she gave up. Whatever her father had placed there was hidden well. She rubbed her temples and vowed to look again later. The last thing she needed was some slave tattling to her father about how much time she spent in his office.

She exited his office, relieved to find no one in the hallway, and went out into the garden. The wind was calm, and the sun warmed the flowers, filling the air with their perfume. It was a perfect day to practice her archery.

"Set up my targets and fetch my bow and quiver," she ordered one of the passing slaves. His deep brown face paled a shade, but he nodded and ran off without asking any questions.

Claudia smiled. At least some people had the good sense to listen to her. Now she just needed to show her father that she wouldn't be the obedient daughter any more. Short of killing him herself, she had no idea how to do that, though, without suffering the same fate as those who defied him.

She cast a glance at the cliffs and shivered. Yes, she knew what awaited her if she pushed too hard too soon. Her plans required patience. The timing had to be perfect. And more importantly, she needed to have a backup plan in case she failed.

The slaves removed the target from its hiding place in one of the outbuildings and set it up. The man she'd spoken to early handed her the bow and quiver, his chin trembling. They all knew what would happen if she got caught.

She smiled. "Relax. My father won't be home for at least an hour."

If only she could follow her own advice. Her conversation with Cotta this morning still churned up her ire. How dare he think she would be his wife? She drew back her bow and pictured his face in the center of the target before letting the arrow go.

It went wide to the right.

She cursed under her breath and grabbed another arrow, taking the time to visualize the point embedding itself right between his eyes, but the arrow missed the target altogether.

"I never pictured you as the archery type," Galerius said behind her.

She jumped, the next arrow tangling up in the bowstring before slipping from her hands. She glared at the slave standing in the doorway. "You're supposed to announce all visitors before showing them in."

"Don't be too hard on him." Galerius came down the

few stairs to the small lawn where she stood. "I told him I'd only be here a few minutes."

Her heart sank a little when she heard that, but she refused to let him know that. She'd hoped he'd be willing to stay long enough to take her into the gardens—or better yet, the bedroom. "My father isn't here."

"Yes, I know that. I waited until I saw him leave before coming over."

Her breath caught. He was trying to catch her alone? "Spying on us?"

He chuckled and held out a small object wrapped in linen. "I'd prefer to not have him take this from you."

She laid her bow aside and took it. Nestled inside the cloth was the most beautiful sapphire she'd ever seen. The deep blue rivaled the twilight sky, with hints of violet fire dancing inside the gem. The stone had been expertly cut so the clean facets enhanced the sparkle, no matter which way she turned it. "It's magnificent."

"I'm glad you like it. You definitely earned it."

An underscored note behind his words ripped the pleasure away from holding the stone. He said she'd earned it like she was nothing more than a common whore, even though she'd won it fairly from their wager. She lifted her chin and tucked the stone away inside the bodice of her dress. "Well, I suppose it's nice enough, considering it came from you."

She grabbed a new arrow from the quiver and resumed her archery practice.

Galerius stood back, watching her with his arms crossed as she missed the bull's-eye over and over again. When she ran out of arrows, he said, "Your slave seems unusually nervous. Have you hit one of them before?"

"Don't be ridiculous. I would never use a slave for target practice. Unlike my father, I don't suffer from a lack of humanity."

"Then why does he look like he'd rather be anywhere than here?"

Claudia laughed, debating whether or not to share the real reason behind her small act of rebellion. "A soothsayer once told my father he'd die by the arrow. He's forbidden any archery on the grounds, even though it's a perfectly respectable sport of a lady of my breeding."

Galerius raised a brow, his grin turning her insides to mush. "So you're openly defying him?"

"Not openly. After all, I did wait until he left for the day. But yes, I am defying his order, which is why the slave looks so worried."

He came closer to her. "And what would happen if you're caught?"

A shiver coursed through her body from his nearness, even though he stood as close as he possibly could without touching her. "Do you really want to know?"

"Yes."

She pointed to the cliff. "Sometimes my father likes to push disobedient slaves over the edge and listen to them scream before their bodies hit the rocks below."

To his credit, he winced. "And would he do the same to you?"

She drew in a deep breath, steadying her racing heart before she answered. She had no doubt in her mind if she pushed her father hard enough, the same fate would come to her. But could she admit that to Galerius? She remembered his reaction when she tried to protect him the other day. "Let's hope I never find myself in that position."

"But you aren't afraid to defy him as long as you don't get caught."

It was a statement, not a question, and the hairs on her arms rose. Had he figured out that she was the one behind the letters?

She took a step forward to increase the distance between them and drew back her bow. "I'm old enough now to be in control of my own life."

Her admission set free a storm of emotions inside her—

153

fear, anger, pride—and her hand shook from the intensity of it. Was she in control of her life? Or was she merely caught between the wills of two very stubborn and powerful men?

The point of the arrow wavered in lazy circles around the bull's-eye. Then a steadying force came from behind her. "Shall I give you a few pointers?" Galerius asked, wrapping his arms around hers like a scaffold.

Her muscles tensed, but that didn't stop the pounding of her pulse in her ears. "You're a soldier who lives by his sword, not a bow."

"But I started out as an archer, as does every young man in the army." His breath brushed against her cheek as he helped her line the arrow up with the target. "There are two things you have to remember. The first is to take a deep breath as you draw your bow, keeping your mind fixed on nothing else but the target."

Her mind was wandering everywhere but the target. The heat of his skin burned through her dress, making her hate the layers of clothes between them. The sun warmed the leather of the bracelet covering his tattoo, carrying the scent from where his hand lay over hers on the bowstring up to her nose.

"Are you focused on the target, Claudia? Or are you letting something distract you?"

She pictured her father's face on the target once again and pulled the arrow back to the just in front of her ear. "Now what?"

Galerius pushed her arms down but kept his body pressed against hers. "No, you weren't focusing like I told you."

She turned around. "What you do mean? How do you know what's going on in my mind?"

"I can feel it in your body—in the hitch of your breath, the tightness of your jaw, the thump of your heart. You cannot let emotions cloud your mind, especially in the heat of the moment."

"But I've heard of soldiers who were blinded by the rage of battle, channeling that fury into every swing of their sword."

His face sobered. "Some do, and many make foolish mistakes because of it."

Was he referring to her as a foolish mistake? Or something from his past? "Don't tell me you are a man devoid of emotion, Galerius. I've seen you consumed by passion before."

"Yes, but there is a time and place for such emotion, and the heat of battle is not one of them." He faced her toward the target again. "Let's continue our lesson."

She wanted to tell him exactly what he could do with his lesson, but once she was back in his arms, her anger faded. His actions were not those of a man who acted like he despised her or a man who was ashamed of his past with her. His touch was gentle, strong, reassuring. She let him guide her movements as she loaded the bow.

"Trust me, Claudia," he whispered.

She gulped, her mouth dry. Could she trust him?

"Take a deep breath in," he continued, his voice soothing her rattled nerves, "focus, and learn to let go."

She did as he instructed, drawing in a deep breath and focusing on just the target. This time, she didn't let the image of her father appear over the bull's-eye. She exhaled, cleansing her mind of her anger and fear, and let the arrow go.

It landed in the dead center of the target.

For a moment, she forgot to breathe. Had she been going about this all wrong? Had her focus on revenge kept her from hitting the target, both now and with stopping her father? Her very core shook from the realization, and the bow slipped from her hand.

Galerius pulled her arms in to her chest, holding her until she gained her composure again. "See, that wasn't so hard, was it?"

His lips brushed against her cheek as he spoke. She turned her head, seeking them out. When she found them, the kiss was different than his previous ones. It was slow, delicate, as though he were frightened to go any further with it.

She twisted in his arms so her fingers threaded through

155

his short hair and pulled him deeper into the kiss. Her tongue grazed the opening of his mouth, begging to be let in. When he surrendered, she lost consciousness of the world around her. Everything came down to a set of dizzying spirals, soft caresses, and a growing hunger she couldn't satisfy.

A moan rose, but she couldn't tell if it came from her or him. His hold tightened around her, his lips never faltering in this new dance of seduction that they were engaged in. But this time, she wanted more than just sex from him. She wanted—no, needed—more.

It would be all too easy to fall in love with Galerius Metellus.

Her throat closed in on her as soon as the thought entered her mind, and she pulled away, choking from it. Love? What did she know of such things? And why him? Why now?

"Claudia…" His voice broke as though he were experiencing the same sensations as her.

He reached for her, but she backed away even more. Of all the times to have her mind clouded by emotions, this wasn't one of them. "Galerius, I—"

Her lungs refused operate properly. By the gods, what was happening to her? She glanced around the garden, finding her focus again when she saw the targets. "I need to clean this up before my father returns."

"Yes, you shouldn't let him catch you practicing."

The pain in his grey eyes matched that in his voice, and her heart ached. She was going about this all wrong, but she didn't know how else to act. Her feet continued to carry her away from him. "The servants can show you out. Good day."

She spun around on her heel and fled into the garden, unable to face him any longer. When she finally stopped, she listened for the sounds of footsteps behind her, but the only thing she heard was the crashing on the waves below.

Tears spilled from her eyes. She covered her mouth, smothering the sob that wanted to break free. Her hand trembled, and her stomach tied itself in knots.

What have I done?

She asked herself that over and over again, wondering when her feelings for him had changed. Everything about him was wrong. He was an Elymanian, a soldier, someone beneath her in society. To admit she had feelings for him risked being shunned by those she knew.

But on the other hand, there were so many things about him that were so right. Things that went beyond the physical pleasure. The way he valued her as a person. The way he was there to steady her when she needed him. The way he held her in his arms like she was something precious.

She pulled out the sapphire he'd given her and stared at it, using it as a focal point until she regained control of herself. He'd asked her to trust him. Could she? Could she trust him with her role in bringing down her father? Could she trust him with the secrets of her past?

And if she told him the truth, would he still want her?

16

Claudia paused by the fountain, splashing water on her face to wash away the salt that clung to her cheeks. The sun hung low on the horizon. She'd lost track of time while in the garden, paralyzed by indecision. More than just her life hung in the balance. Now that her heart was involved, the stakes were raised. But, after battling with her mind and her emotions, she finally realized what she needed to do.

She had to tell Galerius the truth.

But just how much should she tell him? It was one thing to say, "I've been the one sending you those letters." It was an entirely different matter to say, "I'm falling in love with you."

One step at a time, she cautioned herself. He wants you to trust him. Test him out first before spilling all your secrets.

She wiped her hands on her dress and went inside the villa to change for dinner. Another night of having Cotta openly stare at her chest. How much longer would he wait before trying to force his hand? A day? A week? She doubted her father would stop him. He never had in the past. Once the marriage contract was signed, his protection ended.

"Someone had a visitor today, I understand."

Claudia froze in the doorway and turned to her brother. His mocking smile chilled her blood. What else did he know?

"Claudia, come in here," her father ordered from his

study.

She lifted her chin and walked past her brother as though nothing was amiss. Any sign of weakness, of guilt, and he would pounce on it. "Yes, Father?"

"Verres said he saw Galerius leaving this afternoon. What was he doing here?"

Claudia released the breath she'd been holding. So, someone just saw him from the road. None of the slaves had tattled on her. "He came to bring me the spoils of my bet from the horse races."

Her father stared at her as though he were looking for some cracks in her story. Thankfully, she had no reason to lie about that, and the tension eased from her body. "Show me," he said at last.

She pulled the sapphire out of her pocket and showed it to her father and brother. "See?"

"Hand it here."

"No." She yanked it back, sheltering the stone with her hands. "It's mine. I earned it, and I will not give it to you."

The only response her father gave to her defiance was a slight tilt of his brow.

Asinius was less subtle. "Why, you ungrateful bitch! How dare you disobey our father?"

He reached for the sapphire, but she swung at him. The edge of the stone caught his cheek, creating a red line in its wake. He wiped the blood away. Murder filled his eyes as he charged at her.

"Asinius, halt." Her father's command boomed off the walls, and they both turned in his direction. He rose from behind his desk, his body as hard as a statue, and glared at them. "Leave now."

"But you saw what she did," Asinius protested, his voice shrill. "If we don't teach her her place now—"

"Leave that to me."

Any hope that her father was defending her fled. She held the stone close to her chest and offered a quick prayer to the gods that her father's punishment wouldn't be too harsh.

Asinius's pout turned into open gloating as he closed the door behind them.

"Claudia, come here."

She took a hesitant step toward him, her gaze level. Looking away was a sign of weakness, and she would not back down without a fight.

"You seem rather fond of that insignificant stone. After all, you have jewels that are much larger than it."

She drew in a steadying breath. "But it's something I've earned, not something that was given to me."

"Is that all?" Hostilius came around the desk toward her. "I can't help but think you've formed some emotional attachment to it. Or perhaps, to the person who gave it to you."

Her heart jumped into her chest. "Don't be ridiculous, Father," she said with a laugh, hoping it would hide her lie. "Why would I form any sort of emotional attachment to someone like Galerius?"

"Why indeed?" He stopped directly in front of her. The tone of his voice cut through her like a surgeon's knife. "But you've admitted to me that you are fond of him."

She now wished she could take back the ill-thought words she'd flung at him in her anger. Perhaps this was what Galerius had cautioned her about—letting her emotions rule her in the heat of battle. "Yes, I enjoyed fucking him, if that's what you mean."

"And this afternoon?"

"Please, Father, I am capable of exercising some self-control. He merely delivered the sapphire to me and left."

Her response, no matter how truthful, didn't seem to appease him. "He seems very fond of you."

"I told you I'd have him wrapped around my finger. Did you ever doubt me?"

He took a step back, and her pulse slowed. "If that was your intention, then you've done well." He returned to his chair. "But you're not finished yet."

"Meaning?"

Hostilius held out a piece of paper. "I need you to continue to distract him for me. Invite him on an outing with you tomorrow afternoon."

She took the paper as though it were on fire. "And what do you suggest we do?" *And what do you hope to gain from this?*

"What you do best." The cold gleam in his eyes left no doubt in her mind what he was asking of her. "Just make sure you use discretion. I'm still negotiating your marriage contract with Cotta, and we can't have him thinking your prefer an Elymanian's bed over his, now can we?"

If he married her off to Cotta, she'd be sure to cry out Galerius's name every time he tried to bed her.

She turned to leave, but her father cleared his throat, stopping her. "Write him now. I want to make sure you entreat his interest."

A shock of warning shot down her spine. She couldn't help but think she was setting a trap for both her and Galerius, but she set the paper down on the desk and reached for a pen. When she finished the letter asking him to meet her here tomorrow afternoon, she gave it to her father for approval.

He read it and nodded. "Very good, Claudia. I'll see that he gets this. Now run along upstairs and get ready for dinner."

She climbed the stairs to her room slowly, unease weighing down her legs with each step. When she closed the door behind her, she asked Zavi, "Where's Kafi?"

Her maid grew wary. "I don't know, my lady. Your father ordered him and a few other slaves into town this morning, and they haven't returned yet."

Claudia squeezed the sapphire in her hand, fighting back the guilt that plagued her over the young slave's absence

"Is something wrong, my lady?"

Zavi's worry came more for her son than for Claudia. "No. I suppose I don't need Kafi tonight."

She didn't need to involve the boy in her plot anymore and risk his safety. Her father wanted her to spend time with

Galerius, and she could do that. She just had to make sure she took him some place secret, some place safe. Some place no one knew about but her.

And once they were alone, she'd tell him the truth.

17

Galerius waited in the entryway of Hostilius's villa, wishing the tingling along the back of his neck would subside. He wished he could make sense of everything that had happened yesterday, but he couldn't. After the way Claudia had fled from him, he never expected to hear from her again. Instead, her letter arrived a few hours later, inviting him to join her today.

Something seems wrong about this. Very wrong.

Inside the villa, it was as quiet as death. The owner was nowhere to be seen, yet the way the slaves moved with silent, fearful steps told him Hostilius was still somewhere on the grounds. Could he be working on his device? And if so, where was he hiding it?

Before he had a chance to ponder those questions, Claudia appeared from the garden. Her blue dress was simple, and she wore her hair down like a young maiden, letting the sunlight catch it and surround her with its glow. The effect mesmerized him. She held out her hand to him. "Good day, Galerius. Thank you for accepting my invitation."

The relief in her voice eased some of his hesitation. He brought her hand to his lips and studied her. Gone was the scared woman who had run away from him yesterday. A poised, confident lady stood in her place. "How could I refuse?"

She rewarded him with a smile. "Shall we go? I've

arranged for one my father's carriages to take us on a drive today."

"If you wouldn't mind, I'd rather take my own chariot." He led her outside and inwardly grinned when she gasped.

"This is a Deizian chariot. You can't drive it."

"Shall I prove you wrong?" He helped her inside and moved behind her, wrapping his body around hers as he reached for the helm. A quick trickle of magic, and the chariot rose off the ground and started down the drive.

She grasped his arm. "Since when can an Elymanian use magic?"

"When an Elymanian has Deizian blood."

That shut her up for a few moments as she tried to figure out how that was possible. She looked over her shoulder at him. "Your mother?"

He shook his head.

"But your father couldn't possibly have been a Deizian. He was nothing more than a common soldier."

Galerius tightened his jaw and urged the chariot forward. If he stayed silent, maybe she would stop asking so many questions.

She continued to stare at him. "At least that explains your eyes, although I find it a bit unusual that they're not blue like most half-breeds."

"I happen to like the color of my eyes the way they are. Most people look at me and never suspect I can use magic."

The corner of her mouth rose. "Yes, I can see where that would be to your advantage."

They came to the end of the drive, and hopefully, the end of this conversation. "Which way?"

"To the right," she replied, pointing south. She cast a glance behind them, her body tensing.

"Expecting someone?"

"Just trying to make sure we aren't being followed." She relaxed and turned her gaze back to the road ahead of them. "I'm taking you some place private."

His cock stiffened at her words. Some place private, eh? Perhaps secluded enough that he could indulge in her once again, taste the sweetness of her skin, plunge into her tight, wet—

Stop thinking that way, his mind snapped. Just yesterday, he was telling her about the importance of keep her mind free from emotion in the heat of battle, and here he was, letting his lust get the better of him again.

Besides, there was more too her than just sex, as he was quickly learning. She knew why he was here, and yet hadn't betrayed him. She also had a serious grudge against her father, making the empress's assumption that Claudia was behind the letters that much more plausible. She could be the key to stopping Hostilius, and this could be her way of confiding her father's plans to him.

And yet she was also much more than that. He experienced an uncomfortable fullness in his chest whenever he looked at her now. His breathed in her scent as though his life depended on it. And that kiss yesterday...

His chest tightened at the memory of it. No, he never wanted that kiss to end. Why had she pulled away?

Her fingers crawled over his hands, covering them at the helm. "You drive this as well as any Deizian."

"A compliment, Claudia?"

She laughed. "Enjoy it while you can, Galerius."

"Care to show me up?" He lifted his palms from the helm and pressed hers against it. She squirmed in his arms. The chariot came to a halt and landed on the ground. "What's wrong? I thought all Deizian's knew how to work magic?"

"We do. It's just that I—I mean, my father never let me—" A sigh of frustration cut off her explanation, and she quit fighting him. "It's not considered proper for a lady of my breeding to drive a chariot."

"I thought you were a woman who liked to defy her father from time to time." He continued to keep her hands at the helm. "I see nothing wrong with letting you drive my chariot for a while."

She drew in a sharp breath. "You trust me with your chariot?"

He lowered his lips to her ear. "Is there a reason why I shouldn't trust you?"

She stiffened against him and looked down at the helm. "No, you can trust me," she murmured.

"Then I hand the chariot over to you." He released her hands and took a tiny step back, giving her some room. Azurha said trust needed to be given in order to be received. Perhaps this small act would lead to a reward later.

The air prickled with magic, much like the charge before a thunderstorm. Claudia flattened out her palms and bit her bottom lip. The chariot rose a few inches above the ground before violently bucking forward.

Galerius grabbed her hips to steady them while the chariot rocked from side to side, moving forward at a faster pace. It was like watching the red chariot in the races last week, only now, he was in it. But soon they leveled out and sped along the coastal road that hugged the cliffs.

Claudia giggled, a sound so foreign from the dignified demeanor she usually wore. "I had no idea driving a chariot was this much fun."

His pulse slowed once he convinced himself she was in control. "I'm surprised you haven't tried it before."

Their speed slowed as she leaned back against him. "I'm just now learning how to defy my father and do what I want."

Her confession puzzled him. He circled his hands around her waist. "And what made you want to defy him?"

She remained silent for several twists in the road before replying, "I refuse to be his pawn any longer."

That was it. No stories. No inciting incidents. No further explanation. But it was enough to satisfy his curiosity for now, even though he was left wondering where he might fit into her plans to defy her father.

Claudia pulled the chariot off the road and set it gently down on the ground. "Follow me."

At first, he thought she was going to fling herself off the edge. She skirted along the cliff, her toes sending pebbles down below, before she came to a trail that seemed to only be visible to animals. As he closed the gap between them, though, he saw the beginnings of a forgotten path to a secluded beach below.

"Is this where you wanted to take me?"

She looked up at him with a playful grin from just below his ankles. "You're not frightened, are you?"

The drop from the cliff to the beach had to be at least a hundred feet, but Claudia showed no fear as she continued to make her way down the trail, occasionally grasping the wiry brush that grew along the sides. "No, but it's not the safest of paths."

Her laughter echoed up to him. "For a former member of the Legion, you seem rather spooked by a cliff road."

By the gods, she was mocking him. He set his jaw and went after her, skidding along the last few feet and nearly knocking her down when he reached the beach. He caught her in his arms and held her close to him. Her smile warmed him more than the sun overhead.

"See," she murmured, pressing her breasts against his chest, "that wasn't so bad."

"No, it wasn't."

He leaned forward to kiss her, but she wiggled away from him and went toward the water. A barricade of rocks nearly twenty feet away created a small pool at the base of the cliff. The waves inside it sparkled in the sunlight, much calmer than their brethren that crashed around them.

She removed her sandals and waded into the water, her skirts pulled up above her knees. The wind whipped her hair around her hips like a shimmering river of gold. A mischievous glint lit her eyes when she glanced back at him. "Do you know how to swim?"

"Yes."

"Then follow me." She unfastened her dress and threw it back on the beach. He caught a glimpse the roundness of her breasts and the curve of her hips before she slipped under the surface. She reappeared in the center of the pool, her hair fanning around her while she swam. "Come on. The water's warm, and the current isn't very strong here, thanks to the rocks."

He shed his tunic and followed her. Her gaze never wavered from him as he came toward her. As much as she smiled, she seemed on edge, stirring up the tingling in the back of his neck. He'd heard stories of sirens leading sailors to their depths—could he be in the presence of one?

She danced around him in the water. "Are you a strong enough swimmer to go underwater?"

He nodded, not sure where her questions were leading.

"Then follow me." She took his hand and dived under the surface, but he pulled her back.

"Where are you taking me?" he asked, not ready to drown quite yet.

Her grin faded, and hurt slackened her features. She squeezed his hand. "Please, Galerius, trust me."

So it was back to trust. It was one thing to let her drive his chariot, but it was something entirely different to follow her into the dark waves below.

Instead of releasing him, her grip tightened around his hand. "Please," she repeated, "trust me."

Trust needs to be given in order to be received. He closed his eyes, wishing he hadn't been placed in such a vulnerable position, and nodded.

"Take a deep breath and hold on to my hand." She took a large gulp of air and pulled him under with her. He barely had time to fill his lungs before the salt water entered his nostrils. It stung his eyes when he opened them.

Her hand still clutching his, Claudia swam toward a dark hole. He followed her, praying he wasn't about to meet his death. His lungs started to burn from the exertion and the lack of air. An icy blast of water swirled around him from the darkness, stiffening his muscles. But he kept swimming down with her.

Just when he thought he'd reached his end, they moved up toward the surface. Coughs rattled his chest as he drew in his first breaths.

Claudia's hand remained entwined with his and continued to pull him along. "I'll lead you to a place where you can touch the bottom and catch your breath."

How could she navigate the place, as dark as it was? But just as she promised, his feet scraped against stone, and he found his footing. A few seconds later, his breathing slowed, and his vision came into focus.

At first glance, he realized she'd led him into a cave. Then, as his eyes adjusted to the dimness, he noticed the walls were sparkling. He gasped. "What is this place?"

She took a step back. "It's my secret place."

Light filtered into the grotto through the water on the other side and a few small holes overhead. The sparkling began to turn deep blue and rich indigo. "By the gods, are these sapphires?"

She nodded, chewing on her bottom lip the entire time. "I found this place when I was child. My nanny used to take me swimming here because it was safer than anywhere else along the coast. One day, I swam through the opening and came up in here."

He raked his hair back from his face and turned around, taking it all in. Just one wall alone could make him one of the wealthiest men in the empire. "There must be thousands of sapphires in here."

She nodded again, still keeping her distance from him. "No one knows about this place except me. I've never taken anyone here." She hesitated, and then added, "Until now."

A rock felt like it landed in the center of his stomach. In two sentences, she'd managed to bring his world crashing down around him. First, to know about this place and not take advantage of this wealth, he knew Claudia valued more than material things in life. Secondly, she trusted him enough to share it with him.

He swam toward her, rewarded once again by a glimpse of the shy, uncertain Claudia that she normally kept well hidden from everyone. Everyone but him. *What have I done to earn such trust from her?* Whatever it was, it was still very fragile, and he chose his next words with care. "Thank you for bringing me here."

She remained wary, still searching him for a sign of betrayal. Who could blame her? Her whole life had been spent in a world where she was a pawn in her father's games.

He took her hand like she had done at the beach, holding on to it and wordlessly trying to reassure her. "This place is as precious to me as its owner. Your secret is safe with me."

Slowly, her lips spread into a grin, and she closed the gap between them. "Thank you."

"You're welcome," he replied before bending his head toward her. His kiss started out gentle, but she responded with enough passion to consume them both until they slipped under the water.

"Perhaps we need to be more careful." She laughed softly like she had that night in the theater and moved to edge of the grotto. "There's a vein of pink sapphires over here."

He followed her, letting her guide him through the wonders of the cave. Claudia had said she wanted to be free of her father. The treasures inside could have easily financed her freedom, but she left it alone. Once glance at her face told him why. Despite growing up in a wealthy Deizian household of wonders and magic, this grotto mesmerized her more than anything else.

An errant thought probed at the back of his mind. If she could be happy in a place like this, was there a chance she could find happiness with a man like him? He had no land, no wealth, no prestigious bloodlines. Nothing to offer a woman like her. And yet deep inside, he yearned for her.

First I need to prove myself honorable enough for her. The last thing he needed was to hear his father's censure coming from her lips.

Claudia placed her hand on his shoulder, her brows furrowed together. "Is something wrong?"

"No, I was just thinking."

If she'd been any normal woman, she might have nagged him to share his thoughts with her, but she let it go and gave him his space. "We should probably leave soon, before the tide comes in."

He looked up at the high ceiling of the room. "Does the grotto fill up completely?"

"No, but it does make it harder to get out. You have to swim deeper." She moved toward the glowing aqua-hued light that marked the underwater opening to the cave. "Do you need my help?"

"I think I know where I'm going this time."

She dipped below the surface. The shadows of her long legs played along the waves before disappearing from view. He cast one more glance at the glittering walls before sucking in a deep breath and following her.

When he came out on the other side, she was already walking to the shore like some water goddess emerging from the sea. Her golden hair clung to her curves in damp waves, concealing the creamy flesh beneath. She moved with confidence and grace rather than seduction, but the effect was the same to him. His cock hardened, and his throat went dry with desire.

He ran toward her, catching her in his arms and covering her mouth his own. He needed to taste her, to hold her, to feel her respond to his touch. He needed to breathe her in and consume everything she was to satisfy the hunger inside his soul.

She kissed him back with the same hunger, luring him back to the beach until they tumbled onto the pile of clothes they'd left behind. His body pressed hers into the pink sand below, stretching along her entire length. He savored the sensation of her silky skin as it surrounded him from head to toe while he got drunk off her kisses. This is what he craved—this connection between them that made him think the gods had created her especially for him.

171

At last, his lungs burned for air, and he ended their kiss.

Claudia stroked the sides of his cheeks, cupping his face in her hands. "Do you want me to scream your name again when I come?"

"No." He'd already erased any doubts in his mind about her wanting him. "I just want you."

Now it was her turn to kiss him like she was starving. Her fingers ran up and down his back. Her tongue coiled and twisted around his own, making him whimper from want. Her body yielded to his, her legs opening to allow him into the slick recesses of her sex.

He slid into her and knew the feeling of coming home.

***

Claudia lifted her head from Galerius's shoulder to find him snoozing in the afternoon sun. She hated to wake him up after he'd made love to her slowly on the beach.

Made love to her. That's the only way she could describe it. Instead of being rushed or hurried, he'd taken his time with her, drawing out each stroke of his cock until she shivered with delight. Kissing her lips, her neck, her breasts. Holding her in his arms and gazing into her eyes as he sent her over the edge. Pulling her alongside him afterward so their naked bodies still remained in contact with each other.

None of her husbands had treated her this way. None of them had even seemed to care about her feelings, about her desires. None of them had made her feel as precious and wanted as Galerius had in the few short weeks she'd known him.

And he'd even called her precious this afternoon, comparing her to the sapphires she'd shown him.

Her heart thumped against her ribs. As much as she enjoyed her time with him, she needed to face reality soon. There was no future for them other than these stolen moments. She couldn't boldly declare her feelings for him in front of her peers. She couldn't appear alone in public with him. And she couldn't dare think about becoming his wife without being ostracized by everyone she knew.

A bitter laugh rose from her throat. If she even dreamed of eloping with Galerius, her father would send them both tumbling down the cliff rather than acknowledge their union.

And yet, if the emperor could marry a former slave, then perhaps she could hope the rigid rules of society were loosening enough to allow her to be with him.

She ran her fingers across his face, his stubble as rough as the sand beneath their clothes.

He cocked one eye open. "Yes?"

A declaration sat poised on the tip of her tongue. She wanted to tell him she was falling in love with him, and yet she held back like a coward. She had to know for certain he felt the same way before risking her heart.

She lowered her gaze to his chest. "We should probably get dressed before the sun burns us."

He propped himself up on his elbow and pinned her to the ground with his knee. "And what if I want to stay a bit longer here with you?"

"I thought you'd be exhausted by now."

"Never underestimate a man who holds a beautiful and charming woman in his arms." As if to prove his point, the evidence of his growing desire nudged her thigh.

As tempting as it was to linger, she replied, "I have no desire to face my father's wrath by being late for dinner."

He glanced down at the bruises on her arm. Even though they had faded to yellow, their outlines were still visible. A muscle rippled along his jaw. "There's no excuse for him to turn his anger on you."

"Then let's not test him." She pushed Galerius back and tugged her dress out from under him. "I'll need a bath to wash the salt from my hair before I can get ready for dinner."

He remained silent as they dressed and climbed back up the narrow trail to the top of the cliff. Her palms grew clammy from his sudden change in mood. She'd said something to upset him.

It wasn't until they were back in the chariot and heading

toward her father's villa that he spoke again. "I've heard a rumor that your father means to marry you to Atius Cotta."

Her gut clenched. "Unfortunately."

"So you are not in agreement with his plans?"

"I never have been." Her betrothals had always been the same. She'd fake a smile of happiness as her father gave her hand to her future husband. She'd act joyful on her wedding day, even though she hated every moment of the pomp and ceremony. She'd lie in bed as a man who made her skin crawl huffed and puffed over her. And she'd pretend to shed widow's tears when she found them dead within a few months, even though she felt little pity for the men foolish enough to fall into her father's traps.

If she were forced to marry Cotta, it would be no different with him.

Only now, she knew what she wanted. She knew pleasure in the arms of a lover. She knew what it felt like to be wanted and cherished. And this time, she was willing to fight against the arranged marriage because she knew there was more to relationships between men and women than what she'd experienced before.

"What do you plan to do about it?" he asked quietly.

"What can I do? It's not like I have another man vying for my hand. I'm the Black Widow of the Empire, after all. I'm surprised Cotta is desperate enough to marry me."

The warm feelings that had bathed her all afternoon vanished. It was foolish of her to think she was worthy of happiness, anyway. Her path had been cut for her from the day she was born.

She waited for Galerius to say something to cheer her up, for him to fall on his knees and beg her marry him instead. But like her, he'd been well-schooled by life to not chase after foolish fantasies.

That didn't stop her from asking, "Do you ever plan on marrying?"

"No."

"Why not?" It seemed like such a waste. He would make some woman a good husband.

"Because as you've been so kind to point out time and time again, I'm a soldier at heart, and I saw how miserable my father made my mother. I refuse to do that to a woman."

She wrapped her hand around the leather concealing his tattoo. "Is it so hard to let go of that life?"

"Yes." He paused and added, "and no."

"Meaning?"

A heavy sigh sounded behind her. "I suppose one day I could settle down and pretend to be a gentleman and not a soldier, but I'd always worry that I'd neglect my wife, and she'd follow the path of my mother."

The clues fell into place. "Your mother found comfort in the arms of another man."

A grumble radiated through his chest. "Yes."

"And you were the product of that affair, weren't you?" His silence confirmed her suspicions. "No wonder you are hesitant to talk about your Deizian blood. Or to marry."

Her hope wilted as she admitted that. At least she knew now there was no chance of anything more developing between them. It would make it easier to eventually push her feelings aside when needed.

"May I ask what happened to them?"

His grip tightened around the helm, and his body stiffened behind her. "He tired of her, and she took her own life."

She covered his hands with her own, wishing she could ease his pain. "I'm sorry I made you talk about the unpleasantness in your past."

"I think you deserve to know the truth about me."

It still doesn't change the way I feel.

The villa came into view, and the carriage slowed. "Wanting to spend a few more minutes with me?" she teased.

He buried his nose in her hair and inhaled deeply. "Do you doubt your appeal to me?"

She wiggled against him and felt his cock stiffen in response. "No, there's no doubt there. I just wish we had more time."

He jerked out of his haze. His voice was serious as he replied, "So do I."

Once again, she was torn on whether this was the right time to tell him the truth about everything—her letters, her feelings, her fears—but before she reached a decision, they'd stopped in front of the entryway.

Galerius helped her down from the chariot. "Thank you for one of the most memorable afternoons of my life."

A flush stole over her entire body. "Mine, too."

He leaned in to kiss her, but a movement in the shadows caught her eye. She held out her hand, her gaze darting in that direction so he'd know they were being watched. He gave her an almost imperceptible nod and brought her hand to his lips. "I hope to see you again soon, Lady Claudia."

He seemed to carry all her joy away with him as he drove away.

Her attention turned to the shadow along the columns, watching it as she entered the house. It was time to resume the role of the dutiful daughter. She'd barely reached stairs when someone grabbed her from behind and pulled her toward her father's study.

Fear squeezed her heart so tightly, she thought it would burst. She fell on the richly woven carpet and heard the door slam behind her.

"She's back too soon," Asinius growled.

Her father looked up from his papers, creases forming around the downturned corners of his mouth. "You disappoint me, daughter."

She pulled herself up to her knees and glared at her brother. "Will one of you explain to me what I've done wrong now?"

Hostilius looked down his nose at her. "You were supposed to distract Galerius this afternoon."

She'd been right. Her father had used her once again, although it wasn't the trap she'd suspected. "And I did as you said. I wrote him the letter, and when he came, I went on a drive with him."

Asinius grabbed her by her hair, tilting her head back until she looked in his angry blue eyes. "You didn't keep him occupied long enough. What are you, some kind of quick fuck?"

Tear stung her eyes, both from the pain of his hold and his insult. She elbowed him and freed herself from his grasp. "How am I supposed to do something if you don't tell me about it?"

Her father and brother exchanged glances before the former went back to his papers. "We can only hope my men found what I was looking for and are gone before Galerius returns."

A chill wrapped around her throat like an ice-crusted palla. If Galerius caught her father's men in his home, he'd probably suspect she'd had some part in it. The trust she'd worked so hard to build with him would be crushed. "What did you do, Father?"

They both ignored her question as though she didn't exist.

Asinius grinned. "And if he does catch them, they know what to do."

The evil in his voice told they wouldn't commit suicide like so many who failed her father did. These men had orders to kill Galerius if he returned too soon.

Her brother circled her like viper coiling up to strike. "What's wrong? Worried for your lover?"

"Galerius is too fine a solider to let any of Father's men strike him down."

"That's what you think. It'll look like a robbery gone wrong." He stepped back from her with a smirk. "And then you'll have to learn to spread your legs wide for another man."

His jibes tried to tear her confidence apart until she believed what he said, but she held on to the words Galerius had

177

spoken to her earlier that afternoon. She was precious to him, and he wanted her. "You're wrong," she whispered.

Asinius brought his hand back to strike her, but her father intervened, "Control yourself, son. We can't have her bruised and battered in front of Cotta while we're trying to work out the details of the marriage contract."

For the first time in her life, she was thankful her father wanted to marry her off to someone.

"Claudia, you have disappointed me today," her father continued.

She stood and lifted her chin. "How can I please you when you keep your plans hidden from me?"

"Very well, I'll tell you this much. You are to go upstairs and get cleaned up. You are to dress appropriately for dinner. And you are to do everything in your power to charm Cotta, even if it means inviting him up to your room tonight."

Bile rose into the back of her throat. "And what I refuse to go that far?"

Her challenge hardened his expression. "Then I'll have no further use for you."

The coldness in his voice told her what lay in her future once she became useless to him. Banishment would be kinder of the two fates that awaited her.

She let herself out of the study and went up to her room. Once there, she lit a stick of incense at the abandoned shrine to a goddess and dropped to her knees. Her eyes squeezed shut, she prayed to the goddess for protection. Both for her and for Galerius.

18

The tingling at the back of Galerius's neck grew stronger as he approached home. It started when Claudia drew his attention to the man lingering in the shadows when they returned to her villa and worsened with every mile. Was she trying to warn him about something, other than the fact they were being watched?

He'd gladly pay the equivalent of the emperor's treasury if he could've just stayed on the beach with Claudia. Things were just about perfect until she'd insisted they leave. Then he had to bring up her possible marriage to Cotta. *Fool!* If it hadn't been for the little jealous voice in the back of his mind, he never would have said anything. Then she would have never probed into his past.

At least I know she doesn't want to marry Cotta. That was one small blessing.

The streets were crowded with last-minute shoppers gathering ingredients for their evening meals, and his chariot crawled at a snail's pace for the last few blocks. When he reached the front gate of the wall that enclosed his home, the tingling intensified. It wasn't like Carbo to leave it unlatched.

He pushed it open, thankful the hinges had been oiled recently, and slid into the courtyard. The house seemed too still. Red drops sprinkled the front step. His pulse jumped, and he reached for the dagger he kept on the chariot. It wouldn't be as helpful as his gladius if he were attacked, but it was still a weapon.

He nudged the door open and peered inside. The contents of his house had been turned upside down and strewn about as though a storm had rolled in from the sea and concentrated its winds there. He tightened his grip on the dagger's hilt, his palms growing damp. Someone had been searching for something inside. He prayed the letters and the communication orb were still hidden beneath the floorboard.

The door eased open a few more inches, enough to allow him inside. His gut churned as he followed the trail of blood into the room to the left. It formed a pool around Carbo, who was lying on the ground with his eyes open wide. Galerius didn't need to check for a pulse. His servant had long since passed into the afterlife.

The smash of crockery came from the very back of the house. Galerius turned toward it, his muscles flexing. The metallic taste of vengeance filled his mouth. Whoever had broken into his home and murdered Carbo was still here, and he would make them pay.

He crept through the house, hoping to keep the element of surprise on his side. He paused at his bedroom, nothing the overturned mattress and scattered papers. His sword lay hidden inside the secret compartment under the floor. He weighed the risks of retrieving it versus possibly losing the criminals, and opted to have the weapon. They'd already proven capable of bloodshed, and he had no desire to become their next victim.

Everything seemed to go according to plan until the front door creaked. The movement in the back of the house halted, and Galerius cursed under his breath. They knew he was here, and worse, someone else was entering the house.

With the dagger in one hand and the gladius in the other, he crouched on his knees and hid behind the door.

"There's no one here, I tell you," a voice said from the inner courtyard. "The old man said his daughter would keep the

Captain out all afternoon."

Galerius bit down so hard, his teeth ached. Claudia knew about this. She'd pulled him out of his home this afternoon so these men could search it.

I can't believe I was such a fool. Despite her words, she had been and would always be her father's pawn.

"No, I heard something. I swear," another voice replied, coming toward him. "I'm going to have a look."

The first man laughed. "I doubt it was the servant. I made sure he was good and dead."

"But what if the Captain's returned early?"

The sound of a blade sliding out of a scabbard echoed off the plastered walls of the inner courtyard. "Then we'll just have to give him a proper greeting, won't we?"

Footsteps rumbled toward the front of the house. Galerius watched the shadow of the first man slither across the hallway. "The front door's open."

Galerius wished he knew where the second man was, but attacked anyway. The first man stood by the door, a thin Elymanian with hardly any substance to his frame and a crudely hammered blade in his hands. He barely had time to lift his weapon in self-defense before Galerius plunged his sword into his chest and finished him off with a swipe of the dagger across this throat.

One down.

Galerius barely had time to turn around before a blade raked across his upper back. The second man was far more of an adversary than his comrade. Scars crisscrossed his beefy face, and a murderous light shone from his eyes. This was a man who had no problem killing and had done so countless times before.

Galerius blocked the next blow with his dagger, his shoulder screaming in pain from the force of it, and delivered a counterstrike with his sword. The man managed to jump back beyond the reach of the blade and retreated to the inner courtyard. There, he would have more room to maneuver than in the narrow hallway and could use his girth to advantage.

Galerius gave chase. Although he already had a good idea who had sent the men, he needed to hear the thug confirm it. He needed to know Hostilius had sent them. Then he had to come to terms that Claudia knew all about it.

His tunic clung to his back, the salt from the sea mixing with the blood and stinging his wound. His arm protested with every movement, every swing, every parry. The man attacked like a wolf snapping at injured prey, but his breath grew more labored as they danced around each other.

Years of combat had taught Galerius how to seize the moment his enemy showed a sign of weakness. He waited patiently for his opponent to make that critical mistake, to open himself up for attack.

It came with a wide swing. The man missed Galerius, and his sword kept moving away. His chest opened up, and Galerius delivered a quick jab of his dagger just below the man's heart.

The hulk of the man stiffened, his breath hitching.

"What was Hostilius looking for?" Galerius asked, lowering the man to his knees. When no answer came, he twisted the dagger, earning a grunt of pain from the man. "Answer me."

The man grinned. Red rivers of blood poured from between his teeth, but his tongue remained silent.

Galerius yanked the dagger out. Disgust and frustration singed his skin as he watched the man take his secrets with him to the grave. When he saw the man's dying breath leave him, he flung his weapons down and sank onto a nearby granite bench. The men hadn't found the letters or the communication orb, but he had bigger problems to deal with.

Hostilius was on to him.

Claudia had betrayed him.

And both had him as jittery as a man about to face the executioner's axe.

He curled his hand into a fist. He had to be close if Hostilius was resorting this kind of desperation. Very close. Either that, or the device was nearing completion. Either way, it was time to ask for reinforcements and stop Hostilius now before he used it.

His muscles ached in protest as he stood and washed the blood from his hands. He'd have to find a surgeon tonight to stitch up the wound on his back. Hopefully Rufius could recommend a good one. Then there was the problem of the three dead bodies in his house. But first, he needed to contact the emperor.

A shadow flickered past the doorway as he entered the front part of the house. A surge of adrenaline race through his veins, and he bolted for the front door. If someone was poking around his house, chances were that they worked for Hostilius. Maybe he could get the answers he needed.

He managed to catch an Alpirion boy by the tunic, dragging him back into the house. The door slammed behind them. "Who are you, and what are you doing in my house?"

The boy looked up at him with sullen dark eyes and said nothing.

"In case you failed to notice, two men were robbing my house and murdered my servant." He pointed to where Carbo lay in the other room. The boy's eyes grew round. "Tell me what you know, or I'll have to assume you are part of the robbery."

"I'm not a thief," the boy shot back.

"Then what are you doing here?"

The boy squirmed, his gaze flickering from the body to Galerius.

His clothing marked him as a slave. Galerius searched for any piece of gold that would mark him as a freedman, but found nothing. "Who do you belong to?"

"My mistress."

"And who is your mistress?"

The boy once again refused to answer, treading on the last threads of Galerius's patience. Just like every other person he'd faced, the boy would rather die than reveal his secrets.

He sighed and tried a different approach. He knelt in front of the boy, keeping his voice calm and reassuring. "I'm not going to hurt you as long as you are telling the truth. What's your name?"

The boy hesitated for a moment. "Kafi."

"And what are you doing in my home, Kafi?"

"You're the one who pulled me into it."

Galerius tried to hide his grin. The boy was clever. He had to be on his toes if he wanted to glean any information from him. "You were inside the walls of my home. I could have you arrested for trespassing."

The boy's jaw jutted out as if daring him to call the magistrate. "I was just curious."

"Did you see the two men enter my house earlier?"

Several heartbeats passed before Kafi gave a slight nod.

"Do you know what they were looking for?" When the boy looked away, he added, "Please, I need to know why they were here and why they tried to kill me."

Kafi flicked a piece of straw off his coarsely woven tunic.

"Your silence speaks for itself. By keeping this information from me, I have to assume you were working with them."

He rose to his feet, and panic flashed in the boy's eyes. "Please, sir, I'm not a thief."

"Then answer my questions."

Kafi drew his knees up to his chest and rocked back and forth. "My mistress will kill me if she finds out you caught me."

His statement caught Galerius off guard. "Why is that?"

"Because she told me not to let you see me."

"Do you fear your mistress that much?"

"No." Kafi glared at him. "My mistress is a good woman. She's been trying to protect you." His mouth formed a perfect circle and then clamped shut.

Galerius chuckled. He'd gotten a slip of information from the boy, but he doubted he could trick him again. "Who is your mistress? If she's been trying to protect me, then I'd like to thank her."

Mistrust flickered across the boy's face. "If I tell you, I'll

184

place her in danger."

The air whooshed out Galerius's lungs as he guessed the identity of the boy's mistress. How long had Claudia known about his mission? How long had she been looking out for him? "Did she ask you to follow me?"

Another moment of hesitation, followed by another nod.

It was time to ask the one question that had been on his mind since he left Emona. "Has your mistress been sending me letters?"

Kafi's lips thinned, and he looked away. "I will not betray my mistress."

So the empress had been right all along, and now he had the proof he needed. But it still did not explain Claudia's part in this afternoon's events. "Did your mistress know about the men coming to my house today?"

Confusion muddled the boy's features. "I don't know."

"Are you telling me the truth, or are you just trying to protect your mistress?"

"The truth, sir."

Dozens of questions filled his mind, but he doubted he'd learn anything more from Kafi. The slave was obviously devoted to Claudia. "Is there anything else you'd be willing to tell me about these men? Who they worked for? What they wanted?"

"They said something about sapphires," he offered.

"Anything else?"

The boy shook his head, but the stubborn set of his jaw told Galerius he knew more than he was willing to reveal. He squirmed once again. "Are you going to kill me, too?"

The boy was still frightened, despite his bravado, and Galerius saw an opportunity to win him over. "Will your mistress harm you when she finds out I caught you?"

"She might."

"Then let's keep this a secret between us." He held out his hand to help the boy up from the floor. "If your mistress is worried about me, then you can tell her about the thieves and let her know I took care of them. Leave out that we ever met. Does that sound acceptable to you?"

Kafi started to nod, but then asked, "And what do you want in return from me?"

Galerius forced himself to keep a straight face. The boy's wiliness amused him. He thought for a moment before coming up with something he'd easily get the boy to agree to. Claudia had asked once if he would defend her. Even though he still had no idea where she stood between him and her father and what her motives were, he replied, "If your mistress is in danger, let me know."

Kafi nodded and squeezed past him, his eyes not leaving Galerius until he reached the front gate.

Galerius closed the door and bolted it securely behind him. The evening shadows veiled the wreckage of his belongings in deep blue, softening the edges of the disaster, but his soul still remained troubled. He made his way back to the secret compartment in his bedroom and pulled out the communication orb.

He would report the events to the emperor and await orders.

But one thing was certain—he risked both his life and his heart if spent any more time in Claudia's company.

19

Claudia stared blankly at the room full of people.
General Galeo was holding a party to celebrate the completion of
his new villa, and the elite of Tivola's society were there. Wine
flowed freely, and servants carried elegant gold platters filled with
food. The din of voices drowned her ears, but she could not join
the revelry.

Two days had passed since her father had used her to
lure Galerius out of the house. Thanks to Kafi, she knew he was
safe, but he'd made no effort to contact her. Word had spread
through town that he'd stumbled upon a couple of thieves in his
home and killed them, but he hadn't left his house since then.
Only those in her family knew the truth.

Deep inside, she yearned to act. She'd thought about
sending Galerius a letter, apologizing for being tricked by her
father into participating in his plan. She still toyed with telling
him the truth, even though she doubted he would believe her
now. She even considered catching the next airship to Emona
and going straight to the emperor himself, but would he believe
her?

"I hear congratulations are in order, Claudia," Salvia, the
general's wife, said as she maneuvered beside her. "Cotta has
been a widower for a long time and needs a young wife like you."

Her stomach clenched. "Forgive me, Salvia, but as far as

I know, my father and Cotta are still finalizing the details of the marriage contract. Nothing is official yet."

"It's just a matter of time. Once a man makes an offer for a bride, he's usually willing to agree to the terms set by her father. Perhaps the fourth time will be the charm for you." She gave Claudia a saucy wink and left to mingle with her guests.

The news only added to the hollowness in Claudia's chest. Galerius was ignoring her. Her father was going to marry her off once again and possibly overthrow the emperor. And she was trapped where she could do nothing to stop him.

She emptied her glass and watched her father follow the general and six other men into a hallway. The conspiratorial nods and hushed words amongst them said they were up to something. She wove her way through the crowd, watching them until they disappeared into a room at the end of the hallway.

Her gaze traveled across the other partygoers. No one seemed to notice their host was missing, or the fact she'd followed them. The door appeared to be made of thick wood, and the bronze plate beside it announced access was controlled by the owner. She wouldn't learn anything with her ear pressed against the door.

She spun around and moved back through the crowd, heading for the garden in the hopes there might be an open window to the room. She'd almost made it to the door when a man's hand clamped around her wrist.

Her heart jumped. At first, she feared her brother had caught her, but the man's hold was firm, not cruel. She lifted face and found herself staring into familiar grey eyes. "Galerius, what are you doing here?"

"The general invited me." His tone was flat, emotionless, but the heat of his gaze betrayed him.

Her breath hitched, and the room became too warm. "Let's step outside."

He nodded and led her into the gardens, still holding her wrist. Once he found a secluded place, he let her go.

"It's so good to see you again," she began, but stopped

when he took a step back and crossed his arms over his chest. She gulped, hating the lump forming in her throat. Now was as good a time as any to beg for forgiveness. "I suppose I should explain a few things."

"That would be appreciated." He remained an unmoving wall. The soldier in him had taken control and wouldn't yield until she gave him the answers he sought.

She rubbed her hands on her dress. "Let me begin by telling you that I knew nothing of what my father planned the other day. He asked me to invite you for a drive, and I was so anxious to see you again—"

"Spare me your lies, Claudia."

His words hurt more than a slap to her face. She blinked back tears. "You think I'm in league with him, don't you?"

"The evidence points in that direction. What else am I to believe?"

And just like that, all the trust she'd worked so hard to build with him crumbled. He'd always regard her with the wariness, the suspicion, she saw now. But as much as her heart ached, she refused to back down and miss this opportunity to convince him she was on his side. She took a deep breath to hide her emotions. "Very well. I can see how you'd feel that way, but please believe when I tell you I'm finished being my father's pawn."

"So you've told me before."

"What do I need to do to prove it to you?"

"Stop playing your games, Claudia." He started to walk away, but then paused and added, "I can't believe I was foolish enough to…" His mask broke, and she saw the hurt play across his face.

Her spirits lifted. Maybe he still cared for her. "Galerius, I'm going to give you a choice. If you are here to stop my father, then I can tell you he's locked away in a small room that way." She pointed toward the beam of light that fell from the last room in the wing, the room that was most likely where they'd gone. "There's a chance you can hide under the window and maybe

189

learn what they are planning."

His face returned to the blank mask. "Or?"

"Or if you are not here to stop my father…" Her voice shook. What if she'd been wrong about him? Had she'd just betrayed her father to one of his allies? "If you are not here for that, then you can follow me farther into the gardens and let me show you how much I want you."

Galerius opened his mouth to speak, then clamped it shut. His shoulders tightened into a straight line as though every muscle in his body tensed. His gaze traveled down the length of her body, and there was no missing the lust in his eyes. "Claudia, I—"

He sounded like someone was strangling him. He blinked and glanced over his shoulder to the room she'd pointed. When he turned back to her, he'd found his voice again. "Please understand."

The ache inside her doubled in size, making it hard for her to maintain her composure. Her hands trembled, and her vision blurred. She'd given him a choice, and he'd chosen duty over her. She did not need to show him how much his decision hurt. "I do. Once a member of the Legion, always a member of the Legion. I expected no less from you."

He closed the space between them and ran his fingers along her cheek. "I trust you, Claudia."

A sob threatened to rip out of her lungs, but she pressed her jaw closed and merely nodded. She couldn't let him know how much her heart was breaking. She'd given it to him, but he would never claim it. He was first and foremost a soldier and would always be one.

He turned and crept toward the room, leaving her standing there. She forced her arms to remain at her sides, her posture rigid, while he walked away from her. She'd stay there until he disappeared from sight. She'd watch him leave knowing she'd done something to protect the empire.

Just please don't turn around.

But when he reached the edge of the house, he looked

back at her one more time before rounding the corner. A sharp, stabbing pain filled her chest, but a glimmer of hope lingered. Yes, he'd turned her down because of his duty, but he still cared for her. He trusted her, and she wouldn't let him down.

Claudia swiped the back of her hand across her eyes and went back into the villa, cutting her way through the crowd. There's was still a chance Galerius may not overhear what he needed, but she knew of one place that contained the answers.

The hidden drawer in her father's desk.

***

Galerius crept toward the beam of light and the muffled voices that came from the other side of the now-shuttered window. He'd taken a gamble, sneaking into Galeo's party uninvited, but it hopefully would pay off if he could learn more about Hostilius's plan.

His heart pounded, but not from fear of being caught spying on Hostilius. He hated the look on Claudia's face when he turned around. She was trying so hard to hide her pain, but he knew her well enough. Having to choose between her and his mission was one of the hardest decisions he'd ever made.

If you can stop her father, then you can help her be free.

It was the only way he could make her happy in the end. And then maybe, just maybe, there would be a chance to discover something more between them.

The sound of men talking over Hostilius grew louder. Galerius raised up on his knees and peered through the crack. A jumble of togas swirled inside, all richly trimmed with gold threads that matched the hair on their Deizian owners, but he couldn't see their faces.

"Why are you doubting me suddenly?" Hostilius roared. "The device is complete and ready to test. We won't fail."

"That's what you said last time," one of them replied.

"And I've learned from that experience. If we combine all our power, Sergius will not be able to stop us. And we need to act now before his brat is born."

Galerius sucked in a deep breath. They knew of the

191

empress's pregnancy.

"But what about the new company of troops that landed today?" Cotta countered. "The emperor suspects something, or he wouldn't have deployed them here. Face it, Hostilius, you've been caught. It's time to think of something else."

Silence filled the room with the exception of the slow slapping of sandals against the tile floors. The men parted, offering Galerius a clear view. Hostilius moved toward Cotta. "Are trying to tell me and everyone else here that you're a coward?"

Cotta's voice seemed a bit higher than normal when he replied. "I'm no coward, but I do think we need to exercise caution."

"Doesn't it anger you to know the man who drove your only daughter to her death has raised a slave up as his empress and now breeds with her? Do you want to see an Alpirion sitting on the throne, in the spot that would have been held by your grandson if Sergius hadn't disgraced Lucia with the threat of divorce?"

"Sergius will pay for what he's done to my family, to our empire, but I'm not willing to throw my life away on a scheme that's doomed for failure."

"Perhaps you are not man enough for my daughter after all." Hostilius swung his arm, and a gasp rose from the room. The lights flashed along the blood-stained blade in his hand. When he walked away, a red streak bloomed across the pristine white linen of Cotta's toga. "Consider that a warning to you all. I let Cotta live because I need the magic of everyone in this room to make my plan work. But if any of you try to cross me, my next blow will be deadly."

The tension in the room was palpable, even from where Galerius stood in the garden. Cotta remained standing, though his face had grown pale. Whatever wound Hostilius had inflicted on him appeared to be superficial.

"I will test the device within the next day or two. Once I know it is working, I will send for you. And if you do not come,

I suggest sleeping with one eye open for the rest of your days, as short as they'll be."

The men exchanged nervous glances, but no one spoke. Hostilius had them all in his grasp, and history had shown his enemies didn't live long.

"Now go out and enjoy the party General Galeo has been so kind to throw tonight," Hostilius continued, his voice deceptively light and carefree. "Do not let anyone guess that something is wrong. In a few days, the empire will be ours, and we'll enjoy many nights of celebration."

The locks clicked, and the door opened. The men shuffled out like prisoners with their ankles still shackled. Only Hostilius, his son, and the general lingered.

"I thank you for not leaving me a body to dispose of," Galeo said.

"Blood stains are easy enough to clean up." Asinius came toward the window.

Galerius ducked back down, pressing his body against the cool plaster wall before the shutter swung out above his head. Sweat dripped down the small of his back, but he remained as still as a statue.

"I cannot believe Cotta challenged me." Hostilius's voice moved around the room as he paced. "You'd think the recent news from Emona would have made him all the more eager to destroy Sergius."

"Or his upcoming wedding to Claudia," Galeo offered.

A lump formed in Galerius's throat. He'd kidnap her himself before he saw her married to Cotta.

"I'm not worried about that. He signed the contract this morning. I could kill him now and inherit his estates."

Galeo paused for a moment before saying, "Perhaps he's worried about the rumors your daughter has formed a certain attachment to an Elymanian."

Asinius snorted. "Claudia's nothing more than a stupid whore. She's just keeping Galerius occupied until Father can carry out his plan."

Galerius curled his hands into fists, the nails biting into his palms. No wonder Claudia felt no remorse for betraying her family.

"Still think he's working for the emperor after what I told you?" Galeo asked.

"You know what they say about members of the Legion, even ones who left in disgrace." Hostilius continued to move back and forth across the room. "I find it hard to believe Galerius would be motivated to leave his life of wine and *lupas* without some influence from the emperor."

"Which is why Claudia was perfect," Asinius finished. "She'll fuck him into oblivion, giving us more time to carry out our plans. After all, he may have been the Captain of the Legion once, but now he's nothing more than a wastrel who luckily stumbled across a few sapphires."

Galerius's jaw tightened. He may have been a man like that before he left Emona, but now he had a mission, a purpose.

"I was wondering what you hoped to gain by letting her be seen with him, especially while you were negotiating your contract with Cotta"

"I never do anything without cause." Hostilius stopped pacing. "What can you tell me about the men who landed today?"

"Only that they are from an attachment stationed in Emona. I'll find out more tomorrow." The door opened again. "Now, if you'll excuse me, Governor Hostilius, I need to attend to my guests before they worry."

"Yes, I suppose we should all return to the party," he agreed. Their footsteps faded from the room.

Galerius released a long, slow breath, letting his anger wane with it. He'd show them that they were all wrong about him. But first, he needed to report his information to the emperor. He'd hoped the troops who had arrived from Emona would go unnoticed, but he'd lost that element of surprise. The only thing he could do was make sure the conspirators were watched closely. When Hostilius sent for them, he'd follow them and act.

He stood, releasing the cramps from his legs and returned to the garden. Claudia was gone. The ache returned to his chest as her face flashed across his mind, but he pushed it away.

A man without honor didn't deserve a woman like her, and he knew what he needed to do.

20

Claudia held the light orb up to the bottom of the desk, searching for the way to open the secret compartment. Her heart fluttered in her chest. She had no idea how much time she had or when her father or brother would choose to return from the party, but she wasn't going to waste it.

When her search yielded nothing, she banged her palm against the wood. "Damn it!"

The contents inside the drawer shuffled, mocking her incompetence. If it wouldn't leave any glaring evidence of her presence, she'd be tempted to take a saw to the desk and cut it open.

Think like your father. He built this desk for a reason and used it to hide his most secret documents. But he'd need a way to easily access them. A lock that he could control.

Her gaze traveled to the bronze plate by the door. A lock. Instead of looking for a hidden latch, she needed to be looking for a similar bronze plate made of ore. A search of the bottom revealed nothing. She crawled out from under the desk and carefully lifted the papers on top. Still nothing.

She cursed under her breath and collapsed into her father's chair, the glowing orb still in her fingers. The dim light bathed the office in long shadows, but something flashed on the side of the desk. She dismissed it at first, thinking it was just the gold leaf embossed over the carved wood panels, but as she peered closer, one of the roses looked different. The hue was darker, duller.

The exact color of ore.

She ran her fingers over it, noting it felt cooler than the surrounding carvings. This had to be the lock she'd been searching for. When she released a trickle of magic, the rosette vibrated, but the locks didn't release. She slowly increased her magic, focusing on overriding any protective measures her father might have placed on his desk. Sweat beaded along her brow. Her arm ached from the amount of magic she channeled along it. But after several seconds, she was rewarded by the click she'd been listening for.

A drawer slid out toward her, filled with loose papers and scrolls. She glanced to the closed door, making sure once again she was alone, before thumbing through the contents.

The top letter looked recent. Her jaw dropped as she read it. The empress was expecting a child, according to the writer. At the bottom of the paper, scrawled in her father's distinctive handwriting, were the words, "Need to make sure it never lives," followed by a list of assassins her father had hired before.

Her stomach knotted. It was one thing to kill an adult, but a helpless child. *All the more reason to stop him now.*

She turned to the scrolls and opened one. A drawing of the planet, complete with the outer rings and wide base, covered the parchment. It looked similar to the globe in the emperor's throne room. On the side of the page were a series of calculations that meant nothing to her, but she grabbed a piece of paper and copied them down.

The next scroll was a map of the empire, marking where the troops were stationed and measuring the span of miles between each regiment. A chill crawled down her spine when she noticed the greatest distances were circled.

The last thing she pulled out of the drawer was bound stack of papers. She untied the string and started reading. The first pages were letters from other powerful Deizians to her father, discussing ways to overthrow the emperor. Her spirits lifted. This was the evidence she needed to convict her father, the proof she'd been looking for.

She grabbed a new sheet of paper and listed the name of each conspirator in the stack. But as she got to the bottom of the letters, a new set of papers made her blood run cold. It was a series of journal entries in her father's handwriting. Over and over again, it mentioned a device.

The first set of entries was dated over a year ago, around the time of the former emperor's death. "The device is completed and comparable to that in Emona," her father wrote. "Will test tomorrow."

The next entry dated a few days later read, "Flicker in the border noted, but it did not fall. Will need to reassess."

The next few entries told of increasingly successful attempts to weaken the border in various locations. She pulled the map back out and noticed each location corresponded to the circled areas along the border.

Her hands began to tremble. She'd known for months her father wanted to jeopardize the barrier, but she now had proof that he'd successfully done so. But how? She knew he'd been gathering ore and had mentioned something about improving the conduits, but it still meant nothing to her.

The next entry was dated the day he told her they were going to Emona so he could offer her to the emperor's harem. The day a small earthquake had rumbled through the villa. It simply said, "Device exploded this morning from an unknown magic. Will need to reassess."

What if the explosion caused the earthquake?

Her mind reeled with too many questions to answer. One thing was certain—she needed to get this information to Galerius as quickly as possible. She frantically scribbled down her notes, not trying to her disguise her handwriting any more. If her father had managed to rebuild this device, then he'd either succeed in bringing down the barrier or cause an explosion large enough to make part of Tivola crumble into the sea. Either ending would results in hundreds, if not thousands, of deaths.

Her hand shook as she pressed the wax seal to the papers. She offered a quick prayer her information would help Galerius act quickly enough to stop the worst from happening. Then she replaced the contents of the drawer back the way she had found them and slid it shut.

The house was still cloaked in darkness when she opened the study's door. Her father had yet to return. She crept across the atrium and up the stairs to her room, her pulse pounding in her ears. "Zavi, I need Kafi immediately," she hissed as soon as she entered her room.

Her maid nodded and slipped out into the hallway, returning a few minutes later with her very sleepy-appearing son.

Claudia pressed the letter into his hands. "I need to you to deliver this to Galerius immediately. Please take care that you aren't followed or seen. It's a matter of life or death."

If someone caught Kafi, it would most certainly mean his death, closely followed by her own. She released the letter as though it were soaked in poison and added, "Please be careful."

Wide awake now, the boy nodded and dashed out of the room.

Zavi followed her son with worried eyes. "I hope you know what you're doing, my lady."

"I do, too."

***

Galerius had just finished washing his face when a knock sounded at his door. Rufius barged in a second later, not waiting for permission, and shoved an Alpirion youth into the room. "Look at what we found lurking around the front gate."

Galerius immediately recognized the boy's sharp eyes and stubborn jaw. "I know who he is. Leave him here with me."

"We already searched him. No weapons. Just this."

The boy snatched the letter from Rufius's hands. "That is for Captain Galerius only."

The soldier raised his brow in surprise. "Quite a tongue

on this slave."

"I cannot blame him for that," Galerius replied with a shrug. "He learned it from his mistress."

Rufius laughed and closed the door behind him.

Galerius held out his hand. "What does Claudia have for me tonight?"

Kafi's eyes widened for a second before a blank mask settled over his features. "My mistress sent me to give you this letter and to let you know it was a matter of life and death."

He took the letter and broke open the seal. "Life and death?"

"Those were her words." The boy shifted from one foot to the other.

"Then I will pay special attention to what she's written. Would you like something to eat or drink?"

Kafi shook his head. "I need to get home before I'm missed."

"Very wise." He reached into his purse and pulled out two coins. "I appreciate your discretion." He didn't need to explain that he wished Claudia to think her notes were still anonymous.

The boy edged to the door. "Your men aren't going to follow me, are they?"

"Not unless you give them a reason to." He winked, and the boy took off.

Rufius reappeared a moment later. "You want us to follow him?"

Galerius shook his head. "I know who his mistress is, and I have no desire to endanger her or the boy."

"You think my men would be caught?"

"I'm not taking the chance." He opened the letter and scanned the contents. His chest tightened until it was difficult to draw in his next breath. Claudia had finally given him what he needed.

"I don't like that look." Rufius leaned over his shoulder. "What does it say?"

"It puts everything together." He handed the first sheet to his friend and began reading the next few pages. All his questions were being answered. All the strange issues with the barrier last year were being explained. And the threat for a larger attack became more imminent. "I need to contact the emperor immediately."

"At this hour? Surely he's probably in bed with his lovely wife by now."

Galerius shifted from the innuendo implied by Rufius. Based on what he'd seen between the emperor and empress, they were probably still intimate together, even this late in her pregnancy. "Fine, I suppose it can wait until morning. I doubt Hostilius will make an attack on the barrier tonight based on what I overheard. But we need to form a plan to stop him before he does act."

"No argument from me, Captain." Rufius took the rest of the note and read it. "This device Hostilius keeps referring to—what do you think it is?"

"I think he's built a replica of the imperial globe that's in the center of the throne room, the one the emperor uses to maintain the barrier." And the one Hostilius was using to weaken it. "I expect he's hidden it in the tunnels somewhere under the villa."

"And your informant couldn't provide us with that information?" Rufius laid the papers on Galerius's bed. "Seems like she's holding out on us."

Galerius picked up the note, noticing the quickness in the script. "Or maybe she's just discovering this for her herself."

He went to his desk and pulled out a piece of paper. He needed to speak to Claudia immediately, to find out what else she knew, to make sure she was safe. He scribbled a vague invitation for her to join him for dinner tomorrow and sealed it. "Have one of the men deliver this to Claudia Pacilus in the morning."

Rufius's mouth fell open. "You mean the Black Widow's your informant?"

"Yes, and not a word of this to anyone else. If her father

finds out—"

"Say no more." His friend took the letter and went toward the door. "We all know what Hostilius is capable to doing, even to his own daughter."

Galerius picked up Claudia's letter and read it once again. He had the proof he needed, and he knew what Hostilius was planning. The only problem was that she was caught in the middle. If they attacked the villa to hunt for this device, she could get hurt. He didn't dare arrest Hostilius—the governor had too many local allies to stay incarcerated for long, and he would surely retaliate against his daughter once he found out she was the one who had supplied the evidence against him.

No, the only way he could ensure Claudia's safety was if he removed her from Tivola entirely. He'd have an airship waiting to take her someplace safe. Emona. One of the emperor's palaces. Any place where Hostilius couldn't find her. And once she was safe, he'd personally make sure her father would never be a threat to her again.

He only hoped she'd accept his invitation after he had rejected hers this evening.

21

"My lady, this letter just arrived for you."

Claudia took the letter the slave held out for her. Unease shimmied up her spine as she noticed every person in room was watching her, including her father and brother.

"Who is it from?" her father asked.

She glanced at the handwriting. "Galerius, it appears."

Her father popped a ripe fig in his mouth. "Read it aloud to us."

Her blood chilled. What if he'd written a response to her letter from last night? Any hint to it would mean her death. She opened and glanced at the single line inside, a sigh of relief escaping from her lips. "He's inviting me to dinner at his home tonight."

"A formal dinner invitation to all of us?" Hostilius took a sip of wine and waited for her answer.

"No, Father. Just me."

"I think he wants more than just dinner," Asinius joked, earning a harsh glance from their father.

Cotta cleared his throat and shifted in his chair. The last thing her possible suitor wanted to hear was that another man—an Elymanian—was scheduling a liaison with her.

Her father swirled the contents of his cup, appearing to weigh the consequences of letting her go. He leveled his gaze at

Cotta, who jutted his bottom lip out for a few moments before finally looking away. "Very well, I shall let you go."

Her mouth went dry at his decision. "Surely, you jest. I can't be seen going into his home."

"Then I suggest you be discreet about it." He watched her through narrowed blue eyes. "You can be quite the snoop when you choose to be and perhaps you can succeed where my men did not. Use this as an opportunity to search his home."

Something in the tone of his voice set her every nerve on edge. "Father, he isn't going to stand back and let me do such a thing."

"Then I suggest you find a way to incapacitate him. Kill him, if you must."

The ink smudged under her damp fingers. He was testing her. It wasn't the first time he'd asked to her kill someone. She'd never had the stomach to do it before, and certainly did not now. Her heart was too tangled up with Galerius Metellus.

"I think I can incapacitate him in other ways, Father."

Asinius snickered, but thankfully, he refrained from making some crude comment about using her body to do so.

She stood, the letter still clutched in her hand. "In the meantime, I'll need to prepare for the evening. Please excuse me, Father, Lord Cotta."

Her muscles twitched like they'd prefer to run away, but she paced herself, keeping her movements calm and steady until she was well out of their sight. What was Galerius thinking, inviting her to dinner at his home tonight? Did he have any idea how much trouble his absurd presumption could place her in?

She glanced at the letter again. A foolish thought danced through her mind. Maybe he wanted to apologize to her. She laughed at the silliness of it. Galerius was a soldier and cared for nothing but his mission. He'd probably figured out she was the one behind the letter and only wanted to question her further, perhaps even turn her over to the emperor.

It was silly to think he'd want anything more from her.

***

Claudia pulled the palla lower around her face. She'd taken a litter to the baths, but decided it was better to walk discreetly to Galerius's home rather than have the distinctively ornate vehicle parked in front of it for the entire city to see. Her dress tonight was simple, something fitting a middle-class Elymanian rather than a Deizian, and her palla hid the color of her hair as she wove through the crowded streets.

She hadn't eaten since breakfast. Her stomach had varied between feeling like it contained fluttering butterflies to slippery eels all day, leaving no room for food. She was trapped. Her father's decision this morning still unnerved her, especially with Cotta witnessing the exchange. Either he'd withdrawn his suit, or her father had found a way to force him into submission.

Hostilius never acted with a reason, though, and her mind reeled from the possibilities. Perhaps he wanted her out of the house tonight while he tested his new device. Perhaps he wanted her to "distract" Galerius again. Perhaps he wanted to let Cotta know he had complete control over everyone in the room, especially her.

But it was his use of the word "snoop" that kept echoing in her mind. Her hand gripped her palla until it felt like it was choking her. Did he know she'd found his secret drawer? Was he planning on sending her to Galerius's home so he could exterminate them together?

Claudia pressed her back against the wall surrounding Galerius's home, gulping for air. Maybe she should just go home and forget about dinner.

But then Father would punish me for disobeying him.

Still trapped. No matter what she tried to do, her father kept her on a tight leash.

Do not let anyone see your fear. She drew in a slow breath through her nose, waiting for her heart to slow before exhaling. She had to make her father believe she was still working for him. And she had to make Galerius think his rejection from last night still didn't haunt her.

Once she collected herself, she rang the bell at the front

gate.

An Elymanian man answered. He was tall, well muscled, more of a soldier than a common servant. "Good evening."

"I'm here at the invitation of Galerius." She kept her tone sharp, crisp. He may not have been a common servant, but she was determined to treat him like one rather than dwell on the truth.

He studied her face, his gaze then traveling down her body as though he were searching for weapons rather than admiring her curves. "The Captain is expecting you."

Her guard heightened. So, he was the Captain to his man. She checked his wrist for the Legion's tattoo, but saw nothing. That still didn't mean that Galerius wasn't acting as a member of the Legion. She followed the man inside, fully expecting to be arrested for her father's crimes the minute the door closed behind her.

Instead, the man led her through the home, past the inner courtyard Pontus had once filled with statues of himself as different gods, and to the back wing of the house. She kept her face forward, but her eyes glanced through every window and doorway she passed. The house was full of men, all of them like the man in front of her. Galerius had turned his home into a fort full of soldiers.

But why? Because he feared another attack by "burglars?" Or because he was planning an attack of his own?

The man stopped at a closed door and knocked. "She's here."

Claudia rankled at the man's crude manners. She was a Deizian. She deserved a formal announcement befitting her station, not one suitable for a common *lupa* or washer woman.

Galerius opened the door, and her breath caught. The intensity of his gaze left her feeling like they were the only two people in the world. "Leave us alone, Rufius," he said to the man, his attention never leaving her.

Rufius nodded and took a step back. "If you need anything—"

"I doubt I will." He took her hand and led her inside. "See that we're not disturbed unless it's absolutely necessary."

She wanted to laugh. Always a soldier, always devoted to his mission. But the way he looked at her said that the barrier had better be falling before Rufius disturbed them.

The room was sparsely decorated with simple furniture. Still, it was clean and inviting. The oil lamps cast a warm glow on the walls, so different from the harsh light created by the illumination orbs that filled Deizian villas. Several cushions surrounded a low table where a platter of bread and cheese waited. A small clay urn sat next the plate, and a pot simmered over a copper brazier beside it. It was not the feast she was accustomed to, but her stomach growled at the site of it.

Galerius brushed past her and blocked her view of dinner. She noticed that for the first time since he came to Tivola, he no longer bothered to cover up his Legion tattoo. He ran his fingers through his hair, glancing at the floor before finally saying, "Thank you for coming tonight."

"Did you think I wouldn't?"

He licked his lips, his attention back on her. "I wasn't sure."

Desire stirred within the pit of her stomach, warming her blood. Despite what had happened last night, she still wanted him. She unwrapped her palla and pretended to examine the room with her back to him, scared he'd take advantage of her weakness if he saw it. "I suppose you want to question me about the information I provided last night."

He stood fixed in the center of the room. "No, I wish to apologize for my behavior last night."

A lump formed in her throat, making her eyes sting. She swallowed past it. "There's no need to apologize. Once I knew why you were here in Tivola, I didn't expect anything less from you. So please, there's no need to play any more games. I've told you all I know, and if I find something else—"

Heavy footsteps closed in on her, and a pair of warm hands wrapped around her shoulders, cutting her off mid-sentence. "What is it that you want, Claudia?"

The low, husky way he asked his question shattered her defenses. It was the same question he'd asked her weeks ago, and just like then, she couldn't bring herself to tell him what she wanted. What started out as revenge had turned into something unexpected. Then, she risked revealing herself as her father's traitor. Now, she risked betraying her heart.

I can't let him know what kind of power he has over me. I will not trade one master for another.

She squared her shoulders. "What I want is of little consequence."

He lowered his head, his lips brushing against the back of her neck and sending delicious shivers through her body. "It matters to me."

Her breath hitched. If he continued like this, she'd certainly surrender to him. Every second was pure torture. They had no future together. No chance at happiness. But when he held her like this, she almost believed the impossible was possible.

I can't surrender to him.

She jerked forward, the skin along her neck now cold without his touch. "Please, Galerius, don't try to seduce me with the hope that I'll tell you more about my father."

His fingers dug into the soft flesh of her arms, forcing her to turn around. She closed her eyes, terrified she'd take one look and him and be completely lost.

He cupped her chin and lifted her face. "Open your eyes and look at me, Claudia."

Her voice barely rose above a whisper as she replied, "I can't."

"Why?"

Her heart quivered, unable to fully beat. She knew she shouldn't have come here tonight. Galerius was a vice that would destroy her if she continued to indulge in him.

His thumb rubbed against her bottom lip. More torture. By the gods, the man must have been skilled at interrogation

when he was in the Legion. He already had her on the verge of spilling her deepest secrets to him.

"Claudia." The way he said her name deepened the growing ache inside her. It pleaded with her, luring her out from behind the walls she'd built around herself. "Please don't hide from me."

But she had to hide herself—from him, from her family, from everyone she knew. If they saw how weak she really was...

His breath tickled her forehead, his lips tempting inches from hers. "Look at me."

She couldn't fight it any longer. His face loomed in front of her as she complied with his command. The struggle playing out on it mirrored the one churning inside her.

"In all your marriages, have you ever known love?"

The stinging in her eyes intensified. She didn't want to admit the truth. "Deizian marriages are purely political. They are meant to strengthen our power, to keep our bloodlines pure."

He nodded, accepting her answer. She prayed that would be the end of their conversation, but he asked, "Have you ever been in love?"

She broke free from his grasp, her emotions now naked and exposed before him. "Why are you asking me all these questions?"

"Because I want to know the truth."

She backed away, but he pursued her until she was caught between him and the wall. Her breath came quick and short. She was like a rabbit caught in the path of a wolf, helpless, with nowhere else to go except into the clutches of his jaws.

She tried to push him away, but he refused to budge. "I want to know if you have feelings for me, or if I'm just a pawn in your game."

Something inside her snapped. All this time, she'd worried that he was using her, that all his seduction was nothing more than a means to an end. But the pain, the desperation in his words told a different story. He was the one who feared he was being used. He was the one who feared she was merely seducing

him to get what she wanted.

Lie to him, her mind whispered. *Hurt him like he hurt you last night. He'll recover. Maybe he'll even thank you later when he realizes how ridiculous the idea of a relationship with someone like you is.*

But her heart overruled her mind, and she ran her hand along his cheek, pulling him closer to her until their lips met.

He remained hesitant, retreating from her after a few seconds instead of kissing her back.

Are we both so untrusting that we'll ruin everything between us?

She searched his face, wanting him to show her that he was willing to take the same risk that she was. "I could ask you the same question."

His grey eyes flared to life, awakening like a sleeping dragon. "Then let me show you."

He gathered her up in his arms so quickly, she first thought he was going to carry her out of his room. But instead of moving toward the door, he went in the opposite direction—to his bed.

He tossed her on the simple linen covers and crawled on top of her. "It's time someone made love to you properly."

This time, he attacked with his kiss, his lips making demands of hers, his tongue conquering the space of her mouth. When he'd left her breathless, his hands shoved her dress off her shoulders, exposing her breasts to his hungry gaze. "It's time someone worshipped you the way you deserve to be worshipped."

His mouth trailed kisses along the hollow of her neck, searing her skin from the passion of them. He cupped one breast in his hand, bringing up to his greedy mouth. A moan broke free from her throat as his tongue slowly circled her nipple, catching it between his teeth and teasing the sensitive flesh.

He repeated he same on the opposite breast, reducing her to whimpers before coming back to claim her mouth. Neither of them could deny their desire for the other. There was no turning back now, no stopping what they'd started. She held on to him for dear life, drowning in the heat of his embrace, the

seduction of his caress.

He broke away again, his breath coming as quickly as hers. Lust played out front and center on his face, but underneath it appeared a softer emotion, one that had her wanting him all the more. "It's time someone filled that heart of yours with something other than vengeance."

She held his face in her hands, her heart overflowing with the emotion she'd feared for so long. "You already have."

22

Those three little words seemed to satisfy Galerius as much as "I love you," because he smiled and kissed her again. This time, he moved slower, his actions more of a man full of contentment rather than a man searching for answers.

Claudia tilted her head back, savoring the feel of his lips as they trailed along her jaw, her neck, her collarbone. He worshiped her like he had said he would, leaving her feeling like a goddess in his arms. His touch was light, reverent, as he continued lower to her breasts. This time, he didn't devour them with the ferocity that he did before. Instead, he covered them with wispy kisses and tender caresses.

Even though his approach changed, it still managed to fill her with the same heat, the same longing she knew in his embrace. It doubled in intensity as he pushed her dress lower, exposing her stomach. His calloused hands fanned the flat expanse before reaching under her hips, raising her to his mouth. Anticipation rippled through her while his tongue played in the recesses of her navel, teasing her with what she knew he would do her sex if he continued lower.

Galerius massaged tiny circles into her hips with his thumbs, matching the movements of his tongue, and she shivered in delight. His lips continued along their path to the place between her legs that grew slick waiting for his touch. Her hands gripped the crisp linen sheets to keep from pushing him toward it. He said he wanted to make love to her, to worship her, and she feared her interference would ruin his plans, halting them before she knew the pleasure only he could give.

She murmured his named over and over again like a fevered patient, wanting him to know how much she needed him. When his breath bathed the skin of her thighs, she opened them to him. A cry of delight rose from her throat with the first flicks of his tongue. But unlike the night in the theater, he took his time making her come. He teased the sensitive nub until she reached the brink, only to return to the slow, languid movements he had shown the rest of her body.

Claudia raked her fingers through his hair, holding him close to her while the lower half of her body rebelled against his ministrations. Her pelvis bucked every time his teeth raked across her clit. Her breath caught every time he drew it into his mouth.

She longer knew her body. It tightened and released at his command. It rose and fell to the rhythm he set with his kisses. And when it fully surrendered to him, the world melted away to a series of pulsating waves that racked her body with ecstasy. She was his in every way she could imagine—heart, soul, and body.

The next thing she knew, he was pulling her up higher on the bed so that her head was nestled between the down pillows. Her hair had long since fallen free from the pins that confined it, sticking to her cheeks. His tunic was gone in a flash, and he lay down beside her. Her heightened nerves magnified the heat of his skin, the prickle of the hair on his chest and legs, turning such ordinary things into erotic sensations. Her legs reflexively wrapped around his waist when he moved on top of her. Everything felt so right, so perfect.

His erect cock waited at the entry of her sex, and yet he didn't move. Galerius brushed her hair back from her temples and stared into her eyes. "I love you."

"With you, I believe it." She placed a gentle kiss on his lips before whispering, "I love you, too."

She pressed her heels against his buttocks, guiding him as he slid into her with toe-curling slowness, welcoming his hard fullness that stretched her inner walls. He continued to making love to her in the same slow, easy motions he'd employed since he'd taken her to bed. His eyes never left hers as they moved together. They were joined by more than just their bodies. He belonged to her as much as she belonged to him, eliminating any fears or doubts that lingered in her mind.

The exquisite friction of his strokes had her on the brink of climax before she knew it. Her muscles tightened, raising her hips off the mattress. Her fingers dug into his shoulders. Her lungs seized, allowing only short, quick pants. Her sex squeezed around his cock until it released a pounding rush of pleasure that vibrated to the tips of her toes.

He cried out her name in a guttural rasp as he came, collapsing into her arms. The heavy weight of his limp body pressed her into the mattress. She was too weak to move—not that she wanted to, anyway. Exhaustion crept into her arms and legs as though she'd been swimming for hours against a riptide. Now it was time to stop fighting and simply flow with the current.

A few minutes later, Galerius rolled to his side, taking her with him. She cuddled next to him with her head resting comfortably on his chest. She now knew what love was, and she had no regrets confessing her feelings for him.

***

Galerius reached for Claudia while he dozed, only to find a warm spot on the sheets where she'd lain. He bolted up and called her name.

"I'm right here," she replied, her calm voice instantly soothing his worry.

The room came into focus. The soft light from the oil lamps had dimmed as their fuel ran low, but they still provided enough light to make Claudia's hair shimmer like the finest gold. She sat on the cushions around the table, wearing absolutely nothing while she sliced a piece of bread off the loaf on the platter.

"I hope you don't mind that I started dinner without you." She dipped her bread into the stew, licking the gravy off her lips after she ate it. "I was starving."

He eased out of bed and sat down behind her. The scent of her favorite oil lingered on her silky skin. He took her into his arms and pressed his nose against the hollow of her neck, soaking in all in. "You mean I didn't satisfy you?"

A low chuckle vibrated through her chest. "You satisfied everything but my empty stomach."

"Then I was glad I had something here for that." He kissed her shoulder, noticing the lack of tension, of hesitation he'd noticed so many times when he'd held her. She no longer hid her true self from him.

"So am I. After all, you did invite me here for dinner." She laid a piece of cheese on a slice of bread and fed it to him. "Good boy. We need to keep your energy up for the rest of the night."

Making love to her had left him sated and exhausted, but her teasing reawakened his desire. He tightened his arms around her ribs, cupping her breasts in his hands. "Are you telling me you want to go back to bed?"

"Yes, once I'm done eating."

Her playful banter and soft curves almost had him forgetting about the real reason he'd invited her here. Yes, he had wanted to apologize to her for last night, but he was more worried about her safety than anything else. And as much as he hated to destroy the easy afterglow of the moment, he needed to get back to business.

"There's an airship leaving for Emona in the morning, and I want you on it."

Just as he expected, she pulled away from him. "You know I can't leave."

"Why not? You know what your father is planning on doing. You know that I'm here to stop him. Why would you want to be in harm's way?"

She turned and tapped her fingers into the center of his forehead. "Because you are thinking like a soldier and not like a Deizian. If I disappear, it will only raise my father's suspicions and make him ten times more difficult to stop."

"And what if you get hurt?" He knew what the plan was, what measures would be used to invade the villa and hunt down Hostilius and his device. Visions of Claudia lying amongst the rubble, blood staining her pretty face, haunted him. "Please, I need to know you'll be safe."

"I'm a grown woman, Galerius. I haven't survived this long in my father's home without knowing how to protect myself." She smiled and ran her fingers along his jaw. "Right now, he believes he's invincible, that no one can stop him. It's better if he continues to believe that than to have him become paranoid that the emperor is on to him."

He caught her hand in his own, pressing it against his cheek. "Then please promise me you'll stay some place secure, a place where you won't be hurt when we come for your father?"

"I promise." The gravity in her eyes betrayed the levity in her smile. "As long as my name isn't on the arrest warrant, I have nothing to fear, right?"

"I'm being serious here."

"So am I." She reached for her glass of wine and took a long sip. "I must say that although this is considered peasant fare, I find it very tasty."

Her attempt to change the subject didn't sway him. He captured both her hands and waited until he had her full attention. "If anything happens to you, I—"

His voice broke as another image of her corpse filled his mind. He shook it away. "Please, don't go back. Stay with me."

A look of hesitation flickered across her face as though his plea had her wavering on her decision, followed by a look of remorse. "You know I can't. I'm not afraid of what I have to do, and neither should you be. In order to defeat my father, you have to let me go and trust me."

Once it again, it came back to trust. Only this time, every

216

ounce of his being protested in giving it. The hairs on the back of his neck stood up. "And what if I decide not to?"

She stiffened, and remnants of the old Claudia resurfaced. "You can't force me to do anything I don't want to do, Galerius."

The wall he'd worked so hard to bring down was being rebuilt right in front of his eyes, threatening to destroy everything he had with her. "I'm sorry. I didn't mean it that way."

Her expression softened. "I know, but please try to see things my way. In a few days, all this will be behind us. You just have to be patient until then."

A rueful laugh broke free from his chest. Patience was never one of his virtues. He was a soldier, a man of action. But she'd been right in saying he needed to think like a Deizian if he wanted to stop Hostilius. He needed to immerse his mind in a world of scheming and plotting, to wait for the perfect moment to attack.

He kissed her forehead. "Then if you insist on being so stubborn, stay with me tonight."

"And after tonight?"

It was the one question he didn't want to answer. They were both still in danger. The attack on Hostilius could end with one or both of them dead. And even if he succeeded, he'd destroy her family, her home, her world. She'd be left with nothing. But surely, she'd known that when she started writing her letters.

What troubled him more was that even if the emperor left her some of her father's fortunes to support herself, there could never be anything permanent between them. More than just their class difference kept them apart. His fear of turning her into his mother was stronger now than it ever was before.

"I don't want to make promises I can't keep."

She nodded, seeming to appreciate his honesty, and wrapped her arms around his neck. "Then let's take it one night at a time. No more lies. No more deception. No more tricks." She kissed him and slid her body against his in a way that made her desire apparent. "Just me and you. A man and a woman. Nothing more, nothing less."

Her low, seductive plea had him hard and thinking of only one thing. He'd deal with the consequences tomorrow. Right now, he was more than happy to comply with her demands. He picked her up and carried her back to bed.

***

The sky was beginning to lighten outside his window, chasing away the darkness that had filled the room hours earlier when the oil lamps burned out. Galerius was lying on his side, watching Claudia sleep. Her hair splashed across the pillow like streaks of sunshine. The peaceful expression on her face made him loathe waking her, but he'd agreed he would when the time came.

Part of him regretted keeping her in his bed all night. It made it that much harder to let her go. He could get entirely too comfortable sleeping next to her every night. He leaned over and kissed her.

Her eyelids fluttered open and a sleepy smile formed on her lips. She stretched, moving her curves in a sensual way that had him growing hard from watching. "Is it dawn already?"

"Unfortunately."

The smile morphed into a pout, but she sat up and made a futile attempt to comb some of the tangles from her hair. "It's a long walk back home."

"I'll have one of my men drive you." He nuzzled the top of her head, savoring what time he had left with her.

"As long as no one sees me, that should be fine."

He pulled back from her. After everything they'd said last night, was she still ashamed to be seen with him?

She laughed and patted his cheek. "Do look so worried. I promised my father I'd be discreet about coming here, and that includes going back home. Remember, I still want him to think I'm the dutiful daughter." She slid out of bed and started dressing.

He stayed under the covers, watching her. The unease

218

returned, stinging the back of his neck like a nest of hornets. "My offer still stands, Claudia. I can have you on that airship within an hour."

"And my decision remains the same. I know the risks involved, and I'm willing to take them if it means the barrier won't fall. I need to continue to play my part in this. That includes lulling my father into a false sense of security. Besides, I need to find out where he's hiding that device."

"You think it's somewhere on the grounds of the villa?"

She chewed her bottom lip. "There are passages under the main house. I don't know how to find them from the inside, though. Not yet anyway."

"I know about the passages, and I can tell you they're blocked."

"I could have told you that." She paused, the corner of her mouth perking up. "In fact, I think I told you about the landslide in one of my letters."

"You did." It was so refreshing to know who his informant was, to be able to have an open conversation instead of relying on a handful of vague details. "But that would lead me to believe your father would be using them now if they were closed off."

"Again, you're thinking like a soldier and not like a Deizian. My father has an army of slaves at his command. If he wanted mountains moved, he'd get them to do it. He's already invested too much ore in the first device. With the emperor interfering with his smuggled shipments, I can say with absolute certainty he's reusing whatever he had before."

She picked up the strap of leather he'd used for weeks to cover up the tattoo on his wrist and used it to bind her hair back. "I'm ready to go."

The heaviness in his chest made it hard to breathe. He climbed out of bed and put on a clean tunic. "Are you sure you'll be safe tonight?"

"Tonight?" Her lips parted, and a brief moment of panic flashed in her eyes before she covered it up. "Yes, I'll be safe. I'll feign illness and lock the door to my room."

He tilted her chin so her gaze met his. "Stay there until I come to get you."

"I will."

He bent down to kiss her one more time. She clung to him, letting him know she hated leaving as much as he did. "Maybe I should come home with you and make my own marriage offer to your father. If I could get him to agree to it…"

She shook her head and stepped back. "He'd never agree to such a thing, even if he knew how much we loved each other. Remember, Deizian marriages are all about keeping the blood pure."

"I think the emperor would disagree with you on that matter."

Her eyes grew wistful under a veil of moisture. "Yes, I can see how tempting it would be to forget bloodlines when you've found someone who completes you." Without warning, though, her expression hardened again. "But let's be realistic. My father would never agree to our match, so forget that silly scheme to get me out of the house."

It was more than some scheme to get her out of the house. He was actually so foolishly in love with her, he'd consider renouncing his vow never to marry. He took a deep breath. One night at a time, she'd said.

Outside the room, the men were already stirring, no strangers to rising with the sun. He ordered one of them to fetch a carriage for Claudia. They strolled through the house, her arm linked with his, until they came to the front courtyard. She walked to the horse and rubbed his flank. "It's a sturdy animal, but he definitely wouldn't win any chariot races."

"I'll keep that in mind."

"You should. Remember, I'm an excellent judge of horseflesh." She kissed him one final time and whispered, "Don't worry. If I find myself in danger, I'll let you know."

He hoped he wouldn't see Kafi again until all this was over with. He helped her into the carriage and watched her disappear into the early morning fog that had rolled in from the sea.

Rufius came up behind him. "She refused to go, eh?"

"Stubborn woman."

"That's what you get when you get mixed up with the likes of her. She'd used to having her own way."

Normally he'd crack a grin at his friend's remark, but his emotions seemed dulled, as though he'd drank too much wine. "Make sure the men leave her room alone when we go in tonight."

"You told her about our plan?" Worry furrowed Rufius's brow. "Are you sure we can trust her? I know you're thinking with your dick, but if she was still working you for information—"

"She's not." His friend's insult rankled him to the point that the two words came out as a snarl. "I trust her. She won't betray us."

"I hope you're right. It's more than just our lives on the line tonight."

He knew the real Claudia now, and he had no reason to doubt her loyalty.

But the back of his neck continued to sting, and his gut told him he'd made a mistake by letting her go.

23

Claudia was thankful for the thick fog that obscured everything greater than a five-foot radius around her. If her father had posted any guards looking for her return, they wouldn't see her until she was practically on top of them. It would make sneaking back into the house that much easier for her. Hopefully, by the time her father rose for the day, she would have created some good lies to feed him about Galerius—anything to lower his guard for the evening.

A nervous energy hummed through her veins. Galerius would be attacking tonight. If everything went according to plan, she'd been free of her father by dawn, and the barrier would be safe again. But she had also seen the hint of fear in Galerius's eyes when he talked about the plan. He was worried about himself—what man in his position wouldn't be—but he seemed more fearful for her. His concern unsettled her. Yes, he said he loved her, but the ways he showed it were so foreign to her world.

And so unexpected from the man who claimed to be a solider first.

The hazy outline of the villa appeared through the fog, and Claudia stopped the driver. She'd walk the rest of the way, preferring the silence of only her steps rather than the clopping of the horse's hooves and the creaking of the wagon's wheels.

She snuck around to the gardens, thinking she'd attract less attention if she entered the house through those doors.

A slave stood waiting for her. "Your father wishes to see you."

Her tongue turned to clay as she followed him. What was her father doing up at this hour? Every inch of her fought the urge to run away and chase down the driver who'd brought her.

Don't let him see your fear, her mind cautioned. *You cannot betray Galerius, especially now.*

She managed to fix her cool, emotionless mask into place before she entered her father's study. When she saw the scene before her, though, it immediately slipped.

Asinius stood beside her father's desk, holding a knife to Kafi's throat.

"What are you doing to my slave?" she demanded, her stomach knotting with worry for the boy.

Her father remained still in his chair. His glittering blue eyes seemed intent on tearing her disguise apart. "Sit down, Claudia."

"Not until Asinius lets my slave go." Anger churned through her veins, tempering her fear. It was one thing for them to take their vengeance out on her, but there was no need to involve a boy in it.

"Your slave?" Her brother pressed the knife against Kafi's throat. A trickle of red flashed under the shiny metal blade, and the boy's dark eyes widened. "Everything here is Father's."

"No. Kafi is mine through my first marriage." She balled her hands into fists, hoping her outrage would spare his life. "My slave. Not his."

"If you want him to live," her father replied, his voice low and even, "then you'd best obey my orders and sit down."

She glanced from him to Kafi and back again before complying with his order. "What has he done to deserve this treatment, Father?"

Hostilius leaned forward on his desk, his gaze never

leaving hers. "I always knew you were good at spying on people. I just never expected betrayal from you."

She opened her hands and discreetly wiped her palms on her skirt. "Why would you think I'd betray you, Father, especially after all my years of faithful service?"

Her heart pounded with such force, it threatened to make her voice quiver and her hands shake. She cast a quick glance at Kafi, wondering if he'd confessed to her father. One look at the boy's defiant eyes told her that her secret was safe with him. He'd never betray her. All the more reason to spare his life.

"All this time, I thought you were gathering information on Galerius for me like a dutiful daughter." Her father held up a piece of paper. Red chalk had been brushed over the surface, providing a clear outline of her handwriting. She didn't need to read it to know what it said. "Instead, I find a traitor in my own house."

Every muscle in her body locked to keep her from swooning. She'd been caught. But she'd never admit guilt. "I have no idea what you're talking about."

"You may have played me for a fool once, but I know your handwriting." Her father turned the letter over. "Shall I read aloud what you wrote to Galerius?"

"Are you certain it's my handwriting?" She was stalling, trying to figure out a way to convince her father to let Kafi go. "How do you know Asinius didn't forge the letter to implicate me when he's been the one feeding the emperor information?"

"Why, you little bitch!" Her brother lunged at her, lowering the knife from Kafi's throat long enough for the boy to make an attempt to escape. Unfortunately, Asinius managed to grasp his tunic and jerk him back, placing the knife where it had been before. Hatred seethed from his sneering face. He'd be all too happy to kill the slave out of spite.

The fear in Kafi's eyes burned in her chest. "Your quarrel is with me. Let the boy go."

"He's nothing more than a slave," Asinius sneered. "I

wonder how long it will take for him to hit the rocks when I push him over the cliffs."

She turned her attention back to the one man who held both their lives in his hands. "Father, this is not a proper conversation to be having in front of a slave."

A murderous grin spread across her father's lips. Blood would be spilled before the day was through. She only hoped she'd live long enough to warn Galerius. "You're quite fond of this little slave, aren't you?"

"He's probably been fucking her just like everyone else has," her brother muttered.

She took a deep breath, refusing to let his insult distract her. "His mother has been a faithful servant to me for years, and I promised her I'd look out for him."

"And what would you do to save such an insignificant thing like him?"

Her father's question made the hair on the back of her neck stand up. He was trying to get a confession from her. Or worse, wanting her to betray Galerius. She decided it was safer to maintain her façade as the dutiful daughter. "What do you ask of me, Father?"

"What is Galerius planning?"

She swallowed hard, trying to come up with a response that would appease him. "I don't know."

"You mean you spent all night in his bed, fed him information, and gained nothing in return?"

Her father would never understand what she'd gained from her time with Galerius. She now knew what it was like to be loved, cherished, adored. Even though she was facing her own death, she wouldn't trade those moments for a lifetime of misery. "He's as tight-lipped as you are."

Her brother laughed. "You're not only a stupid whore, but apparently not good enough to even fuck a confession out of him."

Anger rippled down her spine, but she kept her mouth closed. She needed to stay calm if she wanted to outwit her father.

Hostilius drummed his fingers on the condemning evidence. "It's quite obvious Galerius has become fond of his little informant. Perhaps we can use that to our advantage."

At last, some leverage, something she could barter in exchange for Kafi's life. She mirrored his calculating smile. "Depends on what you want me to do and what I'll get in return for it."

Her father raised a brow at her audacity. "I want you to write him another letter, this time inviting him to join us for dinner."

Dread coiled in the pit of her stomach, making her grateful she hadn't had breakfast. Did her father know about the impending attack? She reached across the desk for a piece of paper and a pen. "And why should I tell him you're inviting him?"

"I don't care, Claudia. Just make sure he comes tonight."

She could already see her father plotting the various ways to kill Galerius. A poisoned cup. An assassin lurking in the shadows. Perhaps even something bold, like shoving him off the cliff himself. The gruesome images filled her mind as she stared at the blank page. She needed to find a way to let Galerius know it was a trap.

She looked up to see Asinius still holding a blade to Kafi's throat. "If I write this letter, you will let my slave go."

Several long thumps of her heart passed before her father looked at Asinius and nodded.

At least she was able to do one thing correctly. She started writing, inviting Galerius to dinner as her father had instructed. She remembered their conversation from this morning about marriage and added "*My father is agreeable to our marriage and wishes to discuss the terms of the contract with you.*" If anything seemed out of place, it would be that line. Hopefully, he remembered their conversation, too.

She handed the letter back to her father. "There. That should make sure he comes."

Her father read it and chuckled. "He actually thinks I'd allow him to marry you?"

"That's what he spoke of this morning." She sat straighter in her chair, hoping her father would allow Galerius to receive her letter with the hidden warning intact. "I've done what you've asked. Now release Kafi."

Her father folded the letter, sealing it with wax. "Asinius, you heard your sister. Release the slave."

Her brother grinned, and Claudia's breath caught. In less than a second, the blade sliced through Kafi's throat. The boy's eyes bugged out. A stream of red poured down his neck, staining his rough tunic.

Claudia wasn't sure if her cry broke free of her tightened throat or not. She lunged for Kafi, catching him as he fell to the floor in a heap. Tears blurred the image of his dying face. "I'm sorry," she repeated over and over again, cradling him in her arms and brushing his shaggy black hair back. "I'm so sorry."

As the life drained from his eyes, she caught a glimpse of what she hoped was forgiveness.

"You disgust me, crying over a stupid slave." Asinius struck her, the knife still in his hand. Her cheek burned as the salt of her tears mingled with the fresh cut he left on her skin. He followed it with a second blow, knocking her away from Kafi's body.

She was too overwhelmed with guilt to fight back. Kafi had died because of her. She only hoped her letter would be enough to spare Galerius.

But her salvation came from an unexpected source. "Asinius, control yourself," her father ordered.

He came around the desk and sat her up. Warm magic tingled along her cheek as he ran his fingers over the cut. "We have to be careful with her. After all, we can't have her badly bruised when Galerius arrives."

All her life, she'd known him to be a man with a heart as icy as his eyes. He never showed mercy unless he had something more sinister planned.

She couldn't stop her bottom lip from trembling. "What are you planning to do, Father?"

He stood back, towering over her like some vengeful god. "I want him to witness the fall of the empire before I kill him. And I want to you to watch his death, knowing his blood is on your hands."

No mention of her death. He wanted her to live in guilt. She slowly pushed herself to her feet, her battered ribs protesting each movement. She had nothing left to lose now. "You'll fail, just like you did before."

"I wouldn't be so certain of that, daughter."

She stepped back, calculating the best way to escape this madhouse before either plan could take effect.

Asinius grabbed her arm, his fingers leaving new bruises where her prior ones were beginning to fade. "Going somewhere?"

Before she could answer, something connected with the back of her head. Her knees went weak. Blackness closed in on her like a curtain, completely enveloping her consciousness.

***

Galerius sharpened his blade, his eyes focused on the insignia engraved near the hilt. Once a member of the Legion, always a member of the Legion. And after tonight, he'd either have redeemed himself or died trying.

The tingling along his neck revived, practically burning his skin. He rubbed it and wished it would subside. Ever since Claudia had left, he hadn't been able to shake the sensation. The man who drove her home said that everything went smoothly—no signs of trouble. No evidence that she was in danger.

I probably won't feel comfortable until I have her safely in my arms again. He drew a steadying breath and resumed his preparations for tonight.

A knock sounded at his door. This time, Rufius didn't wait to be invited in.

Galerius laid his sword aside. "Ready to go over the plans one final time?"

"Sure, but this may change them." He handed Galerius a letter.

He knew the paper, the wax seal. His pulse quickened. "When did this arrive?"

"Just now. Different messenger, though."

He took the letter and read the contents. "This doesn't make sense."

"Let me see." Rufius peered over his shoulder. "Marriage, eh?"

"Exactly."

His friend laughed. "You give a woman one good night of lovin', and they immediately think you're ready to be tied down to them for the rest of your life."

"No, it's not that." He stood and paced the room, trying to remember the details from his conversation with Claudia this morning. "She has no desire to marry again, nor would her father allow it. It's a warning."

The grin fell from Rufius's face. "Do we need to abort the mission?"

"No. We've invested too much time, too many resources to back out now. We have to stop Hostilius before he activates that device again."

"But if she's trying to send you a warning, chances are her father's already found out about our plans. He'll be waiting for us."

Galerius read the letter one more time. "No, he'll be waiting for just me."

Rufius closed the space between them, his voice rising. "And who's to say that little princess hasn't spilled her guts to her father?"

Galerius refused to back down. He kept his tone quiet, calming as he said, "Like I told you before, I trust her. She started this, and she's the type of person who will see it through to the end. Even if it means endangering her own life."

The last few words shook his soul more than he realized. *By the gods, if I manage to get her out of this alive, I'll never let her go again.*

He glanced outside at the midday sun. He had only a few hours to adjust the plan. "Do you think you can take over for me?"

Rufius's jaw dropped. "You can't be serious. You'll be walking into a trap."

"I know that, but I can't bear the thought of her suffering because of me."

His friend swore under his breath. "She's really got you by the balls, doesn't she?"

"Answer my question, Rufius. Can you take over for me, or do I need to appoint someone else to be in charge?" He leveled his gaze on the soldier and waited for his response.

"I can do it," he replied, "but I still disagree with you going in alone. It's practically suicide. And for what? For some woman?"

"Not just some woman." He grabbed a dagger and strapped it to his thigh under his tunic. "*The woman.* The only one I'll ever need or want."

Rufius shook his head as though he were talking to a madman. "I'll let the others know about the change in plans. How much time do you think you'll need?"

"If I can get there around sunset, hopefully I can get her out before we attack." He found a clean toga and held it up to his scabbard, wondering if it would be big enough to hide his sword if he strapped it to his back. Better to be well armed than to be caught wishing he had another weapon, especially in a situation like this.

"And what if she's already dead?"

His friend's question paralyzed him. What if Hostilius had already punished Claudia for her betrayal? His lungs burned for air as the image of her bloody corpse filled his mind once again. He closed his eyes and offered a silent prayer to the gods for her safety. "If that's the case, then her father's head is mine."

"If you live long enough to catch him."

Galerius tightened his jaw and resumed looking for ways to conceal more weapons on him. "Don't you have something better to do?"

"Fine, I'll start briefing the others." His friend left the room, muttering about what a pig-headed fool he was.

Galerius picked up the letter and read Claudia's words one more time. He wasn't the only pig-headed fool around here. If only he'd convinced her to stay with him. Or better yet, gotten her on board that airship to Emona...

He crumpled the letter in his fist, knowing no good would come of him asking "what if." She was alive a few hours ago. He only hoped he'd get there in time to keep her that way.

24

Galerius rode up the driveway to Hostilius's villa at a cautious pace. He wanted to appear like an excited bridegroom-to-be, but in the back of his mind, he was cataloging possible escape routes, the best place to park his chariot, anything that would make getting Claudia out of there easier.

Dark figures moved along the shadowed balconies, the sun having already dipped behind the back of the house on its journey beyond the sea. Overhead, the purple glow of the neighboring supernova began to fill the sky. Once the sun had completely set, his men would attack. He scanned the horizon for any airships, but saw none.

Please let her still be alive.

He pulled up in front of the villa. A slave appeared as soon as he climbed out of the chariot. "They're expecting you in the gardens, Captain Galerius."

He studied the Alpirion for any hint of fear, of deception. The slave appeared ill-at-ease, as though the neck of his tunic was too tight, and Galerius sharpened his senses. Whatever trap lay waiting for him was back there. He adjusted his toga to better conceal the gladius strapped to his back and followed the slave.

Claudia and her brother stood at the edge of the gardens near the cliff, their bodies silhouetted by the sun. The evening breeze rushed in from sea, whipping the hair that had come loose from her pins around her face. Her posture was stiff, mirroring the slave's, but at least she was still alive.

The tingling along his neck now burned along his entire spine. He remembered what Claudia had told him about the cliffs and eyed them warily. The last thing he wanted was to end up at the bottom of them like so many of Hostilius's enemies.

He focused his attention on Asinius, who stood mere inches behind his sister. Like father, like son. The closer he got to them, the more Asinius inched closer to the edge.

Claudia's eyes grew bigger, and Galerius swore he caught an almost imperceptible shake of her head. She wasn't out of danger yet.

He stopped several arm's lengths in front of them. His fingers itched to grab his sword, but first he needed to know the source of the fear he saw on her face. "Claudia, I received your letter. Does it mean what I think it does?"

She answered with a subtle nod. She'd been caught and had been trying to warn him. Now, it was up to him to rescue her.

Asinius angled his head so his mouth was inches from Claudia's ear. "It seems you've become rather fond of my sister's talents, to want to marry her. Not that you're the first man who's fallen for her wiles. She can be quite the seductress."

Claudia winced as her brother twirled his finger around a lock of her hair.

Galerius's stomach heaved from the way Asinius stared at his sister, like a man assessing a *lupa* before negotiating the price he'd pay for her. His blood pounded in his ears, his anger rising from the way he talked about her if she were nothing more than a common whore. He flexed his fingers and forced himself to remain calm for her sake. All Asinius had to do was give her a quick shove, and she'd be the one at the bottom of the cliff.

The leather scabbards bit into his skin, begging him to release the weapons they held. "I've come to discuss a marriage contract with your father, not you."

233

Asinius stopped ogling his sister and turned toward him, his brows raised. "You really want this package of used goods?"

Claudia closed her eyes, the pain of his insults flickering across her face. The urge to comfort her, to take her in his arms and carry her far away from here grew so strong, he couldn't breathe.

Galerius vowed that he'd make sure she'd never have to hear such things again. "Yes, I do. I want her more than I've ever wanted any other woman before."

The wonder in her eyes when she opened them eased some of his ire. A faint smile appeared before her brother grabbed her arm and pulled her closer.

"Dear sister, what kind of magic did you work on his dick to make him want you so badly?"

"Don't talk about her that way!" Galerius took a step forward, wanting more than ever to cut the other man's tongue out for insulting her that way.

Claudia's gasp stopped him dead in his tracks. Her eyes widened, and his blood chilled, reminding him her life was still in danger.

Asinius's laughter was colder than the icy winds that blew down from the mountains to the north. As long as he had Claudia, he knew he was still in control. "My, my, my. I'm impressed. He's actually defending you, Claudia. You, who spread your legs so willingly at our father's command."

He narrowed his eyes and turned to Galerius, his amusement morphing into open hostility. "But then you poisoned her mind and convinced her to betray us."

He needed to diffuse this situation now before Asinius harmed Claudia. "I think there's been a misunderstanding," he began, coming closer to them. A few more steps, and he'd easily be able to draw his sword and attack.

Claudia's lips parted, and panic distorted her features.

He froze.

Asinius shifted, concealing himself behind her, using her body as a shield. Then he moved the arm that had been behind

234

her the whole time to reveal a knife. Fresh blood coated the blade, and Galerius's vision turned red.

He took another step, only to hear her cry out in pain. Asinius raked the blade along her arm. A new line of blood trickled down it a second later.

"By all means, keep coming closer," Asinius taunted. "I'm enjoying this."

Time to rethink his strategy. Claudia was more than a victim here—she was being used as bait, someone her family deemed disposable for their own ends. The sun sank lower along the horizon. The attack would begin soon, and he could easily see Asinius tossing her over the edge to save himself. He needed to get her away from the cliff before the airships arrived.

"Why did you bring me here tonight?"

Asinius grinned. "Tonight will be the end of Sergius's reign. We thought you should witness it before you die."

As if on cue, the ground beneath him rumbled. The edge of the cliff crumbled, sending the rocks inches from Claudia's feet tumbling to the crashing waves below.

By the gods, they were using the device tonight. Ever since he'd arrived, he'd been hoping the other men wouldn't arrive until he'd secured Claudia. Now they couldn't get here quickly enough.

"Your quarrel is with me, then, not your sister. Let her go."

"Not a chance." Asinius snapped his wrist, bringing the blade of the knife up to her throat. "I want her to witness the cost of her betrayal."

Finally, the moment he'd been waiting for, a chance to turn this power-play around. "She can't witness it if you kill her first."

Despite having a knife pressed against her throat, a look of relief washed over her when he pointed that out.

The baffled expression on her brother's face vanished as quickly as it appeared. "True. Perhaps she can even redeem herself." He jostled her, scraping the blade against her fair skin.

"What do you think of that, dear sister? Your life for his?"

His pulse jumped as Asinius's knife wavered from her throat.

"Yes, see how simple it would be, Claudia." He gave Galerius an evil grin. "You see, it wouldn't be the first time she'd seduced a man and then killed him for my father. You're no different than her husbands."

Claudia's gaze darted between Galerius and the knife. A twinge of fear wormed its way into his soul as her hand hovered inches above the hilt. Would she betray him to save herself? His heart told him no, but it didn't stop the sweat from prickling along his brow.

She wrapped her hand around her brother's over the knife's hilt and met his gaze. "I'm so sorry, Galerius."

Asinius loosened his grip on her, and she moved a step toward him. The soldier inside him ordered him to draw his weapons and strike them both down instead of standing there waiting like a helpless fool. But he just stood there, his eyes never leaving hers. *I have to trust her*, his heart repeated with each beat.

Then an emotion flickered across her face, and his fears ebbed. She was looking at him the same way she had last night when she had told him he'd filled her heart with something other than vengeance. She bit her bottom lip, tightening her grip on the knife.

He came closer to her and held his arms out to his sides, his palms open to show her he wouldn't try to stop whatever she was planning.

The scent of calming lavender wafted on the breeze toward him. "I meant what I said last night," she whispered.

"I know," he replied. "I did, too."

The ground rumbled under them again, distracting her brother enough to free her from his grasp. She whirled around, burying the knife in her brother's chest.

Asinius shrieked, a mixture of both pain and rage. His arms flailed, hooking around Claudia's shoulders and shoving her toward the edge of the cliff. She teetered on the brink, trying to maintain her balance.

Galerius lunged for her as another wave of thunder rolled under their feet. Claudia screamed. The ground gave way beneath her, sending her toward the jagged rocks below.

And then, by some intervention of the gods, his hand clasped hers. He fell to the ground. The impact forced the air from his lungs, but his grip held. "Don't let go," he ordered her.

"I won't," she replied, her voice high with panic.

He began pulling her up when a movement out of the corner of his eye caught his attention.

Asinius sank to his knees and pulled the knife out his chest with agonizing slowness. His breaths were labored, but he still had the strength to stand and stumbled toward them, the blade raised. "You traitorous bitch."

Galerius shifted to the side to shield Claudia, freeing a hand to block the blow. The blade sliced across his palm. His breath hitched from the searing pain, but he managed to hold on to Claudia with his other hand.

Asinius fell toward them. Galerius managed to get his bleeding hand in the center of Asinius's chest, using the momentum of the assault to catapult him over the edge of the cliff. It was almost too easy, the way he sailed over their heads.

Then Claudia cried out again, her fingers slipping from his.

Asinius dangled above the rocks, holding on to his life by one of her ankles as she tried to kick him off.

Galerius wrapped both of his hands around hers. "I have you."

A tear streaked down her dust-caked cheek. "Don't let go, please, don't let go."

"I promise."

But keeping his promise proved more difficult than he imagined. The cut along his hand weakened his grip and coated it with slick blood. The earth rumbled again, slipping beneath his feet, showering her with more rocks and dirt.

A roar of rage echoed from below. Asinius spat out the

rubble from his mouth and shook Claudia, pulling her further from Galerius's grasp.

He gritted his teeth. "Do you trust me?"

Her eyes remained wide with fear, but she nodded.

He shifted his leg out to the side, making the dagger strapped to his thigh as accessible as possible. He removed his injured hand from Claudia and felt his way to the hilt, his gaze focused on Asinius the whole time. He had only one shot, and he needed to make it count.

Focus on the target and free yourself of any emotions. He blocked out his fear, his anger. All that mattered was killing Asinius so he could save Claudia.

He saw confidence glowing in her eyes. She tightened her hold on him and said, "I trust you."

He flicked the dagger. The blade landed perfectly in the soft flesh of Asinius's neck, severing his windpipe. A gurgling noise came from his mouth, and his hand released Claudia's ankle. A few seconds later, his body smashed against the rocks below. A wave crashed over it, carrying him out to sea.

The ground continued to rumble. "On the count of three. One, two, three."

With the final word, he hoisted her up the cliff and into his arms. They fell back against the grass, the earth beneath their feet still crumbling. It wasn't until he had crawled several yards from the edge that his pulse slowed.

Claudia sobbed quietly in his arms, his tunic bunched in her hands.

He kissed her forehead. "It's over, Claudia. We're safe now."

Her shaking eased, even though she clung to him as though she were still dangling from the cliff. "I'm sorry, Galerius. I never meant—I mean—"

He shushed her and wrapped her in his embrace. "You did all you could."

"But why did you come?" She lifted her tear-streaked face from his chest. "Didn't you catch my warning?"

"I did, but I couldn't abandon you, not when you needed me."

Her eyes welled up, and she pulled him into a kiss that stole his breath away. He allowed himself a moment to savor the taste of her lips, the feel of her warm flesh beneath his hands, the scent of lemon and lavender that rose above the blood and dust that covered them. They'd faced death and won. Now he had all the time he needed to show her how much he loved her.

The drone of airships filled the silence, tearing him away from her. The soldiers were approaching and would soon swarm the grounds. "We need to leave now, Claudia."

She looked to the sky and the six flat-bedded airships that flew toward them. "What are they going to do?"

"Stop your father." He rose to his feet and helped her up. "Let's go before we get caught in the crossfire."

But she remained planted where she was, watching the airships hover over the grounds of her home. The soldiers tossed ropes over the sides and rappelled to the ground, drawing their weapons as soon as their feet touched the ground. Shouts filled the villa, followed by the clang of swords as the men loyal to Hostilius inside fought to defend their master.

He tugged on her again, tempted to throw her over his shoulder and carry her away if she continued to resist. "We can't stay here."

She whirled around, watching the ensuing battle with her mouth agape. "They won't be able to find him."

"They will. Come on."

"No." She wrenched her hand free from him. "Don't you see? I'm the only one who can find him."

Claudia turned and ran toward the house, leaving him no choice by to chase after her.

25

Claudia screamed as the soldier in front of her plunged his sword into the mercenary hired by her father. The metallic scent of blood turned her stomach, making her gag. She held her hand to her mouth and ran past them. She needed to get into her father's office before they closed it off.

Someone grabbed her from behind, hauling her toward the front door. "Stop trying to make martyr of yourself," Galerius growled. "You're going to get both of us killed."

"No, we have to get to the device before my father brings down the barrier, and the only way we can get to the tunnels is through me." She wrestled against him, but his grip held.

As if to prove her point, the ground shook with such force, the plaster along the walls cracked and shattered as it fell. The earthquakes were becoming stronger, correlating to the amount of magic her father and his accomplices were using to fuel the device. At this rate, the barrier would fall within minutes.

Galerius turned her around so she faced him. "Do you know how to get to the tunnels?"

She hesitated. She knew the entrance had to be somewhere in her father's office, but she had no idea where the lockpad was. Still, it was better to lie and hope the gods sided with her. "Yes."

"Then show me."

She started for the office only to see two of her father's men charging toward her. Galerius jumped in front of her, his gladius drawn, and blocked one. He was joined by another man, the one who'd answered the door at his home last night. Together, they made quick work of her father's men, delivering death blows before the ground rumbled again.

"They seem to be holing up in that room," the man told Galerius, pointing to the office.

Claudia gave Galerius her best *I told you so* glance.

"Then that's where we need to go," he replied.

"Get the girl out of here and let me do my work, then." The soldier grinned and gathered a few more of his men. They launched a wave of attackers at the closing doors.

Galerius pulled her off into the shadows of the atrium. He ripped a strip of material off his toga and started wrapping his injured hand. "It seems you're right about the office. Why else would they be guarding it so closely?"

For the first time, she noticed the blood running down his arm and caking his skin. She slipped the ring made of ore off her finger and reached for his hand. "Let me heal that."

He shook his head. "Save your magic for when we really need it."

She grabbed his hand and dug the ring into the wound along his palm. He hissed from the pain, but didn't fight her anymore, knowing she needed the ore as a conduit. "You need to be fully healed to fight. Now hold still."

The sounds of battle raged around them, but she blocked it out, trusting Galerius to protect her if it came her way. She focused on the gentle of hum of magic that flowed through her veins, calling on it, gathering it in her hands. A golden light formed along the ring as she stroked it along the blood-soaked bandage. Underneath it, she could see the skin knitting back together, the spilled blood returning to the vessels. When she withdrew her fingers, the cloth was as clean as it was when he arrived at the villa.

"Better?" she asked, slipping the ring back on her finger.

He unraveled the fabric and flexed his hand. "Absolutely."

Now that he was taken care of, she needed to return to finding a way to stop her father. The heavy wooden doors remained closed to the soldiers, who continued to ram it with their shoulders.

Galerius crossed the room to the man he'd fought alongside. "Rufius, what's going on?"

"We have about ten to fifteen men inside. I assume they're protecting Hostilius and his device."

The ground rumbled again, sending more plaster chips to the floor.

The muscle along Galerius's jaw rippled, and his gaze became distant as though he were lost in an unpleasant memory. "We don't have time to waste. Send some the men to fetch one of the laser cannons off the ship."

Rufius's eyes bugged. "Are you nuts? This place is already falling apart from the tremors, and you want to blast it?"

"Do you or do you not want to catch Hostilius before the barrier falls?"

Rufius took a step back before ordering four of the men to grab the cannon and roll it into the house.

The orchestrated thumps of the remaining men's shoulders continued in time with the pounding of the blood along Claudia's temples. There had to be a simpler way to get into the office besides blowing the doors away. "Why are they making so little progress?"

"The doors are locked, my lady," Rufius replied.

She laughed at the absurdity of it. Here they were, bruising their bodies over something she could easily remedy. She pressed her hand against the bronze plate by the door. "All brute and no brains."

With a trickle of magic, the locks clicked, and the next blow sent the soldiers tumbling into the room. Galerius shielded her behind him as the rest of the men rushed in to vanquish the remaining mercenaries. She was glad she couldn't see the slaughter, but she still heard the clang of swords and armor, the cries of pain, the crash of furniture.

It wasn't until things quieted down that Galerius moved forward, allowing her a glimpse of the destruction. Bodies littered the room, staining the fine carpets and mosaic floors with their blood. Her father's massive desk, which had once gleamed with gold and marble, now lay shattered. Spatters of blood concealed the decorative scenes painted on the plaster walls.

Claudia stared at the mess, unable to swallow. This had been her home—one of the grandest villas in Lucrilla—and now it lay in ruins.

Galerius wrapped his hands around her shoulders. "We can leave now, if you want."

She shook her head. She'd made a vow to stop her father, and they'd barely scratched the surface of the barriers protecting him. "I'm not leaving until I see that device destroyed."

"What are we looking for?"

"An ore plate, another lockpad." She lifted her dress and stepped over a body. "It will be well disguised though, like a sconce or rosette. It won't be like what you saw outside."

"You heard Claudia." Galerius had been transformed from her lover to every inch the military leader she knew him to be. The authority in his voice did not allow any challenges. "Fan out and search the room."

She clung to the walls, running her fingers across the plaster panels while searching for the tell-tale hum of magic that would identify the ore. Out of all the people in the room, only she and Galerius had the Deizian blood to activate it, and knowing her father, he would have added precautions that allowed only those of pure Deizian blood to enter his chamber. That meant it was up to her to lead the men there. For once, her pure bloodlines would be useful for something other than breeding.

She came to a section of the wall where a line of golden

swords and phalluses formed a decorative chair rail. She dragged her fingers across it. Like the golden rosettes on his desk, this would be the perfect area to hide a keypad made of the bronze ore. Near the end, she found what she was looking for—the distinct tingle of magic right beside an almost imperceptible crack in the plaster. "I found it."

But unlike the outside lock, it didn't respond to her magic. She doubled her efforts, hoping to hear the click of the locks, but met a wall of resistance. "Why isn't it working?"

Galerius came beside her and covered her hand with his own. His magic flowed through her, augmenting it, but still nothing. He pulled away. "Perhaps your father figured out how to set the locks like the ones in the imperial palace."

If that was the case, then only those he'd granted permission to would be able to enter. People like her brother. Too bad his body was probably already far out to sea. "I'm his daughter, though."

"Yes, and he'd kept you ignorant of his plans even before he learned of your letters."

She forced one more river of magic into the lockpad, determined to overpower it. A shower of sparks filled the room, knocking her back into Galerius. Her knees buckled from the effort, and if he hadn't caught her, she would have fallen to the ground.

"Save your energy," he said, his words soothing her wounded pride.

"But we're so close. Behind that door is the way to my father. If we can't get past it…"

"We will. There are more ways to open a door than just magic." He winked and turned toward the laser cannon that was being rolled into the office. "Line it up over here. We still have a door to knock down."

Claudia stood back and watched as they lined up the cannon with where the door would be, partly mourning the fact they'd have to cause more destruction to her home. A crew of two half-blooded Deizian soldiers stood behind it and shouted for everyone to clear the area. Galerius pulled her out of the office, but not before she heard the whirring of magic building up inside the cannon. A flash of blue light filled the room, followed by a loud boom.

If her father hadn't already known about the invasion going on above him, he would now.

She waited until the dust cleared before going back in. A gaping black hole was present where the red and gold decorated wall once stood. Beyond, it the pull of magic called to her. This was only the beginning.

The soldiers rushed in, descending into the dark staircase. It only took a few seconds before the first screams of agony echoed back to her.

Rufius remained at the door. "What happened?"

"It was a bolt of lightning, sir," one the men replied, helping his singed comrade up the stairs. The soldier was still alive but stunned, with little tendrils of smoke still curling from the blackened edges of his hair.

Galerius and Rufius turned to her as though they had expected her to warn them about this. She lifted her chin. "My father is no fool. He would have set traps along the way, ones that would prevent undesirables from entering."

"Undesirables like non-Deizians," Galerius finished for her. "How do we get past them?"

"I'll go in first and try to disable them."

"How?"

"You're thinking like a soldier again. It takes magic to disable magic." She just hoped her logic was sound. "See, I told you that you still needed me."

He caught her before she entered the staircase and said in a voice meant only for her, "I do need you. Please don't do anything stupid."

She slid her arm through his grasp, pausing at the end to give him a reassuring squeeze, even though her heart fluttered fast enough to send shivers through her body. "Have them wait for my signal before entering."

One step at a time, she let the blackness swallow her. The lack of light sharpened her other senses. The hum of magic grew stronger, and she hadn't gotten very far before her skin tingled as though she'd just passed through a silk veil. The first trap. She focused her mind on finding the source of the magic, running her hands along the damp limestone until they touched the two warm ore plates on either side of the tunnel.

She released her own magic, and the tingling along her skin vanished. "I disabled the first trap," she called up.

Several sets of footsteps came toward her, and the familiar scent of Galerius surrounded her. "What was it?"

"A small barrier." She continued down, listening to see if anyone else suffered the same effects of the unlucky soldier who'd run into before. So far, so good. "I think it would be best for you to stay a few steps behind me in case we come across another trap."

"As you wish." His scent grew weaker, and she continued down the steep staircase.

A layer of water coated the stairs, making them slick beneath her feet. When the ground trembled again, she dug her fingers into the loose stone of the walls to keep from falling into the darkness below. There were no more problems, no signs of other another trap, until her nose smacked into a cold metal door. "We've reached the end for the moment."

"What did you find?" Galerius asked.

"A door." She reached her arms up, trying to feel for the outline of it. "I need a light."

Her request was granted within seconds as Galerius produced an illumination orb. "Is it trapped?"

She waited for the tingle to reappear, but felt nothing. "No, but it is locked. Help me find the lockpad."

A few seconds later, the light reflected off the dull bronze plate. This time, the locks easily yielded to her magic, and they continued on.

The air practically crackled with magic now. Her muscles twitched from the intensity of it. More tremors shook the earth, showering them with dust and rubble, yet she kept her slow pace down the stairs. They'd get to her father soon enough. It was up to her to make sure it was safe for the others to follow, though.

Another metal door blocked their progress. This one felt different than the other—heavier, more daunting, more dangerous. She half expected to find a lyger guarding it. But the increasing magic that surrounded her told they'd find the chamber when they opened it, and that meant the possibility of another trap.

Galerius stood next to her, his expression grave. "It's on the other side, isn't it?"

She nodded, glancing up the stairway at the shadowed figures lining up behind them. "I'd be careful entering the chamber when I open the door."

"Do you sense another trap?"

The air was too charged for her to answer with certainty. "I can't say for sure, but remember, my father has already set one. It would be foolish to think he wouldn't have another placed to guard his device."

Galerius shifted on his feet. "Then we'll proceed with caution."

His body betrayed his words. His hand tightened around the hilt of his sword. His eyes burned with vengeance. He wanted to storm the room, to cut her father and his allies down as quickly as possible to keep the barrier from falling.

And it all fell to her to take them to the next step. She pressed her palm against the plate, restraining her magic. "Remember what I said, Galerius."

But as soon as the locks clicked, he plowed past her into the room. A scream froze in her throat as bolts of lightning rose from the ore-inlaid floor, wrapping around him like a cage. He cried out, a mere grunt, before collapsing to the ground.

26

Galerius was dreaming his flesh was on fire, and prayed to the gods for rain to douse it. His pleas were answered by the touch of cooling hands. They bathed him in their mercy, starting with his face and working down his body before returning to cradle his cheeks.

"Galerius, wake up." As calm as the touch was, the voice was more urgent. "Open your eyes for me, please."

When he did, Claudia's face hovered over his, her sternness softened by worry. "What happened?"

"Another one of those Deizian-only traps," Rufius answered. "Just be grateful your lady pulled you back before you were reduced to cinders."

A whiff of smoke filled his nose as he drew in a deep breath. He looked down at the singe marks adorning his tunic and the soot coating his skin. "It wasn't a dream."

Claudia shook her head and raised him up to a sitting position. "Why do you insist on acting like an idiot and not heeding my warnings?"

The aristocratic arrogance had edged back into her words, but the worry still lingered in her touch. "Remember, I'm a soldier, not a Deizian."

"Yes, and you almost got killed again for it, you stubborn fool."

"You have some nerve, calling me stubborn."

Rufius peered over her shoulder. "I'm sorry to interrupt this little lover's spat, but we have bigger problems to deal with. They're tearing down the barrier, and we can't even get close to them."

He moved aside to show Galerius the situation. Four archers crowded into the doorway, firing arrows through the opening. The room beyond them was the size of the imperial throne room and entirely coated with ore—the walls, the tiles, the ceiling. In the center stood a globe twice the size of the one in the imperial throne room, slow rotating to reveal the flickering red outline of the barrier.

Anger diluted his pain. "Where's Hostilius?"

He tried to rise, but Claudia pushed him back down. "He's on the other side of the globe."

"The cowardly bastard's hiding behind his device." Rufius spat on the ground. "None of my archers can hit him, and none of my soldiers can set foot inside that room without ending up fried like you."

The ground shook, and the barrier fell over the southern edge of the empire for a few seconds. When it reappeared, it was faint. Emperor Sergius must have been pouring all his magic into keeping it up against Hostilius and his allies.

His gut twisted, and anger coiled in his muscles. They were so close, had sacrificed so much, only to find themselves unable to save the empire when they needed to. "How many Deizians are in there?"

Rufius pointed to the arrow-riddled body of Atius Cotta. "Three now."

Three. Less than the men who'd joined Hostilius the other night. Either they'd bowed out, or Hostilius had decided to act without having his entire team assembled.

Claudia stared at the globe, her jaw hard. "We have to find a way to stop them from attacking the barrier."

"Any ideas, princess?" Rufius asked. "After all, it's your father causing all this chaos."

Claudia's eyes flashed, turning the same cold shade of blue he'd seen when Hostilius was angered. She stood in one graceful motion and closed the space between her and Rufius. Magic rippled around her, distorting the air. "Don't you ever take that tone with me, you insignificant Elymanian."

Much to Rufius's credit, he didn't cower before her. "I'm doing all I can to stop him without condemning my men to suicide."

Galerius jumped to his feet to separate them. The room wavered, and they both reached out to steady him. "We need to work together, not stand here and argue."

"We're paralyzed, Galerius." Frustration tightened his friend's voice. "We can't stop the barrier from falling without killing Hostilius, and we can't get to him with that trap he's set."

"But I can."

Claudia's words knocked the air from his lungs. "Whatever you're thinking, don't do it."

She lifted her chin and peered down her nose at him. "Are you trying to order me around?"

"I'm trying to keep you from getting killed." He grabbed her arm, determined to push her as far away from the chamber as he could.

Rufius came and blocked them from escaping. "She has a point, Galerius. When she went to rescue you, she didn't start smoking."

"See, even your second in command agrees with me." She rested her palms against his chest, pushing him away. "The room is designed to keep non-Deizians out, just like the other trap I disabled."

Logic told him he should let her go, but his heart still clenched with worry. He ran his fingers along her cheek. "You shouldn't have to be put in this position."

"I volunteered for it the moment I wrote that first letter." She covered his hand with her own, bringing his fingers to her lips. "I'm not afraid anymore. I know what I have to do. Please don't stop me."

Spoken like a true martyr. Her bravery made him want to haul her back upstairs and keep her under lock and key so he'd never have to see her in harm's way. The ground rumbled again, reminding him there were more important things than his own selfish needs. If the barrier fell, then she'd be in danger from the Barbarians who'd swarm the empire.

He let her go. "Just disable the trap."

She nodded and took a step back, turning to Rufius. "May I have a quiver and bow, just in case?"

"Claudia." His growl did little to intimidate her. "What are you planning?"

"Father is scared of arrows, remember? Besides, if I can get a clear shot at him, maybe I can put your archery lesson to use."

Rufius gave her what she asked for. "When you disable that trap, let me know so I can send my men in."

"You'll know." She looped the quiver to her back and took the bow.

His pulse pounded through his body as he watched her inch closer to the door. The tingling formed at the base of his neck, driving him to chase after her.

Rufius held him back. "You have to let her go, Galerius. It's the only way to stop this. Remember your vow to the emperor."

His father had put his duty to the empire above everything else, losing his wife in the process. Now he was forced to make the same choice with Claudia—his duty to the empire, or his love for the woman who'd captured his heart. "I can't."

"Yes, you can." Rufius shoved him against the wall. "She's made her choice. Now you have to put your personal feelings aside and let her do what she needs to do for all of us. Remember what they told us in training—letting your emotions rule your actions will only lead to your death."

The same thing he'd tried to impress on her last week when he told her to let go of her hatred. He closed his eyes and

251

let go of his fear. He had to let her disable the trap, but as soon as it fell, he wanted blood. "Where's my sword?"

His friend laughed and slapped him on the shoulder. "That's the Galerius I know."

Once he had his gladius firmly in his hand, he felt more in control. The light caught the emblem inscribed on the blade, reminding him of what he once was. "When the trap falls, I'm going to rip Hostilius's heart out."

"I'll let you lead the way." Rufius moved behind him, signaling to other men than Galerius was in charge now.

Claudia gave him a smile and stepped into the room. The ore coated tiles shimmered around her, but she seemed immune to the trap thanks to her pure blood. She took another step, then another, her eyes clenched shut in concentration as she moved closer to the globe. The metal dulled around her, forming a void of magic a few feet in diameter but not enough for him to follow her.

Please find a way to disable the trap. He hated feeling powerless to do anything more than pray, but all their hopes depended on her. If she failed…

The corners of her mouth tilted down, and her breath quickened. The circled widened for a few seconds, only to collapse around her. She opened her eyes and turned back to him. "I can't."

Her confession tore at him like a knife's blade. He swallowed back his frustration and beckoned her back to him. "You've done all you can, then."

Tears glittered in her eyes as her attention flickered between him and the globe. "No, I haven't."

The tingling along his neck turned to fire once again as he watched her kneel on the ground, pressing her palms against the ore tiles. She was planning on doing something stupid, something that would probably get her killed. "Claudia, don't."

She ignored him. Her eyes narrowed, completely focused on the globe.

The air around them quivered with magic, moving at a

different tempo that the one set by Hostilius. Faster, angrier, more powerful. His heart thudded in time with it. His muscles twitched, eager for battle. And yet his body refused to move.

When the Deizians had first arrived on this planet, the native Elymanians thought they shone like the sun when they used their magic. He was witnessing the same transformation in Claudia. A golden aura surrounded her, shining brighter than the magic that surrounded the globe. It blinded him like a flash bomb, forcing him to shield his eyes. Then she sent it racing toward the globe.

Time seemed to stand still for one peaceful second before chaos erupted. An explosion tore through the chamber, knocking them all off their feet. Rocks showered down on him and the soldiers. Darkness filled the void. The hum of magic silenced.

Panic closed his throat as he lost sight of Claudia through the haze of dust. He stumbled into the chamber, not caring if the trap was still active or not. He braced for the pain, but nothing happened.

As the dust settled, he could see the gaping crack that split the globe into two pieces. Two bodies were lying on the other side, their golden hair revealing them to be Deizian, but their faces concealed by the debris. The spot where Claudia had stood was empty.

Sweat beaded his brow. He called out her name. A moan from the far end of the chamber answered him. He spun around in time to see a prone figure moving in the shadows.

Relief washed through him. She was alive, although he still had no idea how badly she was injured. He moved toward her, only to jerk to a stop when he heard a yelp of pain from the doorway.

The soldiers pulled Rufius back into the passageway, the stench of burning flesh filling the chamber. Galerius waited for the same punishment, but nothing came.

"You're of Deizian blood, aren't you?" A gravelly voice asked from behind the remains of the device. Hostilius rose from debris, his eyes glowing in the dark. "A half-blood bastard, I bet."

The room filled with a dim light from the shimmering ore. Prickles of pain crept up from his feet, along his legs, but never reached the intensity of the first time he had set foot in the room. Hostilius had reengaged his trap, but he was too weak to keep all but pure-blooded Deizians out now. Galerius's Deizian blood protected him from what Rufius suffered, but he wondered how long he'd be able to resist.

He tightened his grip on his gladius. "You've failed again, Hostilius. Surrender now, and perhaps the emperor will show you mercy."

The governor laughed, the shrill sound of madness echoing off the walls. "Mercy? I'll show you mercy."

A river of magic, much like what Claudia had sent toward the globe before the explosion, shot toward him. His blood burned, and his vision blurred. He fell to one knee, gasping for breath.

Then it faded, leaving only Hostilius's laughter to mock him. "I'm not finished yet. I'd rather die than surrender."

"I feel the same way." Galerius struggled to his feet and continued toward the man who hid behind the symbol of his failure. "Come out and fight like a man."

"You mean like this?"

Another wave of magic coiled around him and yanked him to the floor, squeezing his chest as though it were trying to smother him. Galerius rolled over onto his stomach, fighting with every inch of his being just to rise to his hands and knees.

"There's a reason why my ancestors conquered this planet centuries ago. The power lies in our blood." To reinforce his point, Hostilius pummeled Galerius with another shot of magic, forcing a moan from him. "The purer the blood, the stronger the magic. That's what the emperor has forgotten."

A storm of magic now engulfed him, smothering him with its intensity. A loud bang filled his ears as the metal door to the chamber slammed shut, cutting off any aid Rufius and the other soldiers could give him. His pulse pounded through his body, pumping out the sweat that drenched his skin.

No longer fearing the archers on the other side, Hostilius stepped out from the rubble and prowled toward him like a lyger approaching wounded prey. "You see, Galerius? I will win. You can't stop me."

The magic's golden light flashed menacingly on the blade in Hostilius's hand. Galerius tried to draw a breath in, tried to rise to defend himself from his approaching enemy, but every effort doubled his agony. He'd failed everyone—Claudia, the emperor—everyone.

You'll never be anything more than a disgrace to me.

He wanted to shout to his father's ghost that he was wrong, that he still had a chance to redeem himself, but the words wouldn't form on his tongue. The magic continued to pull him down, forcing his gaze on his distorted reflection in the bronze tiles below. He tightened his hand around the hilt of his sword until his fingers blanched. If he could muster up to the strength to strike Hostilius when he came into range...

"You're nothing more than a flea to me, and it's time I disposed of you." Hostilius stood above him, the knife raised.

Galerius's gut clenched as though he'd already been stabbed, but it was his enemy who buckled backward with a sharp grunt. The ropes of magic that had pinned him to the floor loosened. He tore his gaze away from the his hands

An arrow stuck out from the center of Hostilius's chest. The Deizian stared at in awe, his eyes wide. The twang of the bow filled the silent chamber, and another arrow imbedded itself less than an inch from the first one. The knife clattered to the floor, and Hostilius staggered back.

Galerius turned in the direction the arrows came from. Claudia stood on her knees with the bow in her hand. Her expression remained stony as she watched her father inch closer to death. Blood dripped down the side of her face, staining her golden hair, but that didn't stop her from loading a third arrow and firing it with the same deadly accuracy. Her eyes shifted from her father to him, and she nodded as though she were giving permission to a gladiator to finish off his foe.

Galerius rose in one swift movement, throwing all his weight behind his sword as he plunged it into Hostilius's chest. "I guess you should have listened to the soothsayer."

The governor's mouth hung open, letting the blood pour out from it. His legs buckled, and the life ebbed from his eyes. The threat he posed to the empire died with him.

Galerius ripped his gladius from his enemy's corpse and stood over it, his breath coming hard and deep. He'd completed his mission.

A gasp ended his moment of celebration. Claudia stared at her father, her face pale, and swooned. He dropped his sword to catch her, pulling her into his arms. "We did it."

She clung to him, her fingers digging into the flesh of his arms, and cried for several minutes. He made no effort to silence her. She needed this release after everything she'd been through today. Instead, he held her close and stroked her hair, reveling in the knowledge she was alive. Her hot tears washed away his fear, and the gentle shaking of her chest made him thankful she still breathed.

"Please," she whispered, lifting her face to him, "take me away from this place. Promise me that I'll never have to see it again."

He brushed the tears back from her eyes, his chest tightening. This was one vow he'd keep until he drew his last breath. "I promise."

27

"Wait." Claudia caught Galerius and turned him around, adjusting the drape of his toga. "You can't go into the imperial throne room looking like that."

He captured her hands. "I don't think the emperor cares about my clothing."

"And you're still thinking like a soldier, not a like Deizian." The twinkle in her eyes told him she was teasing him.

"I am what I am." He kissed her fingertips. "Would you have me change?"

She grinned and shook her head. "But I would like it better if you made a good impression in front of the emperor."

Varro cleared his throat behind them, a gentle reminder that the emperor was waiting for him.

Claudia glanced at him over Galerius's shoulder and gave his clothes one final pat. "You'd best go now. I'll wait here for you."

She retreated to the grand fountain in the center of the atrium and sat on the edge, staring into the water. Melancholy still tempered her movements. A week had passed since they'd stopped her father, and last night was the first night she hadn't been haunted by nightmares that left her screaming at the end. Even when he made love to her until they collapsed in exhaustion, her sleep was still troubled.

He frowned as he watched her, regretting that he'd allowed her to witness all she had, that he'd allowed her suffer. Part of him wished he'd forced her onto the airship that morning rather than allowing her to return home. Would things have turned out differently?

He took a few steps back, continuing to watch her and reassure himself she'd be safe here within the walls of the imperial palace, before he turned to face Varro. "Thank you for waiting."

Varro chuckled. "I'm not the one who's waiting for you."

He followed the steward through the entryway and into the throne room. The royal couple sat with their thrones in front of the entry to gardens, the sun streaming in behind them and illuminating them in its glow. The contrast between them—the golden-haired Sergius and the raven-haired Azurha—made them appear to be day and night, two halves of a whole.

He came to the center of the room and knelt before them. "Good morning, Your Imperial Majesties."

Sergius lifted his hand, palm up, to indicate he should rise. "We owe you a great deal of gratitude, Galerius. Because of your efforts, the barrier still stands, and the empire is safe."

His voice broke with pride. At last, he had redeemed himself. "I am honored to hear your praise."

"Your report was fascinating," Empress Azurha said. "I am still astounded by the amount of ore Hostilius was able to obtain to build the chamber you described."

"He was a man with many connections, many resources, and many ways to obtain what he wanted." Galerius had spent over a day going through the papers hidden in the desk, awestruck at the number of accomplices the governor had. He had sent them back to Emona with his report, allowing the emperor to do what he wished with the other men listed.

"And yet the one person who initiated his downfall was his own daughter." Sergius leaned forward. "How is Lady Claudia faring?"

"As well as can be expected." Galerius refused to sully her reputation sharing what he'd witnessed when they were alone. He knew how important it was for her to not reveal any sign of weakness. "She has lost her family, had her wealth and titles stripped from her. But she is bearing it all with the dignity I've come to expect from her."

"We shall come to her later." The emperor nodded and leaned back. "Your report makes quite a few references to Rufius. He seemed to play an instrumental part in bringing down Hostilius. What are your thoughts on him?"

The questions seemed odd to Galerius. He was a soldier, not an advisor. Yet, he didn't feel any tingling along his neck to suggest there was something sinister about the emperor's inquiries. "He is a good soldier, Your Majesty. Brave, intelligent, and resourceful."

"What do you think I should do with him? Give him a promotion? Offer him a place in the Legion?"

Galerius snorted. "Rufius is breed of his own. I know him well enough to honestly say I don't think he'd be happy in charge of thousands of men. He is a man of action, not of paperwork."

Sergius nodded. "Marcus and I have been discussing the possibility of gathering a group of resourceful men like Rufius and having them investigate any rumors we hear—similar to what Marcus has done for me in the past, but with more anonymity."

"I think that would be something Rufius is well suited for. He has been stationed around the empire and is capable of blending in where needed." *Such as drinking at bars in the seedier areas of town and weaseling information out the drunkards there.*

"Good. Then we'll invite him to Emona and discuss this idea further with him."

Galerius shifted on his feet, wondering if the conversation was finished. Why would the emperor order him here this morning if he only wanted to discuss Rufius? "Do you have any other questions for me, Your Imperial Majesty?"

Azurha's brow rose. "Anxious to leave, Galerius?"

The growing roundness in her belly did little to soften her demeanor. Her unwavering gaze made his skin prickle. The emperor may have been pleased with this work, but empress watched him as though she were looking for a weakness to exploit.

He straightened his spine, taking a cue from Claudia's behavior in front of the public. "Not at all, Empress Azurha, but I am a man who prefers to get right the point."

Sergius grinned. "That was one of the reasons my father appointed you to Legion in the first place and why he promoted you to Captain so quickly. You refused to engage in these courtly games that drove him mad."

"Your father was a busy man, as are you. I have no desire to waste your time."

Sergius clasped his hands in front of his mouth, his index fingers pointed in a steeple, and studied him. "We respected your resignation from the Legion, even though we did not agree with your reasoning. However, if you wish to be reinstated, we would be honored to have you as our Captain again."

The air whooshed from his lungs. Everything he'd lost could be his again. All he had to do was accept the offer.

And yet, he hesitated. Was that what he still wanted? "I am honored by your offer, Your Imperial Majesty, but I believe you already have a good Captain in Horatius."

A moment of wordless communication passed between the imperial couple before Sergius replied, "Then perhaps you could serve as a general in our army. We need men we can trust, men who know how to read our enemies, men who inspire others to follow them. In short, men like you."

He almost laughed. What would his father have thought to know that his disgraceful son could have risen to the rank of general? It was tempting. His mind raced with the possibilities that position offered. He could make the army more efficient, change tactics, ensure the empire was protected.

But still he hesitated, and his chest tightened when he

realized why. He could never give Claudia the life she deserved if he was a soldier. He wanted to chase away her demons, to show her what it meant to be loved and cherished, and he couldn't do that if his life revolved around war and combat. He'd seen what that had done to his parents.

"Again, I am honored, Emperor Sergius, but I have to decline your offer."

The emperor's mouth fell open, and rightly so. No man in his right mind would have refused such a generous offer, but Galerius knew nothing but peace from his decision.

Sergius regained his composure. "We wish to reward you for your service, Galerius, but you seem to want something more than what we offer."

"Not something more—just something different."

A hint of a smile played on the empress's lips as though she was reading his mind. "And what would that be?"

What would he need to offer Claudia happiness? Could a woman born into one of the wealthiest and most powerful families in the empire be happy with a simple life? She seemed to be content lying in his arms every night for now, but what would the future hold?

He cleared his throat. "If you are in a generous mood, Your Majesties, I want nothing more than a home and some land that would allow me to start a family and provide for their comforts."

Again, his reply caught the emperor off guard. The Galerius from two months ago would have been puzzled by his request, too, but so much had changed since then. "You do not strike me as a man wishing to retire in the country, and in truth, I think it would be a waste of your talents if we allowed that."

The hint of anger in the emperor's voice set him on edge. Had he pushed too far?

The empress reached across the space between their thrones, covering her husband's hand with her own. "Titus, dear, I think I may have a solution that would satisfy you both."

She fixed those unnaturally colored eyes on him. "The

261

emperor wishes to keep you in his service, Galerius, because he knows he can trust you, and that makes him value you all the more when we are faced with so many potential enemies." She rubbed her swollen belly as if to prove her point, reviving his memory of all the spiteful comments he'd heard from the Deizian lords about having a child of mixed blood in line for the throne.

He bowed his head. "I appreciate the faith you have placed in me, but I regret to say that I no longer desire the life of a soldier."

"I can see that," the empress replied. "Therefore, let me suggest a new role for you. Lucrilla is without a governor now. We will need to appoint a new one to replace Hostilius, a man we can trust, a man who is familiar not only with the area but with the threats still hidden there."

Sergius smiled at his wife and squeezed her hand. "An excellent idea. What do you say to that, Galerius?"

As much as he risked gaining the ire of the emperor by refusing another position, his promise to Claudia remained as strong as ever. He would never take her back to Tivola, never make her live in the home that held such painful memories for her. "Again, I must decline your generous offer."

A panicked look passed between the imperial couple, and Galerius almost laughed. Just like before, they had scripted this entire meeting to convince him to take the position. Only this time, he hadn't reacted the way they expected.

"May we ask why?" Sergius asked.

"I made a promise to someone, and I intend to keep it."

The empress gave him a soft smile, one that belied her reputation as a deadly assassin and revealed her to be more of a romantic than he would have expected. But then, he'd witnessed the same thing with Claudia. Under the tough exterior was a woman with a heart of gold, and he could see why the emperor had married her, despite her past. But it also added a level of caution to his situation. How much did she know about his relationship with Claudia?

Sergius, however, was not satisfied with his response. "Is that the only reason?"

He could almost hear Claudia teasing him, reminding him he was just a soldier, not Deizian. "I worry that I am not qualified to perform the duties required by a provincial governor."

"We shall see about that." Azurha looked past him. "Varro, please fetch Claudia and bring her here."

***

Claudia ran her fingers across the surface of the water, watching the waves she created merge with the ones made from the gurgling fountain. Nothing had gone the way she planned. She'd set out to gain her independence from her father, and even though she was now free from him, she was left adrift when it came to her future. She had nothing left—no money, no jewels, no family, no home. Nothing except Galerius.

And of course, things hadn't gone according to plan with him, either. What started out as a simple game of seduction had cost her heart. She'd never imagined she could love someone with this kind of intensity. And even though he loved her back, the bittersweet knowledge that he would always be committed to his duty kept her from reveling in the moment. For now, all she could do was embrace the time she had with him until the emperor sent him on another mission.

The tell-tale limp of the palace steward approached her. "Lady Claudia, the empress wishes to speak with you."

Her mouth went dry. The last time she'd seen the Alpirion who'd managed to ensnare the emperor was the day Azurha threatened her with a shard of pottery. She stood slowly, making an act of smoothing her dress while she locked away her fear. "Take me to her."

Varro led her to the throne room. She focused her attention on Galerius, silently asking him why they sent for her, but before he could answer, she'd moved as close to the thrones as she dared and was forced to sink into a curtsy. She lowered her eyes out of respect for the emperor, but she refused to bow her head. "What do you wish of me?"

When she saw the command to rise, she did so. A tremble worked its way into her fingers, intensified by the silence. She clenched her hands into fists and buried them in the folds of her dress. Did they wish to punish her for the sins of her father?

At last, the emperor said, "Claudia, we wish to thank you for having the courage to do something that must have been extremely difficult for you."

She drew in a calming breath. There would be no executioner's ax for her. "I couldn't sit by and allow him to destroy the barrier, Your Imperial Majesty."

"Your aid to Galerius is to be commended," the emperor continued. "You sacrificed a great deal to protect the empire."

Yes, I lost everything, her mind wailed, but she kept a smile plastered on her lips. Perhaps he'd take pity on her and at least give her the villa in Padero she'd wanted. Her gaze traveled to the very pregnant empress, hoping they would stop the pleasantries and tell her why they'd sent for her.

The Alpirion met her gaze and lifted her chin. "Since you've spent a considerable amount of time working beside Galerius, we were wondering if you could answer a few questions we have about him."

In the past, Claudia would've sneered at the idea of an Alpirion adopting the imperial "we," but the empress spoke with such authority that it seemed to suit her.

She turned to Galerius. "What do you wish to know?"

"We are perplexed by his behavior this morning." Sergius cocked his head to the side. "We have offered him both a reinstatement as Captain of the Legion and the position of general in the army, yet he has declined both."

Her brows drew together. Why would a soldier like Galerius turn down what would be the epitome of his career? There were men who would have given their sword arms to be offered what he had. "Did you ask him why?"

"Yes, and he has given us annoyingly vague answers," the empress replied.

The corner of Galerius's mouth rose, and her pulse quickened. What could he possibly want besides those things?

"Then we tried something different," the Emperor continued. "We offered him the position held by your father, but he refused that, too."

Her breath hitched. Lucrilla was one of the wealthiest provinces in the empire. Galerius must have had his mind addled to turn such a prize down.

Galerius's grin widened, but he remained silent.

She turned back to the imperial couple. "Did he give a reason why?"

The empress nodded. "One of the reasons he gave was that he was bound to a promise. Do you care to elaborate on that?"

Her eyes stung. He had turned them down because of her. "Galerius is an honorable man, one who honors his vows."

"Precisely, which is why we are so desperate to keep him our service." Emperor Sergius shifted in his chair. "He claims he is not fit to rule a province. As the daughter of a former governor, what do you say to his abilities?"

She looked to Galerius, hoping he would provide her with an answer, but when he gave none, she was forced to speak what was in her heart. "He is intelligent, loyal, a natural leader. I know of several provincial governors who lack such abilities."

"So if I appointed him as governor, do you think he could handle the demands of the job?"

She weighed the emperor's question carefully along with what she thought Galerius would want her to say. "He's not a pure-blooded Deizian. He was bought up as a soldier, not as a member of a ruling family where protocols and politics are taught from birth."

"True, but perhaps we don't wish to have the empire controlled by pure bloodlines anymore." Sergius turned to his wife, his loving glance speaking volumes. "We intend to build a new empire, and we want men like Galerius to help us build it."

"He embodies many of the qualities one would want in a

provincial governor, but he has no knowledge of how things are done." She was talking circles now, hoping one of the men would speak with his decision and end this discussion. "He would need to be educated, guided during his first few years as governor until he'd learned enough to run a province and all it entails."

Azurha gave a sympathetic nod. No doubt, she was experiencing the same thing, learning to be an empress from her humble beginnings as a slave. "Do you think you would be able to teach him how to be a provincial governor?"

"Me?" She balked at the idea. She was a woman, someone who'd been forced into the periphery when important subjects came up during dinners rather than asked to express her opinions.

"Yes." The empress coolly assessed her. "You were born into a family with strong political ties. Surely you must have learned a few things from watching your father and husbands."

Her blood ran cold, and she wiped her clammy palms on her skirts. She didn't like where this conversation was heading.

"The empress makes a valid point, Claudia," Sergius continued. "With you by his side, I would have no hesitation appointing Galerius to the position of governor."

Her stomach knotted. They were trying to coerce her into another political marriage, one that would send her back to Tivola. But if she refused…

Thankfully, Galerius spoke before she was forced to give them an answer. "Your Imperial Majesties, I appreciate your generosity, but I have already declined Lucrilla. There is no need to trouble Claudia with such a proposition."

She may not have been dangling from a cliff this time, but he still managed to save her.

"We respect your decision to turn down Lucrilla, but may we remind you that Anicium has been without a governor since Pontus was killed?" Sergius paused, letting his offer sink in. "It is a smaller province, not as wealthy as Lucrilla, but also, not as demanding. And the people there have been under the rule of men with mixed blood for several generations."

She waited for Galerius to reply. It was a good offer, one that he'd be a fool to refuse. And yet, as she watched him, he seemed torn by it. Hints of self-doubt hampered his movements, tightened his face and choked his words. "Your Majesties, I appreciate your offer…"

He was going to refuse them, but she wouldn't let him say no. Everything the emperor said was true about the province, and the more she thought about it, the more convinced she became that it would be a prime position for him. "Your Majesties, I think Galerius would be a fine choice as governor of Anicium."

Galerius stared at her as though she'd lost her mind. "But you said yourself that you don't think I could do it alone, at least not initially."

She closed the space between them, taking his hand in her own and rubbing her thumb over the tattoo inside his wrist. The empire needed more men like him, men who valued others before themselves, and she wouldn't let him walk away from the opportunity. "Then I will be there to help you."

"Claudia, I don't want you to be forced into marrying me just so I can become governor. You are free to live your own life now, not to be some prize in a game of politics." He stroked her cheek. "You deserve better than that."

"Who said anything about marriage?" the empress asked. "We were discussing the idea of appointing Claudia as your advisor, not as your wife."

But she already knew her answer. "And what if I want to be his wife? That is, if he'll have me. I know I have a bad reputation when it comes to husbands."

"I'd be willing to take on the risk." A hint of humor danced in his grey eyes. "Are you sure you want a soldier like me?"

"I don't care what you choose to do with your life, as long as you'll let me stay by your side." She meant it, too. She'd follow him the front lines and live the simple life of a soldier's wife if it meant she could fall asleep in his loving arms every night.

He pressed her hand against his chest so she could feel steady beat of his heart. It spoke of certainty, not fear. "I have no intention of ever letting you go."

Epilogue

Ten months later

Galerius felt the fatigue wash away from his muscles as soon as the airship docked. After nearly two months in Emona, he was home at last. Winter hadn't completely faded from Anicium, and the biting chill in the evening air made the warm glow of his villa that much more inviting.

Claudia stood waiting for him the atrium, her golden hair adorned with tiny pearls, appearing every inch the proper provincial governor's wife. She curtsied as he approached her. "Welcome home, my husband."

It was all a show for the household. When she lifted her eyes, he saw the heat burning within them and grew hard. By the gods, he'd missed her so badly, he was tempted to take her right there in front of everyone. Instead, he took her hand and brushed his lips across her knuckles. "It is good to be home with my wife."

She stood and led him toward his office. "I hope all was well in Emona. I took the liberty of making a few decisions in your absence, but there are some matters left that require your immediate attention."

Although her words sounded like something any political advisor would say, her wicked smile left no doubt which matter she wanted attended to immediately. As soon as the door closed behind him, he took her in his arms and kissed her thoroughly.

She moaned, raking her fingers through his hair, clinging to him as her tongue danced with his. Her desire matched his, and the way she tore away his toga left no room for conversation. She wanted him now, and he was more than happy to oblige.

He picked her up in his arms, her legs wrapping around his waist while her lips remained locked with his. He'd go mad if he wasn't inside her soon. His hands dug into the soft flesh of her buttocks, inching her skirts higher as he carried to toward the desk.

"No, not there," she said when she brushed against it. "You'll mess up your papers."

"Do you think I give a damn about my papers when I have you in my arms?" But he spun around, pressing her against the wall. His cock ached from want. He couldn't get his tunic up fast enough.

Her sex was hot and wet as he plunged into her. She gasped and dug her fingers into his shoulders. "I missed you, Galerius."

"Not as much as I missed you." He began moving inside her, his thrusts quick and sharp. He'd take his time making love to her properly later. Now, he just needed to come, to enjoy the way her body shimmied against his to create the exquisite friction that set every nerve in his body on fire.

She moaned his name, urging him to continue. Her pupils dilated to leave only a thin rim of blue. Her lips parted, her breath coming hard and fast. She clenched her walls tighter around him, bringing him closer to the brink of orgasm before becoming lost in her own climax.

He loved watching her come, loved the way she lost control and completely surrendered to him. He'd never seen anything more beautiful. It sent him over the edge. He cried out her name as he spilled into her.

Completely spent for the moment, he sank to his knees with Claudia still wrapped around him. Her scent enveloped him as he buried his nose in the hollow of her neck, breathing her scent in while his orgasm still hummed through his veins.

She covered his face with delicate kisses, easing his head back until he was looking up at her. Contentment softened her face. "Thank you. I needed that."

He chuckled, pressing his lips against hers. "I did, too."

Her legs loosened around his waist, letting her body slide down along his. "Now that we got that out of the way, there are a few things I need to talk to you about."

"I just came home after two months, and you want to talk business?" He pushed her dress off her shoulder, nibbling at the pale flesh underneath.

Her breath hitched, but she continued, "You need to read about the progress they're making on the new aqueduct."

"Uh-huh." He slipped his hand under her dress, cupping one of breasts in his hand. Her nipple stiffened under his thumb, making him want to taste it all the more.

"And then there's a letter from Rufius for you."

"I can read that later." He lowered his mouth to her breast, gently sucking on the pink peak and rolling his tongue around it. She whimpered, but made no effort to stop him. A few more minutes of this kind of foreplay, and he'd be ready to come inside her again.

He turned his attention to the other breast, reducing her to harried whispers of his name. She was his completely, and he wouldn't have her any other way.

His cock began hardening, and his kissed his way back up to her lips. "Shall I take you to bed now?"

She bit her bottom lip, hesitation tightened her features. "There's one more thing I need to tell you."

"Are you certain it can't wait until morning?" He was determined to convince her it was, catching the lobe of her ear between his teeth. He was rewarded by another moan of pleasure.

She nodded and pushed him back. The panic on her face chilled his desire. Whatever she wanted to tell him was serious.

She took drew in a deep breath and said in a rush of words, "You're going to be a father."

He sat back, letting her news sink in. A father. The prospect both thrilled him and terrified him. What if he turned out to be like his own father? Or worse, like Claudia's? No, he refused to be like either of them, but it still left his mind stark with terror. "Are you certain?"

She nodded, watching him with concern. "Do you not want the child?"

He watched the tears well up in her eyes and pushed away any doubts he had. He pulled her into his arms. "Of course I do." He remember their conversation months ago when she revealed she'd taken precautions not to get pregnant during her prior marriages. "But do you want it?"

She laughed and wiped her eyes with the back of her hand. "Yes. I'd rather have a child conceived in love than one bred to keep bloodlines pure. This child is a part of you, and I couldn't want it any more than I already do."

"I feel the same way." He kissed her again—long, slow, and sweet this time—wanting to reassure her of his feelings. "I love you."

She smiled and replied, "I love you, too."

"Is there anything else I should know before taking you to bed?"

She shook her head, grinning. "I think I've told everything that's important."

"Good, because I intend to make love to you until dawn." He helped her up to her feet, leading her into their bedroom. His heart swelled with love as he watched her remove her dress and stretch out alongside him in bed. He savored the feeling of her soft curves beneath him, her tender kisses, the way her eyes shone with love as she stared up at him, and knew he had all he'd ever want here in his arms.

A Note to Readers

Dear Reader,

Thank you so much for reading *Deception's Web*. I hope you enjoyed it. If you did, please leave a review on the site where you purchased this book or on Goodreads.

I love to hear from readers. You can find me on Facebook and Twitter, or you can email me using the contact form on my website, www.CristaMcHugh.com.

If you would like to be the first to know about new releases or be entered into exclusive contests, please sign up for my newsletter using the contact form on my website, www.CristaMcHugh.com. Also, please like my Facebook page for more excerpts and teasers from upcoming books.

--Crista

Books by Crista McHugh

The Soulbearer Trilogy
A Soul For Trouble
A Soul For Chaos
A Soul For Vengeance

The Elgean Chronicles:
A Thread of Magic
The Tears of Elios

The Deizian Empire:
Tangled Web
Poisoned Web
Deception's Web

The Kavanaugh Foundation:
Heart of a Huntress, Book 1
Angelic Surrender, Book 2
"A High Stakes Game", Book 2.5 (a free read)
Kiss of Temptation, Book 3
Night of the Huntress (Print Anthology of Books 1 and 2)

The Kelly Brothers
The Sweetest Seduction, Book 1 (Jan. 2014)
Breakaway Hearts, Book 2 (Feb. 2014)
Falling for the Wingman, Book 3 (Mar. 2014)
The Heart's Game, Book 4 (May 2014)

Other titles by Crista McHugh
The Alchemy of Desire
"A Waltz at Midnight"
Cat's Eyes
"More Than a Fling"
"Provoking the Spirit"
Eight Tiny Flames (part of *A Very Scandalous Holiday* Anthology)

Praise For Crista McHugh

A SOUL FOR TROUBLE

"Book one in the Soulbearer trilogy, this fantastical romance is completely different from the myriad of others out there. It's a great book that pits Trouble against Chaos — two characters that all readers will want to visit again and again!"
— 4 1/2 STARS, RT Book Reviews

TANGLED WEB

"Crista McHugh's **Tangled Web** is sinfully delicious! This erotic feast features one fascinating couple and a killer plotline. It's impossible to turn away from this story after reading the first few pages!... **Tangled Web** is a keeper!"
— Recommended Read, Joyfully Reviewed

THE TEARS OF ELIOS

"The first thing that came to mind upon finishing this book is, 'Holy Crap! Is that it?!' I did not want this book to end."
— Starcrossed Reviews

A WALTZ AT MIDNIGHT

"I love this story! I didn't expect it to be so entrancing and captivating... A WALTZ AT MIDNIGHT is a great romantic story with engaging characters that I didn't wish to end... A must read for romance lovers!"
—The Romance Reviews

HEART OF A HUNTRESS

"Warning: you will not want to put this book down once you start."
— Happily Ever After Reviews

ANGELIC SURRENDER

"The author did such a great job creating my ideal hero that I found myself thinking about him for days."
— Whipped Cream Reviews

KISS OF TEMPTATION

"As Ms. McHugh moves on with her writing of *The Kavanaugh Foundation*, I found this story even more spell binding than first two books."
— Literary Nymph Reviews

CAT'S EYES

"…an excellent plot with oodles of action and suspense. I could not put it down."
— Just Erotic Romance Reviews
"This is a well-paced, enjoyable read complete with action, suspense, humor, and hot sex."
— Night Owl Reviews

THE ALCHEMY OF DESIRE

"Crista McHugh did an incredible job of drawing me into the world of magic, steampunk, and old west that she created."
— Wakela Runen's World

MORE THAN A FLING

"What I liked most about this short story is the fact the main characters, Danni and Ryan, are "real" people… highly engaging and enjoyable."
— Whipped Cream Reviews

PROVOKING THE SPIRIT

"I loved the twists and turns the author threw at me while I was reading and felt my heart racing in my chest numerous times as I was flipping the pages… Overall, this is a fantastic story that's worth picking up!"
— Night Owl Reviews

Author Bio:

Growing up in small town Alabama, Crista relied on story-telling as a natural way for her to pass the time and keep her two younger sisters entertained.

She currently lives in the Audi-filled suburbs of Seattle with her husband and two children, maintaining her alter ego of mild-mannered physician by day while she continues to pursue writing on nights and weekends.

Just for laughs, here are some of the jobs she's had in the past to pay the bills: barista, bartender, sommelier, stagehand, actress, morgue attendant, and autopsy assistant.

And she's also a recovering LARPer. (She blames it on her crazy college days)

For the latest updates, deleted scenes, and answers to any burning questions you have, please check out her webpage, www.CristaMcHugh.com.

Find Crista online at:

Twitter: twitter.com/crista_mchugh

Facebook: www.facebook.com/CristaMcHugh

CPSIA information can be obtained
at www.ICGtesting.com
Printed in the USA
FFOW05n0755181013
2064FF